Dacia Maraini is Italy's most controversial author. Works translated into English include *Isolina, The Silent Duchess* (Campiello Prize 1990) and *Bagheria*. A fearless political and social campaigner, she is hated by the power brokers of Italian society. As *The Guardian* put it: "Once Alberto Moravia's lover, she is now a bestselling writer, vociferous about women and the Left, who has turned detective. No wonder the Italian establishment want to silence Dacia Maraini."

voices

Dacia Maraini

translated by
Dick Kitto and Elspeth Spottiswood

This book was published with assistance from
the Arts Council of England

Library of Congress Catalog Card Number: 96–69699

A complete catalogue record for this book can be
obtained from the British Library on request

First published in Italian as *Voci* in 1994 by Rizzoli, Milan

This edition first published in 1997 by
Serpent's Tail, 4 Blackstock Mews, London N4
and 180 Varick Street, New York, NY 10014

Phototypeset in 10.5pt Bembo by Intype London Ltd
Printed in Great Britain by
Cox & Wyman Ltd., Reading, Berks.

Alice took up the fan and gloves . . . and went on talking: "Dear, dear! How queer everything is to-day! And yesterday things went on just as usual. I wonder if I've been changed in the night? Let me think: was I the same when I got up this morning? I almost think I can remember feeling a little different. But if I'm not the same, the next question is, Who in the world am I?"

Lewis Carroll *Alice in Wonderland*

1

The taxi drops me in front of the gate in the Via Santa Cecilia. But why do I have such a feeling of suspense? I am back home again, I say to myself, I have come back. But how is it that I can hardly recognise this gate, this courtyard, this apartment building with its array of open windows? It feels as if I have a thorn in the roof of my mouth, like the premonition of some disaster. What is waiting for me on this mild morning that brings with it all the familiar smells of returning home? What is it that weighs down my thoughts as if it wanted to twist them and obliterate them?

My eyes search for Stefana, the doorkeeper. At this time of day she is usually in the porter's lodge sorting out the mail but I do not see either her or her tall, lanky husband Giovanni. I cross the courtyard pulling my suitcase behind me; its wheels drag reluctantly across the gravel. I stop for a moment in the middle of the courtyard with its surface of crushed stones and look around me. As always the oleanders and the pink geraniums are still there in the flowerbeds even though they are veiled by a film of summer dust; the little fountain of mossy stone still drips with a noise like the trickle of a broken tap; the two big lime trees are laden with flowers. They seem the only things that are not drooping in the heat and which are impervious to the heavy atmosphere that today hangs oppressively. They stand there with their bundles of downy scented flowers tossing gently in the light summer wind.

The windows overlook the courtyard as if they were watching eyes but today they all seem blind; the stairs too are deserted and strangely silent. With a weary sigh the lift deposits me on the top floor, my floor.

While I am looking for the keys in my handbag, I become aware of a strong smell of hospital disinfectant. I turn round and see that the door of the opposite apartment is half-open. I take a step forward and push it with my finger. I watch it swing back very gently, revealing a passage bathed in sunlight, the fringed edge of a rolled-up carpet and a pair of blue canvas tennis shoes placed neatly beside the door.

My glance lingers. I am puzzled; my eyes are held by those blue shoes so clean and bright in the sunshine, bringing to mind the memory of happy walks, skipping on tiptoe, chasing balls as they fly across tennis courts. Why are they lying there, paired together, motionless, unlaced and undamaged, beside the open door? They are too carefully placed for anyone to have thrown them off impatiently as they came into the apartment. There is something so neat and precise about the way they are exposed to public gaze with the laces wound round the upper part of the shoe.

I can hear voices coming from the other end of the apartment, and then suddenly I see Stefana's face in front of me with her sad, plaintive eyes.

"Didn't you know?"

"Know what?"

"She died five days ago, she was murdered."

"Murdered!"

"Yes, twenty stab wounds from a frenzied attack . . . and they still haven't found him . . . poor us!"

A soft, expressive voice, the pupils of her eyes sliding up to show the white of the cornea. I am reminded of a painting by Delacroix; a look of alarm as if someone has seen catastrophe hanging above them in their mind's eye and has been unable to find words to describe it; an indoor pallor that "feeds off the lives of others", as Marco says. Yet Stefana Mario is an intelligent, well-informed woman. I look at her large capable hands. Can it have been those hands that laid out the body of the dead woman?

"But why on earth was she murdered?"

"No one knows, it seems nothing was stolen . . . it was just terrible, you should have seen it. Then when the police arrived, along with the examining magistrate, forensic scientists, journalists, photographers, the lot; their dirty shoes went trailing up and down the stairs . . . The funeral was the day before yesterday . . . Now we've cleaned up everything but there'll still be police in there measuring . . . they say that today they're going to put seals on the doors."

I am aware how I am clutching hold of my keys with such force that they are hurting my fingers.

"Stefana, would you like to come in and I'll make you a cup of coffee?"

"No, I've got to go back downstairs. There's no one in the porter's lodge."

I hear her quick footsteps as she goes downstairs in her patched shoes that give out a light muffled thud at each step.

I open the door to my apartment and pull my suitcase inside. I sniff the air, which smells shut in and fusty. I throw open the shutters, I bend down to look at the plants. They are flagging, all pale and dusty yet not short of water. Stefana has been watering them every day as we agreed. But being shut away in the silence of an empty apartment makes them lose heart; my plants don't like being left on their own and they are telling me this very clearly, whispering behind my back in husky voices.

I sit down at my desk in front of a pile of letters which have come while I was away. I open one but realise that I am reading the words without taking in their meaning. I go back to the first sentence two, three times, then I give up. My thoughts, like the yellow donkey I once saw in a painting by Chagall, are flying mysteriously out of the picture frame. I ask myself what I know about this neighbour of mine who was stabbed to death. Nothing. A woman living behind the door opposite to mine and I do not even know her name.

I would meet her sometimes in the lift. I would look at her much as one looks at someone on the next seat in a train or a bus, with a feeling of guilt for my ill-mannered curiosity. But why on earth should it be ill-mannered to be interested in the person who lives in the apartment opposite mine?

My neighbour was tall and elegant; her light chestnut hair cut short in the shape of a helmet, a small delicate nose, a well-defined upper lip that when it wrinkled into a smile, revealed slightly protruding infant teeth. The smile of a rabbit I thought when I saw her for the first time, shy and timid like someone who is accustomed to nibbling at secret thoughts. Big grey eyes, a broad forehead, a soft white skin strewn with freckles. Her voice, on the rare occasions I heard it, seemed muffled as if she were afraid of exposing herself or being a bother, a colourless voice lacking expression and surrendering to shyness, yet with unexpected flickers of light-heartedness and daring.

Like me she lived alone while Stefana and her less visible husband watched over us like two indulgent, elderly parents, although in reality they are more or less our own age.

But why did my neighbour often come back so late at night? Sometimes when I was half-asleep, I would hear her door close with a thud and the key being forced to turn in the lock. Even the shutters were bolted with a loud, energetic clatter. Every morning and every evening I'd hear them being slammed open or shut. Why did she go out in the morning so silently, looking tired and dazed? And why did she sometimes leave looking so furtive and carrying with her nothing but a yellow rucksack?

According to our neighbours, both of us were in need of protection because we lived alone, because we had tiring jobs that often kept us away from home, me with my work for radio and she . . . but here I am brought to a standstill because I do not know any more.

I pick up the letter again and start reading it. It is a bill from my accountant. Then there is the electricity bill already overdue and the telephone bill only a few days before it has to be settled. Lastly a chain letter telling me to "copy this and send it off to ten friends. If you do this you will have good luck in the future; if you do not you will have trouble for seven years."

Just like when one breaks a mirror . . . I throw it into the wastepaper basket.

My glance falls on the answering machine, the red eye is flashing imperiously. I press the message button.

"Hullo Michela, it's Tirinnanzi. Are you still not back from your refresher course? Ring me as soon as you get back. 'Bye."

A click, a rustling, a metallic voice that accentuates the syllables. "Thursday June twenty-third twelve-twenty p.m." And then a female voice I do not recognise. "Dear Michela Canova I am . . ." but the message is interrupted by a mysterious click.

The voice reminds me of my neighbour but why should she have wanted to ring me?

Another click, the metallic voice intoning "Friday June twenty-fourth eight-thirty a.m. Excuse me if . . . I'd like to talk to you about . . ." But once again the sentence is abruptly interrupted. It really does sound like my neighbour's voice. But when did she die? Stefana said it was five days ago. But five days would be precisely the 24th of June.

I go on to listen to other messages but I do not hear any more of that hesitant voice with the sudden interruptions. I must find out the exact time of her death, I tell myself. I remove the cassette from the answering machine and put it away inside an envelope.

2

It is hot, my jacket weighs heavily on my shoulders, the water dribbles out of the tap.

I look at the suitcase lying on the floor asking to be opened and unpacked. The glass from which I've hardly drunk any water asks to be put back with the other objects on the shelf above the sink; this morning they are all talking as if they are impelled by an urgent need to be sociable.

Even the soap seems to have a voice, raucous and breathless like someone who has had a throat operation. How the objects are chattering! As a child I used to read again and again a Hans Andersen story about how one night all the toys in a house began to talk among themselves. I had always guessed that toys were endowed with thoughts. Then when I read how eggs can faint when a hand approaches them too roughly, or how trees can feel lonely, or how at night walls are able to talk, I said to myself that I knew it all already. Am I being somewhat animistic?

But what am I doing standing barefoot in front of the closed front door? My eyes are alongside the peep-hole, my gaze explores the empty passage. Now I know what I am looking for; those blue tennis shoes, small, delicate, and so methodically placed side by side on the bare floor. They too are saying something, but what is it?

"In the conduct of daily life in urban areas it is usual to know nothing of the person who lives next door . . . we live in a society of islands rigorously separated by a network of discreet hypocrisy which results in each family remaining cocooned inside its own cultural and linguistic bunker."

Where have I heard this voice? It is obviously from a verbose sociologist, but where have I heard him? Probably on the radio, perhaps even in a programme of mine. My memory is a meeting place for so many voices, pretentious, mannered, speculative, obsessive. I would be glad to forget them all but my ear is endowed with an animal voracity and rummages like a pig, pushing its nose into all the detritus of left-over sounds, casually absorbing manufactured sentences, commonplace statements and erudite quotations exactly as they reach me from the microphone waiting for my stomach to make its drastic selection. How long is it since my neighbour came to live in this apartment building? Six months, a year? Perhaps even longer, yet I never even asked her name. The brass door-plate still bears the name of the previous tenant, Professor Guido Festoni, inscribed in flowing script, black on gold. A big tall man with hair cut in a brush and a voice like thunder.

He had a wife who came from Milan who, according to Stefana, was a stockbroker. No children, only an elderly mother (I never knew if she was his or hers) whom I used to see sometimes in the passage, a grim looking person festooned with rings and bracelets. Then Professor Festoni was transferred to Milan and in a few days all his furniture and papers were taken out. The apartment stayed empty for months. Every so often someone would come to look at it and I would hear voices through the walls.

I thought it was still empty when one evening, coming back from the broadcasting studio, I met a woman in the lift. She said, "I'm going to the top floor. And you?"

"Me too. Have you come to see the empty apartment?"

"No, I've just rented it."

I was on the point of giving her my name and saying that if

she wanted anything to ring my door bell, when the lift stopped with a faint hiss and she got out in a hurry.

"Goodbye."

"Goodbye."

I opened my door and she opened hers. As I went into the kitchen I heard her noisily turning the inside door key several times as if to say, "you're nice and friendly but keep your distance!" Clack, clack, clack . . . the key went on grinding in the lock. But how long can it be, this bolt that fastens the door to the ceiling and the floor? After that day I rarely saw her. In the morning when I went out around eight o'clock to go to the studio there was absolute silence from her apartment. When I came back at lunch-time I would sometimes hear music playing. On my way out at half-past three, there was again a total silence. Occasionally when I came back dead tired at about seven in the evening, I would meet her on her way out all scented and wearing a skimpy white coat that made her look like a little girl, and a black beret slanted sideways on her soft hair.

"What was her name?" I ask Stefana as soon as I meet her in the courtyard. She looks at me with an ironic smile. Like the sociologist on the radio she too appears to think that "the alienation of the contemporary world shuts us away unified and non-communicative within our own particular family environment, and in this situation we find a perverse satisfaction."

"Angela Bari," she answers absent-mindedly.

"Did she have a job?"

"A bit of acting, I think . . . but her family was well-to-do . . . a mother in Fiesole with money. But she wasn't at the funeral. Her father died when she was little."

"And she didn't have any other relations?"

"She has a sister but we didn't see much of her. It's just as well you were away, Signora Michela. It would have been horrible for you, she could have been screaming, who knows, and no one heard the poor thing . . . And you could have met the murderer in the passage."

"Did you hear her screaming?"

"No, I was busy down in the basement."

"Did they take anything?"

"No, nothing . . . the money was rolled up inside a biscuit tin in the kitchen. She kept it all piled up with the notes all crumpled, I bet she didn't know how much it added up to . . . two million lire all told. And they didn't take it."

"Did it happen in the morning or at night?"

"Late, around eleven or even midnight. And the entrance door was shut, we didn't see anyone go out. She came home about seven, and up to the time I closed the door I hadn't seen anyone come down. Afterwards someone must have gone upstairs. But who could it have been? Giovanni found her the next morning when he went to collect the rubbish bags . . . the door was open . . . and she was there . . . dead!"

I am aware of something strange in Stefana's calm pallid face, a hidden thought, a word left unspoken or simply the unconscious act of witnessing the horror of a crime in which she has been involved purely through the demon of chance.

I tell her about the voice on my answering machine but she doesn't seem to find it important. She does not think it is the voice of Angela Bari, then she says, "Did you know each other?"

"No, we didn't."

"Well, in that case . . ."

I watch her move away, crossing the sunny courtyard on her way to meet the postman.

Yet, as I remember it, the voice of my neighbour was oddly reminiscent of that voice recorded on the tape of the answering machine. And it was on the same day as her death.

I too go across the courtyard where I am overcome by the strong fragrance of the lime trees. The fountain, covered in fern, dribbles its tranquil sound of trickling water. I look round for my little Fiat. I can't remember where I parked it. Luckily its unusual colour stands out among other cars even at a distance. I think of it as a ripe cherry colour, as a friend of mine once described it to me, in spite of it being called "dark red" in the handbook.

There it is parked between a small white van and an enormous luxury car with American style fins. I insert the key into the starter and turn it, but nothing happens. After having been abandoned for so many days it seems to feel insulted and remains mute. I try again and again to start the engine, pushing down on the accelerator until at last, after a fit of coughing and a lot of spluttering, it decides to start.

3

On my desk at the radio station I find a note from Tirinnanzi saying: "The director is waiting to see you. 'Bye."

I had wanted to see to my letters, establish if the computer was working, find my recordings, but this note puts me in a rush.

"Tirinnanzi told me you wanted to see me," I begin hesitantly.

"Ah, Signora Canova, it's you. Welcome back! How was the refresher course in Marseilles?"

"Yes, it was good."

The director is younger than any of us. Exceedingly tall, with the appearance of a figure in a comic strip; casually dressed, pink shirts, worn leather jackets, yellow English-style shoes unpolished. On his face there is always a crafty smile that is quite winning.

"I'm needing some rather delicate work from you, how would that be?"

"Why not?"

He is very good at arousing curiosity. As he looks at me his eyes sparkle.

"Do sit down, Signora Canova."

I sit facing him, on the edge of my chair. I am trying to anticipate whether it might really be about some interesting work or only some stupid nonsense he is wanting to hand over to me for reasons of his own.

"Through current market research we're finding that the number of women who listen to the radio is expanding day by day. It's growing by leaps and bounds, I could say 'disastrously'. I see you disagree with my use of that word, but now let me explain. I'm not trying to discredit women, you know me. The fact is that where women are concerned, even if we're talking only about housewives, there are so many emotional needs, the family, jealousy, small talk . . . in short, the greater the number of women listeners, the more we shall have to lower our tone, do you follow me? We've got to be rather low-key, this is what is needed . . . so no politics, no sports commentaries – and you know what an effort we made to bring our cover of sporting events up to a level that has both style and language . . . because it's we who are the creators of language – I've said this many times – we are the linguistic conscience of Italy, a small conscience no doubt, a small part of the whole, but we are it and the feminine public is pre-linguistic, uneducated in the use of language; it has to get hold of crude emotions, that's why I'm talking about catastrophe."

His handsome boyish face leans over the table expressing real suffering intelligence.

"Women want stories, do you understand that, Signora Canova? Love stories above all, and then stories about death, suffering, terrifying things, but they have a chronic hunger for stories."

"One can write stories without having to make them treacle," I comment just to say something.

"No, one can't . . . for the simple reason that women listeners want love, they expect romance."

"One can't be certain of that . . . when a story is well told it doesn't have to be lightweight." I am astonished at my daring. With the previous director there was never any contradiction, he didn't allow it. He'd put his nose in and then he'd take revenge. This one doesn't act like that; he's young, democratic, he allows you a few liberties. Only later does he do exactly what he wants.

"I sent for you because I'm aware of your professional commitment, you, your . . ." I see he is in difficulty over finding the right word. If he starts praising me, God knows what he will be wanting in exchange, probably unpaid extra work; research outside office hours.

"We need to work for women and you know how to do

that. By the way, I've never told you how good your programme on free time was. We received hundreds of phone calls."

"Thank you."

I watch his slender fingers, long and transparent, as they play with a pen. They too seem to be trying to attract my attention, to entice me. "We are little butterflies, we are gentle, we are light as air, we are intelligent. Allow yourself to be charmed by us, let yourself be led along the inaccessible and dangerous path of radio broadcasting."

"Not long ago an official from the homicide section of the police headquarters was here. Did you see her?"

"Was she the woman with braces on her teeth?"

"Yes, that was her. Commissioner Adele Sòfia. I asked her here to verify some statistics. Did you know that 65 per cent of crimes against women go unpunished? A listener had alerted us to this and others followed, bombarding us with telephone calls. It's a burning issue for our public. So I have decided to put on a series of forty programmes about crimes against women, particularly those that go unpunished. And I think you, Signora Canova, are the best person to take this on."

The butterfly hands are suddenly closing up, as if they are being held in a taut expectant silence. The enticement is still at work and has a way of knocking at the heart to get a response.

Out of an old habit that has to do with strategy, I take my time. "Let me think about it," I say knowing already that I will accept.

The director's hands remain firmly placed upon his desk. My answer does not satisfy him, he is in a hurry and cannot wait for me to think about it. His blue eyes stare at me worriedly. "Is that all?" they are saying.

"Dear Signora Canova, I am disappointed. I don't simply want your agreement, that is part of your work here, but I need your sensitive participation, I want your enthusiasm to be communicated to the listeners, since the future of broadcasting in the current state of need appears to belong them by right."

"When I got back from Marseilles, I discovered that . . ." And I am just on the point of telling him about the crime in the next-door apartment, and the odd coincidence of his request coming right on top of something that has happened so close to me. But he cuts me short. "I can imagine it, Signora Canova, I can imagine it . . . I know how good your work is . . . so are we ready to begin?"

I think how I should at least ask how much I might be paid for all the research, but my concern with the disturbing movement of those suspended hands puts me off. It makes me feel uncomfortable in my chair. He knows that I know it is a stupid tactic even if rather a feeble one. It serves to postpone an agreement that in any case will eventually happen with all the enjoyment that is part of such a situation.

"This time we will also pay for your overtime, I promise," he generously informs me, "you can have all the time you ask for and a substantial budget as well."

"I accept."

With alarm I see that his hands are still clasped together as if the current were missing. But it only needs a few seconds and the motor starts up again; his hands rise and begin to fly as before. They are such splendid hands, I have to admit it, never has a director of broadcasting had hands like them, long, pale, without one single hair, wart, or any imperfection, the slender knuckles, the gentle curve of the thumbs.

"Take a Nagra, they're small and portable. Also take two miniature Sonys, professional type D; they're the ones the BBC uses and I've just got them from Japan because they aren't on sale here yet. So now you can get to work straight away, do you agree?"

While I wait for the Nagra, I realise he has already forgotten me. He rests from the effort of seduction by taking refuge behind a printed news-sheet. The phone rings, he answers it cheerfully, and I melt away, saying goodbye with a nod of my head.

4

It is a long time since I walked in the streets around my apartment building. Usually I would stand and look at the tall plants climbing up the façades of the buildings in the Piazza Ponziani, and then I'd rush off to the radio station. Today I am just walking. I go down the Via dei Genovesi and along the Via Anicia until I reach the narrow street of the Tabacchi. The air is faintly tinged with mauve from the exhausts of the cars and the buses. Beneath my feet the asphalt is soft like rubber.

In the Via San Crisogono I stop in front of a butcher's shop and count the small heads of dead sheep hanging on hooks. Shiny as plastic, they dangle against the dirty glass of the shop window: the poor wretched ears have lost all their skin, the teeth are lipless, the eyes stripped of their eyelids, dangling against the dirty glass of the shop window. How could I have passed in front of them so many times without paying any attention?

I see the butcher inside and he beckons me to come in. As I enter I feel a cold shiver. The man is standing behind a raised bench and is intent on cutting up the bones and cartilage of a rabbit. He lifts his small round face and gives me a welcoming smile.

"It's ages since I last saw you. I was afraid you might have become a vegetarian!"

"I don't eat at home much," I say to justify myself. A woman bent double with arthritis is leaning against the small glass case waiting for her piece of rabbit.

"Would you fancy a nice pork chop or some tender beef?"

"I'll have the beef," I say without much enthusiasm. And I seem to hear a murmuring sound behind me. The small hanging heads are being shaken by little malevolent gusts of laughter, hiccups and twitterings. These days the voices have multiplied dangerously; their tone is menacing, as if they were an echo from the murder of Angela Bari reverberating over everything that happens to me.

"Did you know Angela Bari?" I ask casually. The butcher stops with a bleeding pig's trotter in his hand. How secure and happy they seem, those hands that tear, chop and manipulate dead meat. He looks at me with surprise and then answers cheerfully. "Of course I knew her, she often used to come in to buy meat for her dog."

"What dog? I didn't know she had a dog."

"If she didn't have a dog what was she doing buying two kilos of mince every time she came in? And it had to be good mince, top quality."

"Did you ever see her with a dog on a lead?"

"No, that's true, I didn't, But I thought she must have kept it at home. I'd imagine you have a good big courtyard at Via Santa Cecilia with all those lime trees and the corners filled with geraniums. She could have kept the dog there."

"I lived opposite and I never saw her with a dog."

The man looks at me in a dismissive way as if he were asking himself why I was delving into such unimportant details; after all she's dead, isn't she? And in a way so horrible that it made everyone in the neighbourhood shiver when they read about it.

"Here's your piece of beef. Six thousand lire."

He hands me the package of meat wrapped in yellow, blood-stained paper. I say goodbye and go out thinking of Angela Bari's invisible dog. I never heard it bark, nor have I ever seen any imprint of its paws in the passage; no, Angela Bari certainly did not have a dog. But then why did she buy kilos of minced meat? I pass in front of the newspaper kiosk. I see the owner is there. Why not ask him as well?

"Did Angela Bari ever come here to buy newspapers?"

"Who? Oh, the woman who was murdered at 22 Via Santa Cecilia? Yes, she'd come sometimes, not every day. She didn't really read newspapers, just a magazine now and again. She was always nice, always smiling. Do you think it was her ex-husband who did her in?"

"Do you remember when it was she last came?"

"How should I . . . so many people come by here . . . but I think she came Sunday morning, and after that I didn't see her any more."

Continuing on my way I come to the local market. A canti-levered cement roof, a covered space, barrows of fruit and vegetables, a fountain spurting water into a dirty cement basin full of stalks.

I ask the old matronly woman selling vegetables if she remem-bers Angela Bari.

"How wouldn't I, such a lovely girl always dressed in white and with those little bright blue tennis shoes . . . how wouldn't I . . . she was ever so beautiful . . . But why did they kill her? It's always the best people who die soonest; they stir up too much envy, isn't that right? Would you like some of these French beans, they're soft as butter."

"Did she often come here to the market?"

"Who, the girl with the blue tennis shoes? No, only from time to time. I remember once when she bought half a kilo of parsley. I had to get other stall holders to lend me some, I didn't have enough and she was wanting so much. I said to her what is it for, my dear, are you wanting to poison yourself? . . . Parsley is known for its use in abortions . . . when I was a girl I remember that was quite common but not any more."

She laughs, opening wide her big mouth of broken and blackened teeth. Signora Mariuccia is strong and energetic in spite of her seventy years and she can still shift boxes of fruit, dust the apples with her apron, and top and tail the beans with quick movements of her fingers while she waits for customers. But her clientèle is declining because nowadays housewives prefer to go to the supermarket where vegetables are sold wrapped in cellophane and cost a little less, though they are all the same size and look as if they have been blown up with a bicycle pump.

I leave the market with a small bag of beans and some peaches. I continue walking. I go up part of the Via Anicia and turn down Via dei Salumi. I go round the Piazza Ponziani and take the Via della Botticella until I reach the tree-lined bank of the Tiber. But why am I walking through the streets instead of working on this new broadcasting project? I am pursued by the thought of Angela Bari. I ask myself over and over again if it is her voice on my answering machine, did this mean she wanted to tell me something. If so, what?

I think of her leaving the apartment in her light-coloured trousers and her little blue shoes and I try to imagine where she is going. I see her walking across the courtyard of the Via Santa Cecilia, passing close to the small, moss-covered fountain that drips so softly. I see her pausing for a moment in the shadow of a lime tree, overcome maybe by the strong scent of the flowers. Then she sets off decisively for the street.

Something about her light and heedless way of walking worries me; without my wishing it, Angela Bari has entered into my thoughts and pitched camp, waiting, even though I cannot really imagine what she could possibly expect from me.

5

On the crime pages of the popular press the headlines report the murder in Via Santa Cecilia among many others; a young woman named Angela Bari has been stabbed with a knife and killed. Was it her lover? This "lover" is called Giulio Carlini and lives in Genoa but used to come down to see her once a week.

I try to remember if I ever encountered him either in the passage or in the lift, but my mind is blank. I cannot remember anything about him. If it were true that he came every week, then I would surely have met him, but whenever I saw her she was always alone. According to the next day's papers, Giulio Carlini has a cast-iron alibi and now the attention moves to her sister Ludovica Bari and a man living with her called Mario Torres, known to be violent and already arrested once before for getting into a fight and causing a public disturbance. Why did the two of them not react immediately to the news of Angela's death? Why had Mario Torres sold his car only a few days after the girl was murdered? But as someone pointed out, neither had any reason to kill Angela and Torres is a car dealer with plenty of cash. Ludovica is well off with money of her own and the two of them have been living together quite happily for many years. But is their alibi to be believed, demands an insistent journalist from the *Corriere della Sera*, since although they state they went together to the cinema that evening, they have not kept the tickets?

As the days go by, the papers start criticising the police for failing to discover who is responsible for the crime. What are they doing? Why are they not investigating the case more thoroughly? How could someone kill a girl with such ferocity and not leave any traces? Angela Bari was unknown during her lifetime but now her photograph appears day after day and she becomes notorious and talked about: that fragile smile evokes feelings of tenderness, her childlike body which looks as if it grew up in too much of a hurry, her tight-fitting trousers, loose shirts, the helmet shape of her hair style, her little sky blue tennis shoes. The notoriety she had looked for in life through her appearances in films and in heaven knows how much other humiliation and grief, she has now obtained in death.

Now, a week after she was murdered, journalists are trampling inside Angela's life with both feet, without any regard for her. How did she manage to survive without having a job? Why did she keep such odd hours? Is it true that she once acted a part in a pornographic film? No one really knows the answer, yet people say they recognised her. Could she have changed her name? It is hinted she was a prostitute . . . However there is a good interview with Stefana Mario which ends speculation; Angela lived on her own and did not have male visitors except for Signor Carlini who came from time to time, and that was that.

In the *Messaggero* I come across a lengthy interview with Giulio Carlini, who was in Genoa on the day of the crime; there are four witnesses ready to swear to this.

"Were you the fiancé of Angela Bari?"

"No. Well, in a sort of a way . . . we saw each other from time to time . . . but I didn't have any binding relationship with her."

"When did you last see her?"

"A few days before her death, in Florence where her mother

lives. I met her, we had dinner together, then I went to stay in a hotel and she slept at her mother's. The next day I went with her to the station where she took the train for Rome and I took one for Genoa."

"Do you remember what day that was?"

"It was Sunday I think; yes, it was Sunday."

But if it was on Sunday that Angela went to buy a paper from the local kiosk, how could she have been in Florence with Carlini?

"Did you ever hear of Angela Bari having any enemies?"

"No, not that I knew of."

"Did she ever tell you she was afraid of anyone or that she was being threatened?"

"No, she seemed quite calm and confident."

"How would you describe her?"

"Basically she was a shy person with sudden moments of gaiety which took people by surprise because no one expected this from her."

The black and white newspaper photographs portray a tall thin man with a sunken face; two wrinkles across his forehead, small bright eyes, a clearly defined mouth, something indolent and disquieting around his sensitive nostrils. For several days the newspaper columns are flooded with all the various suppositions about the crime in Via Santa Cecilia; it was her lover, no, her ex-husband, but he has been living in America for years. Then it was perhaps a lunatic, or a maniac, and so on . . .

They reconstruct the events. On the morning of June 25th the porter Mario goes to the top floor of the apartment building in Via Santa Cecilia in order to collect the rubbish bags as he does every morning. He finds the door of Angela Bari's apartment half-open, and the light on inside. He rings, he knocks, he calls, and in the absence of any response, he goes in. There in the living room he finds the woman's body. She is lying on her back naked and lacerated by knife wounds. He is astonished that there should be so little blood on the floor. "The girl looked as if she were asleep," says the porter. He rings for the police who, after their initial investigations, establish that Angela

Bari died between ten p.m. and midnight on the 24th of June from an internal haemorrhage caused by knife wounds.

Her sister Ludovica Bari was informed that morning, but does not present herself until the evening. And when she arrives accompanied by her "fiancé" Mario Torres, she refuses to enter the apartment and insists that it should be cleaned immediately. She does not shed any tears and seems more irritable than grief-stricken. A photograph shows Ludovica Bari looking elegant in white trousers, a long shirt of pink silk and a leather jacket falling softly over her hips.

Within the next few days, the accounts in the papers become ever more fantastic and improbable; the police have not succeeded in identifying the killer, so each reporter feels he has the right to invent his own theory. In the popular imagination Angela Bari becomes transformed into the mysterious victim of a mysterious attacker who kills her because she is a spy, or a drug dealer, or perhaps even belonged to a secret society, or on the contrary, was herself a secret agent working for the police.

The one and only photograph, taken on the terrace against a background of geraniums, with her shirt open showing her thin neck, her sunglasses slightly askew on her nose and her mouth widening into a friendly, childlike smile, gets published in one paper after another throughout Italy. Later on, other photographs are found among her things: photos of her taken for a film, seductive, half-nude, voluptuous pose. Yet they have nothing indecent or vulgar about them. It is now realised that although Angela was described by one journalist as being "like so many young girls, eagerly chasing after a contract", in all these poses she maintains a composed and innocent look, dignified yet slightly awkward, and this arouses feelings of tenderness and sympathy for her. And possibly this is the reason for her "failure as a sexy actress", insinuated by one malicious commentator.

6

I wake up with the feeling of a presence in the room.
My fingers hurry to turn on the light which illuminates the
darkness. There is nobody there, yet it seemed as if I were
hearing footsteps on the wooden floor.

I am getting too involved with this crime; why don't I put
a weight on top of it? Thinking about it has brought up clouds
of doubt that I have not known before. That interrupted voice
on the answering machine is one of them. In addition, I have
accepted work where I will have to get to know and become
involved with other slaughtered bodies, other voices hissing
pitilessly. Perhaps it was rash of me to agree to work on a
programme about crimes against women. I should have refused
with a loud "no".

I put out the light and turn on to my side, but sleep has a
hard time closing my eyes. I can hear the voice of my father;
coming back at night he bends over my bed saying, "You've
still got your eyes open, Michela." I used to be unable to get
to sleep until I knew he was home. I would always imagine
him to be in danger, calling for help, and if I were asleep how
could I help him? I used to wait for the click of the lock, the
sound of his footsteps going down the passage.

I knew he would have brought with him the fresh scent of
outdoor breezes, mingled with the aroma of bitter cherries. He
might be wearing round his neck the white silk scarf I liked so
much and maybe he was in the kitchen making himself a cup
of coffee while he listened to the late news on the radio.

He seemed so young even when he became old that when
I saw him dead, I simply could not believe it. And I still can't.
Yet there were so many times when I would have liked to kill
him; for so many betrayals, for his total lack of concern towards
my mother, for his polished and boorish egotism.

He was all grey. Where a delicate blue had once harmonised
with the handsome amber colour of his neck, it was now grey,
such an unremarkable and colourless grey that I could only see

him as a stranger, an enemy. I would never have imagined that
in death he would take on this colour as if he were covered in
cement. It was a homogeneous grey, a surface barely interrupted
by tiny bubbles of air, the grey of liquid cement, a grey without
any possibility of change or remedy.

I told myself that I might perhaps be able to wake him up
again, with my own living breath. And so I pressed my mouth
against his mouth to bring him back to life. I wanted him to
take from my body what the French call "élan" – I have always
liked that word and he used it often. "He hasn't got 'élan'," he
would say of someone, and inside myself I would think of a
crow in flight. I wanted my "élan" to fly and bring air to his
lungs again, make his cheeks soft and pink again, his neck
supple and the colour of amber, his eyes bright and smiling.

Instead, he took my warm breath with his dusty greyness
and turned it into an icy draught. I was afraid, I feared the
greyness would infect me and that I too would become grey,
colourless. I can see now how his greyness was so much stronger
than my tepid warmth, than my "élan".

Thinking about the presence that woke me up, I know it
was not him. My father would never act so stealthily. It was
more like someone unknown watching me asleep. My father
would announce himself, calling me by name, he would take a
chair and settle himself in it noisily. He would lean over me
and start making jokes, "Go on, tell me who has been getting
you into this sort of state and I'll go and give them a good
hiding!"

"I'm just getting older, papa."

"Don't talk such nonsense; you were always such a pretty
little girl. Who has given you those wrinkles round your eyes?"

"I'm not fifteen any more, papa."

"But you're still a little girl! Do you want me to give you a
good-night kiss?"

"Papa, remember that you're dead and your hands can't touch
me."

No, it was definitely not my father. And if it were Angela
Bari with her light, diffident footsteps advancing towards the
boundary edge of safety which separates the dead from the

living? I have a suspicion that it was really her, and that she has been sitting in my imagination like a queen during these sultry days of July.

I try to match the image of her in the photograph reproduced so often in the newspapers with how she looked walking along the passage the few brief times we met each other. I seem to know her so well, yet I know nothing about her. And the fact that she has been so brutally torn apart suddenly seems like something that has been done to me.

Tomorrow I shall ring Ludovica Bari. I must do something, I tell myself. I will go and meet her and ask her about her sister. Little by little I am throwing myself at the mercy of ghosts. With this thought I fall into a deep sleep.

I am immersed in soft, black water; it feels light. I can see lights far away on the curving slope of the river bank; they look so beautiful. I know I have to swim to reach that luminous half-moon, breathing through my nose because my mouth is lapped by small delicate waves. The water is tepid and I am not afraid of its blackness. I swim with a sense of well-being which is reassuring even if the lights do not come any nearer; although I am going towards them they stay remote and unreachable like so many stars shimmering in the water. Swimming is part of a game and I know that eventually something will happen which will reveal its mystery.

7

It feels fresh this morning and unexpectedly it began to rain at dawn.

I gulp down a cup of coffee, slip on a waterproof jacket and rush downstairs. I want to ask Stefana something but the porter's lodge is empty. I cross the dripping courtyard, making a wide detour so that I can pass under the lime trees; I love to smell the scent that gathers round their trunks.

In the street I go round and round looking for my cherry-red Fiat, wondering where on earth I could have parked it. But what do I see? On the wall in front of me is "Mind your own business!" spray-painted on the light-coloured surface.

I stop with a jolt. There is always a lot of graffiti on that wall and it is ridiculous to think it has anything to do with me. But I cannot help feeling a sense of alarm in front of those threatening words which have appeared since yesterday.

The writing reveals a careful, confident hand, it isn't the usual wild and uncertain scrawl. Each letter is precisely drawn. But possibly I'm mistaken, perhaps it wasn't spray-painted but painted on with a brush.

I find my car at last, trapped between a Mercedes and an Alfa Romeo; there isn't room to move an inch. I start to back out, pushing against the bumpers of the two other cars.

"What the hell are you doing, trying to wreck my Mercedes?" the voice outside sounds angry, furious.

I stop turning the wheel and look round at him. A man with an ugly checked hat on his head is watching me intently.

"Why don't you move your car?" I ask. "There's nothing in front and I'm squashed in like a sardine."

The man casts an insulting look at my small car but rather than move his Mercedes, which is the last of the cars parked alongside the pavement, he plants his big legs beside my Fiat as if to say, "let's see you do it again!"

Sweating, I start to manoeuvre, trying not to touch his precious bumpers. "Can't get it right, like all women", I hear him mutter and he stays there, arms folded, fixing me with a punitive stare.

Should I get out and start an argument? It would only be a waste of time. I finally manage to extricate myself; my arms are aching and my back dripping with sweat. "Congratulations on your driving!" says the man in a sarcastic voice and I see him smile, pleased at having taught me a lesson.

I arrive at the radio station a few minutes late. As I come in, the first person I see is Tirinnanzi. "Ah, you're here at last! I was waiting for you . . . there's no one at the control desk. We've got to go ahead with the music but right now the phone calls are coming in . . . can you deal with it all?"

While I sit in front of the desk, my bag still slung over my shoulder, I see him bending over the badly lit table to write the radio news. Three years ago he still had all his hair, now part of his scalp has become completely smooth and reflects the neon lights dotted across the ceiling. What has been happening to him? His gums bleed and he walks as if his feet are hurting.

I answer calls from listeners, I put them in touch with each other. I raise the sound of the music, I lower it. Meanwhile the technician Mario Calzone has arrived. He has an ice-cream in his hand. As he watches me dealing with the control knobs and switches, he shakes his head.

"You're not doing it right, Michela. You've put the speakers on, look!" He laughs, his mouth surrounded by flecks of green ice-cream.

"Instead of criticising why don't you settle in and do it yourself. I've got a lot of work to get on with."

"Just let me finish my ice-cream – you go ahead: the listeners won't notice anything."

I wait till he's finished his ice-cream and washed his sticky hands and at last I'm freed from the control desk.

Tirannanzi comes towards me carrying the pages of the radio news.

"Is it true you're going to do a programme on crimes against women? If you can come round to my place tomorrow, I'll give you some stuff that might be useful."

"Thanks, but couldn't you leave it out for me or else bring it here, isn't that the same?"

"No, it isn't. I want you to see my new place. I've just bought a 'Balletta' painted in 1912, it's lovely."

"What's a Baletta?"

"A little picture by Balla, a delicious painting, would you like to see it?"

"And where's your new place?"

"In Via Merulana, can you come?"

"I don't think I can, Tirinnanzi, I've got so much to do."

I watch him go back to the little table with a sulky look. Perhaps his last girlfriend has ditched him, he must be on his own again. When he looks like that I feel I want to kiss him. He looks like an offended child.

On my table I find a pile of paper which was not there yesterday. It appears that everyone wants to help me with my research into crimes against women: the young actress, Tamara Verde, who comes in now and again to read dramatised stories, has brought me some newspaper cuttings; the director's secretary, Lorenza, has found a book in English about sexual crimes in the archives.

I take a quick look through the press cuttings. I read about a decapitated girl whose head can't be found. And of two sisters drowned in the Lake of Nemi who have taken the secret of their attacker with them. There is the case of a prostitute being hacked to pieces. And of a little girl who disappeared at the entrance to her school and was later found drained of blood in a ditch.

I take the card file and begin to divide up the cases and stick little labels on them. At the first one my hand trembles, but by the tenth I go ahead quite quickly and confidently. Yet a feeling of repugnance lurks in my throat. Why should I be having to deal with these horrors? There is nothing seductive about crime, nothing exciting about the slashing of bodies, only a profound and dismal pain.

And yet the sphinx shows her stone face among the tortured bodies creating the deep and altogether human need to resolve a riddle, to bring our thoughts and suppositions together. There is a psychological pattern that demands explanations, and we find ourselves right in the middle of the labyrinth holding on to the end of the thread, not knowing where we are next going to poke our nose. To whom belongs the potent hand that has ordained a body to be silent? And why does it remain at a distance outside the picture, shut off from conscience like the corpse of a heart inside a living body?

At last the index cards are arranged systematically and everything tells me I shall get used to all these horrors. But can one ever get used to such dreadful and repugnant things without losing something of one's own capacity to feel and to suffer? The bad taste on my tongue is actually telling me no. But the pathetic monotony of these photographs piling up in front of me says "yes". And it is this transition, this crossing from "no" to "yes" which worries me because it happens without giving rise to the painful discrepancy I had imagined.

I lift the phone. I ring Adele Sòfia, the commissioner of police. She answers me in a calm, gentle voice.

"I'm from Radio Italia Viva and I'd like to come and see you,"

"Your director Cusumano has spoken to me about you. Aren't you Michela Canova? Yes, do come, only not today as I'm very busy, but tomorrow would be fine. Is that all right?"

I dial Ludovica Bari's number. I am answered by a tense, apprehensive voice.

"I'm Michela Canova from Radio Italia Viva. Could I come and see you?"

"If it's to talk about my sister Angela, certainly not."

"Well, I actually live in Via Santa Cecilia, at number 22. Your sister's apartment was close to mine, so we met each other."

"Good heavens! You must be Michela, the person who lives opposite, Angela told me about you. Yes, do come soon."

8

In the photographs of her in the newspapers, Ludovica Bari appears small and dark. In fact she is tall, with a long neck, slender arms, fair hair, an impulsive way of walking and a hard face.

She precedes me into the sitting room, stepping lightly over Chinese carpets spread at random on the white tiled floor. Gold-coloured door handles, chandeliers with glass drops, sofas covered in a lovely chintz of blue and violet flowers on a milky white background.

"Would you like a soft drink?" She stretches a thin, bare arm towards a small glass table, uncorks a bottle, pours a reddish liquid into a goblet and offers it to me with a smile.

I notice she has false teeth although she is certainly not yet forty. They are absolutely perfect teeth of gleaming porcelain, just a bit too perfect.

"Can I ask you a question?" she says while she sips the soft drink.

It is as if she wants to reverse our roles so that it is not me interviewing her but her interviewing me.

"Did you ever see a small man, who was always dressed in black and wore ankle boots with high heels, entering or leaving my sister Angela's apartment?"

"I don't remember, wait while I try and think about it." But my memory stays inflexibly blocked and wordless as always happens when I question it point blank.

"Try to remember."

"No, nothing comes to mind, I haven't any idea . . . whenever I saw your sister she was alone, but it's true that my hours were very different from hers. I saw her very little, as a matter of fact."

"Poor Angela, she could never get it right."

Where have I heard this expression? Yes, from the owner of the Mercedes while I was trying to move my car. So Angela, like me, could never get it right? Awkward, slow, blocked? Or simply absent-minded?

"You'll have noticed how fragile she was, how confused and incapable of organising herself. She was always like that, even as a child. Poor Angela, she always got to school late; she used to study but couldn't learn, she got thrown out of class for things she hadn't done, was failed every other year, she was a disaster."

"And you?"

"I was just the opposite, I hardly did any work but I got good reports. They always wanted to make me head student. I did better than the other pupils and every year I got promoted. Yet Angela never bore me a grudge for that; I've never known anyone less competitive than she was. She was such a sweet person, so gentle, so amiable although very insecure. Wait, I'll let you see a photo of her when she was little."

She disappears down the passage and comes back immediately

with a collection of photographs which she spreads out on the sofa beside me.

"Here we are at Fiesole. We used to go there every summer to spend a month with our grandparents. Now my mother lives in the villa ... There's one of me thin as a rake, not that I'm much fatter now, but then I must have been a real fright. And here is Angela, Do you see her hair? She's always been more beautiful and more vulnerable than me ... I don't know why I'm telling you all this, I don't know you, but I remember how Angela talked quite often about you. She admired you. 'She does the kind of work I'd like to do', she often said. And she used to listen to you on the radio, she said your voice 'was like a basket full of snails', she said it just like that ... You must forgive me but I've never heard you on the radio ... perhaps out of some sort of prejudice, I never paid much attention to what Angela said."

I am so astounded that the glass slips out of my hand and spills on to one of the Chinese rugs. I bend down to pick it up, and try to make excuses. She smiles patiently and rushes into the kitchen to get a wet cloth.

I had never for a moment imagined that my neighbour had noticed me or spoken about me to her sister. I never imagined she listened to me on the radio and that she wanted to be doing the same kind of work as I do, or that she could think my voice was "a basket full of snails". Why did she never address a word to me? And why did she lock herself so noisily into her apartment, abandoning me on the landing as if I were an enemy each time we met in the lift?

"Here we are in Vulcano," says Ludovica as she hands me another snapshot, after having thrown away the dirty cloth.

"Do you know Vulcano?"

"No."

"Papa often took us there on holiday. We used to rent a villa there. It overlooked the sea, I still remember it. Here you can't see the villa, but to make up for it you have the dark lava. The island is all black, and the amazing thing is that out of this livid, glassy earth grew wonderful living plants of the most tender green."

With her body stretched out and relaxed, Ludovica Bari wants at all costs to be seen as a nice person. Her soft hair falls over one side of her face. In contrast to her sister who used to wear her hair short, hers is long and snake-like, flowing over her cheeks and her neck. The waves of hair cascade down over her bare arms and her breasts, which are heavy for a body as slight as hers.

"Here we are on bicycles at the Villa Borghese. My father had already died, and my mother had just remarried. Neither of us is looking happy, the point being that we didn't much like our stepfather . . . yes, like in all the best-known fairy stories it's a tradition that stepmothers and stepfathers aren't wanted . . . Although he was kind and caring, he prided himself on being severe with us because he wanted to be a good father. I think Angela was afraid of him, even though she was the favourite daughter, and he showered presents on us all . . . you should have seen Christmas, everything he did . . . Mamma would get up and with her eyes tight shut Glauco would bring her into our room and they'd throw open the shutters and there would be an enormous Christmas tree loaded with parcels of all shapes and sizes. He'd wrapped them up one by one and he always knew what we wanted."

"Is your stepfather still alive?"

"Yes, and in good shape. He left my mother to go and live with a girl thirty years younger."

"When did all this happen?"

"A few years ago. I don't exactly remember when and I'd rather not think about it. Since then my mother has suffered from eczema on her hands and devastating headaches. When they come on she barricades herself in the house with the blinds down. She can't get out of bed and even a glimmer of light makes her scream. Angela used to go and sit with her and hold her hand for hours – her poor hands that are so full of blisters and sores she's had to cover them with gloves . . . I go to see her less because we tend to quarrel. She's such a beautiful woman, she ought to find herself another husband instead of shutting herself up in a room to suffer . . . and I get out of the house as soon as I can so that we don't start quarrelling. I got married at eighteen and I was very naive, I think, a child."

"Your husband is called Mario Torres?"

"No, he came later. I left my husband because I didn't really love him, I realised that after being married for a year; we were too different. Mario Torres is my 'betrothed' as he calls himself, but that's not really a word to describe somebody one loves and with whom one lives without any idea of getting married. Isn't 'partner' too official, and 'lover' too sinful? It seems like a word from the sort of novel my mother reads – and 'comrade' is too political."

"Why don't you consider getting married?"

Now with Ludovica everything seems possible, even such an indiscreet question as this. She is pulling me into her life and I get the impression she wants to talk, she does not even seem to be disturbed by the presence of the tape-recorder which I touch as little as possible so that she is less aware of it.

"Marriage ruins everything," she replies affably. "I tried it once and that was enough. I don't believe I'll ever get married again. A 'betrothed' has something that's attractive; with him I make love, travel, and go to the cinema, but we each have our own home. Don't you think it's better that way?"

"Didn't you say you lived together?"

"Only when we want to – this is understood – but both of us keep our own homes. Do you have a man in your life?"

"Yes."

"And what's he called?"

"Marco."

"And what does he do?"

"Right now he's in Angola working for his newspaper so I don't see him much."

"It's better like that."

Her long tenuous hands are rummaging through the snapshots; she puts some to one side, others she throws into my lap. She seems overwhelmed by a nervous excitement that heightens the colour of her cheeks.

"To give you some idea of my sister's character – after my father died he left us four apartments, two to me and two to her. When she reached the age of twenty she gave one away, I don't know who to. There were times when I thought she was mad. She said having property was nothing but a burden. Here she is in Venice among the pigeons, a photo that's more than just ordinary, though it's quite commonplace in a way, but I do believe this was the happiest time in her life. She'd just got married to a man she was in love with, she thought she was going to America with him. Then it all fell apart and he went off on his own."

"Why?"

"Who knows? Perhaps it was Angela's fault. Men fell head over heels in love with her and then left her. Maybe they were afraid of her or afraid of her secret."

"Her secret? What was that?"

"I don't know. Anyone might feel that Angela had a secret. She gave the impression of a person whose body contained terrible secrets . . . perhaps it was all an act, I don't know. But that was the impression she gave."

I look at her curled up on the sofa as if she were feeling cold.

Her hair falls over her face and her expression grows darker and more intense.

"The trouble was that she got pregnant by that husband. After he left we convinced her she should have an abortion. She didn't want that but she'd stopped eating, her weight had gone down to forty kilos and she'd started drinking. We forced her to have it but it was for her own good. The child would have been born deformed, the doctors said."

Now she looks relaxed again, almost serene. What a strange ability to change her appearance this woman has, I say to myself. One minute she makes herself seem small, dark, almost ugly; at another tall, slender and quite beautiful.

"It was properly done, you see, with an anaesthetic." I understand she is talking of her sister's abortion. "She didn't suffer at all. But then, instead of getting better she got worse, and so we persuaded her to go and see a psychoanalyst. After a month of treatment he said she would recover but that she was quite ill, so she spent a year in a psychiatric clinic. To pay for it she sold the other apartment. So you see my sister was a lovely girl, but incapable, unbalanced, a bit crazy."

"And who might have killed her?" I ask, checking my microphone which is in danger of slipping on to the floor.

"If I knew that I'd feel calmer. Lately my sister had been acting rather mysteriously; it seemed as if she were afraid of us, she didn't tell us who her friends were, who she'd been going out with, how she was living, as if she'd become jealous of her own life, she kept even the silliest things hidden."

"But did she work? How did she live?"

"Yes, she worked from time to time, for short spells. If she happened to get a small part in a film she'd do it, then she'd pack up working for a few months until the money ran out, and then she'd start looking around for work again."

"And did she have any money of her own?"

"She squandered everything she'd inherited, threw it to the winds. My mother gave her money from time to time but never a fixed income. Angela was too proud to ask for money and at times she was reduced to living on potatoes. I begged her to come and see me, there was always food for her here, and money, but she never came . . . I don't think she liked Mario much though he was very fascinated by her. I think she was happier going to my mother at Fiesole. She liked the garden at the villa where she used to play as a child, she would stay for hours and hours lying under a lime tree gazing up at the sky. She used to say how the scent of the limes made her think of paradise."

So Angela Bari loved lime trees and perhaps she wouldn't have chosen to come and live in Via Santa Cecilia if it hadn't been for the two enormous lime trees that grow in the courtyard. On a summer evening their strong sweet scent rises up to the top floor.

"She was unstable, I've told you that, mentally ill. There was a time when she was always vomiting, no one knew what was the matter. She had all kinds of medical investigations but they couldn't find anything wrong. It was her mind that wasn't working right."

She seems animated by a need to demonstrate something.

What does she want me to know or not to know? In a voice of heroic resolution she is putting pressure on me to learn all about her family. Yet while she is showing me the disorder and the failures arising from the breakdown of her small familial world, she is suggesting interpretations and making judgements about it and seems anxious for me to make my own.

"But now it's getting late and I have to go out. Would you like to keep one of the photos?"

"Thank you", I say and reach towards a picture of the two sisters walking together in the street. Ludovica is a little taller than Angela, the sun is in her hair, a proud smile on her thin lips. Angela is softer and plumper with something compliant and despairing in the way she walks. I look at it intently and I think I can distinguish on the feet of the younger sister a pair of blue tennis shoes. Are they the ones I saw behind the entrance to the empty apartment?

9

Going into the lift I meet a man. But weren't the doors shut, so how could he be there standing pressed against the side of the lift as if he were waiting for me? I could still get out, but while I waste time trying to make up my mind, the doors close and the lift begins to ascend. I look at him anxiously; he is quite small and young, although his face looks twisted and wrinkled. He is wearing a black sports jacket and high-heeled boots.

Ludovica's words come to my mind. "Have you ever seen a small man who was always dressed in black and who wore ankle boots with high heels entering or leaving my sister's apartment?" Could it be him? But where is he trying to go? Angela Bari's apartment is shut and locked. The police have put seals on it. My apprehension makes me look at the man again. What does he want from me? What if he is Angela's murderer, is it likely her sister suspected him? Yet it would be stupid for a murderer to show himself so openly. I smile inwardly at my hurried reasoning, and then realise I am merely trying to reassure myself.

The lift indicator continues to light up at each floor but the lift shows no sign of stopping. My anxiety is drying up the saliva in my mouth. Perhaps the best thing would be to talk to him.

"I'm going up to the top floor. Are you?"

"Me too", he says drily.

I notice he has got a Venetian accent. There is something of the perpetual student about him; he is either a student disguised as a villain or a villain disguised as a student.

The lift continues to ascend. I stay close to the alarm switch so I can rush to press it if he shows any sign of moving. But he doesn't move at all. He is looking at me as if he were only half-awake, smiling through closed lips. Perhaps he realises I am scared and is laughing at me. I try to look as self-possessed as I can. I notice his small nervous hands, could they be the hands of a killer? On his little finger a silver ring set with a tiger eye catches my attention. The ring and the hands make me think of a boy from some destitute urban area, brought up with poverty and violence; the look of intelligence in his eyes and the rather snobbish elegance of the way he is dressed make me think of a youth who is rich, spoiled.

At last the lift comes to a halt with a small click and the doors spring open with a hiss. I get out and walk calmly towards my apartment even though my heart is in turmoil. Out of the corner of my eye I see there is no sign of him getting out of the lift. He stays there in front of the open doors and watches me struggling with my keys. Do I open the door or not? Suppose he comes up behind me and tries to follow me in? Will I have time to shut the door before he catches up with me?

But he doesn't seem to be taking any notice of me. He lights a cigarette and throws the spent match on to the floor with a defiant look. While I am inserting the key in the lock and trying to hurry into the apartment, I hear the click of the lift door closing and he is swallowed up together with his boots, his leather jacket and his ring with the tiger's-eye. I breathe a sigh of relief. I go into the apartment and bolt the door. I start preparing a meal. Tonight I have guests and haven't got anything

prepared. It is nearly half-past eight. I decide on spaghetti with
butter and lemon rind; it is so richly flavoured and quick to
prepare, Then I shall serve some ham and melon, and the
cheeses I bought in a hurry this morning on my way to work.

But while I fill a saucepan with water, grate the lemon peel,
open the packet of butter, I can't help thinking of the shifty
expression of the man in black; it continues to go round and
round inside my head.

What was he trying to demonstrate by forcing himself into
the lift with me? Was it a threat, or a warning, or merely some
funny pretence of spying on me, or even a stupid joke?

I must phone Ludovica Bari. It was she who told me about
the man so shouldn't I try to contact her? My hands smeared
with butter, I go to the telephone and dial her number. She
answers immediately, laughing.

"Oh, it's you! We were just talking about you."

"I wanted to tell you that this evening in the lift I saw that
man with the boots and black leather sports jacket."

"He's right here in front of me", she says, sounding amused.

"Do you know him then?"

"I didn't know him at all. Angela spoke to me about him,
that's all. But now I do know him because he's come here to
see me and he's a really nice guy."

"But why on earth did he follow me and then didn't even
get out of the lift? Could you please ask him since he's with
you?" I can hear muttering and then giggling. Ludovica's clear
fresh voice comes back back on the phone.

"He's an odd sort of chap. He only waited for you in the lift
because he wanted to see what you looked like, to know who
you were."

"But why on earth did he want to see me? What's it got to
do with me? And anyway since you say he was looking for me,
why didn't he open his mouth when he found me?"

"He says he hasn't got anything to say."

"But why did he want to see me?" I go on insisting.

More murmuring in a low voice, a sound of giggling, and
then Ludovica's voice saying kindly, "He says he wanted to

come face to face with all the people Angela used to see, myself included."

"Ask him what he thinks about Angela's murder."

"He says he doesn't know," is the laconic reply. "Goodbye, Michela." So the conversation ends.

And I stay there like an idiot without any idea of what to do next and with the feeling that I've just participated in some strange and incomprehensible game.

The door bell rings. The guests have arrived and I have not even laid the table or put the wine to chill or sliced the bread.

10

A pretentious entrance with decorations in terracotta. To the right is an entry phone with golden buttons on the metal plate. I am looking for Adele Sòfia. I find two surnames, Sòfia and Girardengo. Would one be that of the husband? I ring. A faint voice answers, "Fifth floor".

The lift is an antiquated one with a wooden framework and big glass panels that leave the passengers exposed like pigeons in a cage. It slides from one floor to the next beneath the glow of a pale yellow light bulb.

As I open the lift door I meet a woman of middle age; she is thin, dark, and has a welcoming smile. She doesn't seem like the person I met for a brief moment at the radio station.

"I'm looking for Adele Sòfia," I say, "I have an appointment with her."

"Yes, she's here, come in . . . I'm Marta Girardengo, we work together."

She follows me down a passage covered in a lacquer-red moquette. Silently a door opens, Adele Sòfia comes towards me with a kitchen cloth in her hand.

"Excuse me, but I'm dealing with the cooker . . . come in and make yourself comfortable."

I settle myself into a chair of Tyrolean design: inlaid wood with little hearts and stars. The whole of the sitting room is in

Alpine style with furniture of solid wood, antlers hanging on the walls, and a beautiful stove of white and green majolica. Before Adele Sòfia joins me on the sofa, I notice her taking off a large cloth apron. She points to a low divan covered in coarse woollen material.

"Would you prefer the divan?"

"No, I'm fine here."

She sits down in front of me and gives me a friendly smile. I think she must be about forty. She has a sturdy muscular build with something soft and motherly in the way she moves: there is a resolute look in her large bright eyes.

"Have you come for all the data? Your director has spoken to me about it. It's not easy to get precise statistics . . . for instance we don't make distinctions as to sex, crimes against women are seen to be crimes and that's it. I can give you some documentation but more from abroad than from here in Italy. It's really the Americans who have a mania for cataloguing offences according to sex . . . in America they've actually discovered that one of the main causes for violent deaths occurring more frequently in the case of women is to be found in the family: husbands who kill wives, sons who kill mothers. In the case of the 40 per cent of crimes occuring within the family, 72 per cent of the victims are women. I read this only a short while ago . . . and do you know the most curious thing is that there are more whites than blacks, or so they say. But you know how debatable statistics are and how often they can be manipulated."

"Do you know about the case of Angela Bari?"

"I've read something about it in the newspapers. One of my colleagues, detective Lipari, is working on it and the examining magistrate is Boni. But why does this case interest you particularly?"

"Angela Bari lived opposite me in the same apartment building at 22 Via Santa Cecilia."

"And you knew her?"

"Not really, she hadn't been living there for long, less than a year. I saw her only occasionally in the lift."

"Do you suspect anybody?"

"No, not at all."

"Well, then . . ."

I see she is about to get up. Is she wanting to dismiss me? "Would you like to try some *canederli* with a really excellent Reno wine? They're just ready."

"No thanks, I really must get back to the radio station."

"*Canederli* are my speciality. Are you sure you won't try some?"

It is actually lunch-time and no one expects me back before three o'clock. I accept her invitation, I am really hungry and she seems pleased.

She leads the way into a large room that is both a kitchen and a dining room. I notice three places are laid at the table, one for Adele Sòfia, one for Marta Girardengo and one for me, so presumably she had already foreseen I would say "yes".

We sit down. Adele Sòfia serves the *canederli*, which are indeed deliciously flavoured. Out of the oven Marta Girardengo takes a spinach tart covered with melted butter and cheese.

It feels as if I have known them for years. They laugh, eat, pour each other drinks; they are spontaneous and welcoming. Adele Sòfia looks like someone but I can't remember whom. Then, while I split a *canederli* in half, I realise who it is: Gertrude Stein in the portrait by Picasso. The same matronly presence, the same intense hazel eyes, the same abundant mop of hair tied behind her neck in the same easy knot, the same large, clearly defined mouth. The only difference is the tooth band which gives something unexpected and childlike to the maternal dignity of the police commissioner.

"When a murderer isn't found during the first few days, it proves difficult to find them later on," she says with her mouth full.

"How many crimes go unsentenced here in Italy and what do you learn from this?"

"We haven't got precise figures, as I've already said, and they aren't always made known by the police, which is understandable since there's always so much distrust."

"I've heard talk of 40 per cent . . ." Adele Sòfia laughs. Should I be thinking it is higher? She puts another round ball of bread crumbs and smoked ham on my plate, in spite of my gesture of refusal.

"More spinach?"

"Is it true that crimes against women are more often unpunished?"

"Yes, it's true."

"And why is that? Do you mind if I use the tape-recorder?" I ask, positioning my little Sony on the table.

She does not answer yes or no but her voice changes slightly; from sounding conversational, it becomes more explanatory and didactic.

"Because so often they occur in the family," she explains patiently, "and that is a minefield. It is difficult to understand what is going on in the relationships between members of a nuclear family, one gets lost in it and that's a real problem. They all accuse each other in turn and from a legal standpoint it all gets very complicated."

She gets up, goes to fetch a piece of paper and puts it beside my plate.

"Look, here are the crimes committed during the past four weeks. Only two have been accounted for, of the rest we know nothing."

She makes an odd sound like the puff of a punctured balloon and accompanies it with a delicate movement of her hand. I notice a silver ring set with a tiger's-eye on her little finger. I look at her in amazement. Where have I seen exactly the same ring? Yes, of course, on the finger of the man with the ankle boots whom I saw a few days ago in the lift.

Adele Sòfia sees me staring at her ring and slowly twists it round her finger. "This ring was given me by a friend who is now dead," she says, suddenly serious and sad.

"I've seen one exactly the same on the little finger of a man I met," I say and I go on to tell her the story of my encounter in the lift and of what Ludovica had said about him. But it does not seem as if she attaches much importance to it.

"We'll do a check," she says casually.

I go back to the sheet of paper that was put beside me. It is a list of names followed by brief notes.

"Cinzia O., age seven. Found dead with fractured skull in Via Tiburtina. Evidence of sexual interference. Identity of suspect unknown.

"Maria B., age forty-five. Cause of death; strangulation in her house. Identity of suspect unknown.

"Renata M., age twenty-two. Found at Villa Borghese. Cause of death: knife wounds. Identity of suspect unknown.

"Giovannina L., age sixteen. Found at Ostia by road sweepers. Cause of death: bullet in head. Identity of suspect unknown."

I can't manage to eat any more. Adele Sòfia looks at me pityingly.

"You shouldn't let yourself get so upset, or how will you be able to carry out your research?"

I lift a spoonful of spinach tart up to my mouth but my lips stay clenched.

"Keeping one's distance from crimes doesn't mean that they stop being committed," she states sagely, "it's as well to know that in a city like Rome, a violent crime takes place almost every day. If we are able to do something, that's fine, but otherwise we have to be patient. It's important to recognise that we live in a brutal city, above all for anyone who has not got the *conquibus*."

That word rouses me from the state of lethargy into which I had collapsed. *Conquibus*? It's so long since I last heard the word. When I was at high school my teacher of Italian often used it. She would ask me whether I ever found the occasion or the courage to make use of it myself. And today this police commissioner who looks like Gertrude Stein pronounces it during lunch in front of a spinach tart, while talking about unpunished crimes, using the word *conquibus* quite naturally as if it were part of everyday language.

"But does it never happen that years later someone will confess to the crime they've committed?"

"It's extremely rare. It happens more frequently that a fellow prisoner or a previous accomplice decides to denounce a former friend. This can happen, although not very often . . . But you strike me as being much too sensitive to start getting involved in all this. Why don't you drop it?"

"I'm thinking the same," I reply and I am being sincere. The *canederli* are stuck half way to my stomach and I am unable either to bring them up or swallow them down.

I see she is laughing at me, although not in an unkind way, but as one laughs at someone who is being rather clumsy and awkward when they stumble across one's feet.

"I'll help you, if you wish," she says, becoming serious. "But do think it over before you take on such thankless work. Let me know." This time she is dismissing me with a quick but kindly gesture, without offering me any coffee.

"In a quarter of an hour they'll be waiting for me at the office, it's getting late," she says. "Did you like the *canederli*? They remind me of the time I spent in Bolzano. Finish up your wine, it'll do you good."

While she quickly clears the table, I get to my feet and gulp down the sparkling white wine. At last it seems as if I can start to digest my meal.

11

Tonight I am all alone in front of the control desk. The technician has bronchitis and his replacement has telephoned to say he is unable to come because his wife is having labour pains. The director made a big scene over "all these lay-abouts who never want to lift a finger", but he's been careful not to say it to them because he knows that good technicians are rare, cost a lot and are hard to replace, whereas there is no shortage of journalists. And anyway in the evening the control desk is often inadequately staffed.

The late night broadcast is entitled "Talking to You", at least this is how it is described in the weekly listings: the listener telephones, and with the help of Professor Baldi who is sitting comfortably at home, we listen and give advice in response to the anguished voices calling Radio Italia Viva. Few do it for a laugh, most call out of desperation and seem on the point of collapse beneath their burden of loneliness and distress.

"My wife has left me and I can't sleep," says one caller in a hoarse voice.

"You haven't told us your name."

"Giovanni, I'm called Giovanni . . . I've tried drinking brandy, I've tried hot baths, I've tried walking up and down, I've tried doing exercises, but nothing helps. I just can't get to sleep."

"Why did your wife leave you?"

"I don't know . . . that's the trouble, I don't know. One evening she just went out and didn't come back. Then she sent word through a cousin of hers that she wanted her pyjamas. Not her pictures, not her clothes or any of her own things, not even the bits of jewellery she had, no, only her pyjamas. As if to say 'I'm not sleeping with you any more'."

"My dear Giovanni," I hear the professor's voice coming on the line, but it suddenly becomes hoarse and muffled. What can be happening? I try to increase the volume but all I can hear is a sound of crackling. Another disaster for Radio Italia Viva's equipment, which was bought second-hand from the government radio station. "She went off without saying a word . . . surely she ought to give me some sort of explanation . . . I got in touch with her through her cousin and do you know what she had to say? 'Just send me my pyjamas and then we'll talk.' What do you think, will she ever come back?"

"Have you asked yourself what the real reason for your wife leaving you might be?"

I have been able to make Professor Baldi's voice a bit clearer but I can't manage to cut out the background noise.

"There was no reason, Professor, I've told you, my wife went off and now all she wants is her pyjamas."

I am just about to increase the sound of the professor's voice and decrease the listener's when I hear him starting to cough. I turn up the background music to cover the explosions coming down the microphone. I try to get the listener to go on talking, but he is like a mule, he sticks obstinately to the story of the pyjamas and is quite unable to say anything else.

Meanwhile Professor Baldi, after two bouts of violent coughing, comes back to speak quietly into the receiver.

"Dear Giovanni, you must be honest and ask yourself whether you might be in any way responsible for this . . ."

I turn the music right down, I try to lighten the voice of the professor as much as possible at the risk of distorting the voice of the listener. I keep my finger on the sound mixer, trying not to upset the balance of sound.

"I want to know from all of you, from Professor Baldi who is an authority on the psyche, and from Signora Canova who is a journalist in contact with all the bad problems in the world, whether every marriage is fated to break down, to crumble, to go to ruin . . . because around me all I can see are marriages collapsing . . . Until yesterday I thought that my marriage might hold out, but instead my wife sends her cousin to say she wants to see her pyjamas again! So what is the meaning of that?"

"Signor Giovanni, you have already told me . . . but either I heard wrong or you said 'my marriage'?"

"Yes, Professor Baldi, I said that. And why not?"

"There lies the mistake, my dear Giovanni, and this could be why your wife went off. If you had said 'our marriage' things might have been different, but to say 'my marriage' means that in your head you were thinking: my wife, my house, my happiness, my future, my sleep etc. And so what has happened is that her marriage has been quite different from yours. Such expressions, dear Giovanni, demonstrate a profound disregard for the reasons your wife might have . . . are you still there? I don't hear you any more." He comes back to me and says "That idiot has been cut off! Give me the next caller."

I hope Giovanni does not hear this as he was still on line. I switch off the connection and the listener's voice fades away to nothing, I turn on the background music and I ask Professor Baldi whether he wants another telephone call immediately, or whether he would rather have some respite. I hear him sneezing noisily. Suddenly a child's voice pops up saying "Bless you!". But where on earth did that voice come from? I do not know if Professor Baldi has any children; it must be a listener who has got in on the quiet. I hear Professor Baldi coughing again, I shut off the speaker and turn up the music.

Now I come to think about it, this dry irritable cough is always with him. Even the technicians have to work miracles to stop it being heard over the microphone.

Professor Baldi does not seem like a happy man, yet he is willing to give advice about unhappiness. I have never actually met him, I only know his voice on the telephone, sounding crackly when mechanically amplified. Who knows whether he is tall, short, dark or fair? I do not know anything about him but I feel that I know him well because his voice exposes him as if he were standing naked at the end of the telephone line; a person who is calm, kindly and somewhat indolent. His intelligence is slow-moving with a tendency to be cynical and over-critical, and yet with a good analytical capacity. But he has an undoubted hold over his listeners because so many people are always ringing him up. His secret is to continue a challenging severity with a material soft-heartedness.

What I like most about him is an unexpected little laugh that involuntarily pops out from time to time like the sudden jump of a happy child. This clashes with his usual smooth, reasonable voice used to giving advice, imparting lessons, delivering formulas, making diagnoses at a distance.

"This is Gabriella," says a shrill voice down the phone.

"How old are you, dear Gabriella?"

His use of "dear" to everyone puts me off. I told him so once but he has never taken any notice.

"The trouble, Professor, is that I'm jealous, so jealous that it's ruining my life."

She must be young, her voice sounds clear and lively.

"Do you remember that character of Pirandello's who sealed the soles of his wife's shoes with glue so she couldn't go out? Well, I'm like that, obsessed with doubts, only I can't stop my husband from going out. But I watch him all the time, sometimes I even follow him down the street. I spy on him, I stick my hand into his pockets, I go through his wallet and once I found a condom, and you see he doesn't use them with me."

"You are clearly suffering from an obsession, dear Rosanna."

"Gabriella, Professor, Gabriella."

"Ah yes, Gabriella, excuse me. Jealousy is a confession of weakness. You are afraid of losing control of your husband because that control is the only thing which enables you to feel powerful. To lose control is to lose your power. But to focus power entirely on another person is like a population putting everything into a system of monoculture . . . it is asking for catastrophe. You will be enslaved to one single market, and to famine as well."

Where does he find such comparisons I ask, and I laugh to myself at the risk he is taking. I can't imagine what poor Gabriella is making of it.

"Instead of poking around in your husband's wallet, try to do something you can enjoy, take up some activity he isn't involved in, leave him in peace and think of something else."

"That's just what my confessor says."

A moment of silence. The professor is not too happy at being compared with a priest.

"And then you know how jealousy can act like a suggestion, as if you were saying to the loved one 'Betray me'. He will end by doing that even though he may not want to, in order to satisfy your mania for investigation. I don't suppose your confessor will tell you this!"

"But Professor Baldi, what am I to do so that I can think of something else when I can only think of him?"

I hear the professor yawning carelessly. I lower the sound, I step in to announce that the radio news will follow shortly. The professor seems relieved, he did not know how to cope with this young woman and her jealousy. He has no curiosity about the stories people tell him.

I put Billie Holiday on the turntable. This is against the orders of the director who has insisted on songs from this week's Top Ten, but at this time of night I hope he isn't listening. "You must remember that our station keeps gaining listeners because we always provide the top ten." He has told me this so many times.

I have brought the Billie Holiday record from home; the radio archives are full of rubbish and there are no classics.

Probably at this hour the director is having dinner with a new flame, even though once or twice I've seen him arrive during a broadcast at two in the morning with his long blond hair and his beautiful butterfly hands opening out like fans ready to seduce or reproach.

I hear the deep, aching voice of Billie Holiday brushing away from my memory the horrors of those tortured bodies which have obsessed my mind all day. Yet her body was also torn apart.

Meanwhile my eyes are drawn to the reflection of the neon lights on Tirinnanzi's naked scalp. He gives me a sign to say he is ready to read the news. I turn the volume down slowly. It upsets me to have to interrupt the soft, sad monologue. When the seconds count reaches three minutes I give Tirinnanzi the signal to start off with the news.

He has a mellow voice, persuasive, full of nuances even if a little affected. Listening to him, one imagines him to be the most fascinating man in the world. But to see him makes one feel sad; his white face, the way his hands look drained of blood, his bare, swollen ankles which look as if they have been boiled before being put into shoes.

I listen to the news programme without paying much attention, waiting till it comes to the local news: the case of Angela Bari. Yesterday in Genoa the police investigating the case interrogated the victim's "fiancé" Giulio Carlini. It appears that his alibi is not as secure as it seemed a few days ago. The man has lied on several fronts, he had also hidden the fact that he was having a relationship with another woman in Genoa. So that is that. But what a news bulletin, so confusing and incomplete. I should go and see what the press agency has written. At this time of night they allow themselves a freedom which is not permissible during the day. At this time most listeners are presumed to be asleep and those that are listening aren't paying much attention. I imagine Tirinnanzi writing the news seated at his table thinking of other things, feeling half dead from fatigue and boredom.

I would like to talk to this Carlini, but who knows if I shall be able to track him down. Meanwhile I plug in the news signature tune. I take Tirinnanzi off the air and put on some other music, Maria Monti this time, another singer the director would not approve of. Then I dial Professor Baldi's number and he replies, coughing. He sounds annoyed, sleepy and is undoubtedly thinking that considering what he earns, he might just as well give up doing this work. But in fact it isn't the salary that counts; it is the popularity radio gives that gratifies him: even though ours is a private radio station, it has fifty thousand listeners a night who make the professor known. It also brings clients to his consulting room and bolsters his professional prestige.

The telephone rings. I answer, put the voice into the sound mixer and make sure that Professor Baldi can hear it.

"Hullo, this is Radio Italia Viva. Who is speaking?"

"I'm Sabrina. I would like to talk to Professor Baldi."

"This is Professor Baldi speaking. What is your problem, Sabrina?"

A fit of coughing, the voice emerges hoarse and gritty. How can I fade out the sound without losing its strength? If only the refresher course had been more about technique and less about theory.

"Hullo, excuse me, Professor, but I wanted to say something about Angela Bari, the murdered girl they talked about on the news a short time ago."

"Tell me, my dear Sabrina." It is obvious he's bored; the Bari case does not mean anything to him, he feels sleepy and is not hiding it. I am all ears.

"I knew the woman, a year ago, in the house of a friend. Well . . . in short I'd better tell you straight, I am a prostitute."

Professor Baldi gives no sign of being on the line, perhaps he has fallen asleep. I intrude into the conversation and try to get her to tell me more.

"What did you want to tell us about Angela Bari? Why did you phone us?" I tell myself I must not scare her or ask useless questions. I must try to keep her on the line and get her to give me her phone number.

"I think she worked as a prostitute as well."

"Are you sure of this or might you have imagined it?"

"I can imagine it, that's not difficult. But my boyfriend . . . that's to say my man was behind her and he wouldn't back anyone who wasn't earning something for him."

"So you are jealous too?" The voice of Professor Baldi erupts with crackling sounds from the depths of the control desk. I make it louder, adjust it, get it in balance; I am doing my duty even if I don't want to. There is still that hollow cough and then a clicking sound as if he were playing with his tongue against his palate. "Jealousy, my dear Sabrina, is an illicit appropriation of the destiny of another person . . ." Now he is ruining everything; what has jealousy got to do with this story of prostitution? I take a decision to put music between him and the girl. Then I pick up the phone again and on a separate line ask her for her home number.

"Why?" she asks surprised.

"Because I want to talk to you; I'm a friend of Angela's and there's something I want to ask you."

"Okay," she says and although rather hesitant, she articulates the number in a low voice, "five five eight one one six three. When will you call me?"

"Tomorrow, is that all right?"

"Hullo, hullo," I hear the professor's voice, insistent and annoyed, advancing through the sound waves of the music.

"Turn the music down, Miss Canova, I can't hear a thing." And as soon as I release the microphone he goes on undaunted.

"Dear Sabrina, if you are still listening to me, I have to say to you what I have already said to our dear friend Mariella, no, I mean Gabriella, that jealousy has no connection with the feeling of love but sanctions the possessiveness that is under discussion."

It is obvious that Professor Baldi knows about the mechanics of jealousy and has given it thought. In his enthusiasm his voice becomes less pinched and weak; it has a touch of passion which does not seem to belong to it. I listen to him with admiration.

Another telephone call comes in. I put the voice into the mixer and tune in the professor. All of a sudden I feel so tired that my fingers fall asleep on the keys.

I look at the time, it is almost time for the night shift to end. I get the music ready, it will carry on without me till six-thirty in the morning.

I put on my shoes, which I had taken off because of the

heat; they were underneath the desk. I stuff the tapes I brought from home into my shoulder bag and I get ready to turn off the light after having said good-night to the listeners and to Professor Baldi. Tirinnanzi must have already gone home, I see his desk is empty. On it a note written in red ink, "Goodbye, Michela, see you tomorrow."

12

"Did you ever see a small man here who was dressed in black and wearing high-heeled ankle boots?"

Stefana lifts her eyes, eyes which seem to find it difficult to support two heavy eyelids fringed with dark eyelashes; in the quivering shadow the white of the cornea sparkles.

"Did you ever see him?" she says, turning to her husband.

He thinks about it and then shakes his head. But I know how vague Giovanni can be; he never remembers who has come by and who hasn't. His mother, here on a visit from far-away Calabria, looks at me suspiciously. Her skin is studded with freckles, her two eyes are set close together in a furrow and her curved mouth is like that of a fish.

Stefana has told me more than once that her mother-in-law keeps a butcher's shop. When she comes to see her son in Rome she carries two large parcels of meat on her back, and then for several days strong smells of roast meat, boiled meat, and meat rissoles in sauce permeate the stairs.

Looking sidelong past my head with a surly glance, she says, "I have seen him."

"But mother, you're never here, how can you have seen him?"

The son, who has been a university student, is a little ashamed of this mother up from the country who goes around in dirty clothes stained with blood from meat carcases and is in the habit of heaving a quarter side of beef on to one shoulder as she hurries to hang it up in the shop.

"I saw him," she insists and I immediately draw closer to

hear more. I lean towards her and breathe in the smell of roast meat that rises from her neck.

"Did you see him when you arrived and your son met you or later than that?"

"Who knows? But I saw him."

"A small chap, rather pale, and always wearing black?"

"I don't remember."

"But, mother, if you don't remember, how can you say you saw him?"

"Was he short or tall?" I ask.

"No, short."

"Mother, you're mixing him up with someone else . . . I've never seen anyone like that."

"Giovanni, a month ago you asked me three times if I knew the woman who was coming up to see me and she was my mother!"

"Oh, there's so many people in this building, there are ninety apartments and they're always changing, how can I remember?"

"Your mother only comes here occasionally but she strikes me as being a reliable observer."

"Did you really see this fellow, mother, yes or no?"

"I saw him."

"This time or another?"

"Another."

"And when was it?"

"Who knows?"

"I remember," says Stefana and she smiles, happy to be of use to me.

"Another time . . . let's see . . . it was in May, yes, at the end of May, now we're in July. It was almost two months ago."

"And what has this fellow done?"

"But did he say anything to you, mother?" Giovanni asks insistently, and then he explains. "Sometimes when my mother is here she settles herself in the porter's lodge while I go out to do some errands and Stefana stays down below with the child."

"He didn't say anything to me."

"What did he do, mother?"

"He went to the lift."

"And did you ask him where he was going?"

"How would I know, he could have been from here."

"Was he wearing a silver ring with a tiger's-eye?"

"No, no animals."

I can't get her to remember any more. Stefana and Giovanni do their utmost but the woman refuses to respond.

From a cupboard Stefana takes out a hard sweet made with figs and ground almonds mixed with honey. "My mother-in-law brought this. Would you like some?" I try a small piece; it is too sweet but nevertheless I eat it to please her. Meanwhile Giovanni pours some wine, fragrant with the scent of pine, into a mauve crystal glass.

"She was such a nice girl."

"Angela Bari?"

"Yes, Angela Bari. Do you know that every time she came back from being away she used to bring a present for Berengario?"

Who is Berengario? I think for a moment and then I remember that it is the rather unfortunate name they decided to give their son in honour of his father's graduate thesis.

Stefana was also at university in Reggio. And there they knew each other and loved each other and decided to have a child. Then the absolute impossibility for him of getting work, together with her pregnancy, drove them to Rome where the only job they have been able to find has been in the porter's lodge at Via Santa Cecilia with ninety apartments to look after, three flights of stairs to clean and the courtyard to keep in order. They are here, as they are always saying, while waiting for a better job.

"What sort of presents did she bring Berengario?"

"Well, a little blue plush kitten, a Pinocchio made of lacquered wood, a box of coloured pencils. From Sweden she brought a little spinning top that plays a tune as it spins round – do you want to see it? Berengario doesn't play with it any more but it must be in the box with the Christmas things."

She comes back in a moment clutching a small metal top decorated with a design of red and yellow diamond shapes. As it spins, the toy gives out a cascade of high notes, almost like a

Clementi sonata. "You can keep it if you like," she says kindly. "Berengario has gone on to playing with footballs by now."

"Thank you," I say. "Did Angela Bari come down to see you often?"

"Not really, she'd come occasionally for a cup of coffee. She used to say that Stefana made the best coffee in the world. She'd sit where my mother's sitting now, she'd have some coffee and then she'd start singing."

"She used to sing?"

"Yes, she liked singing."

"What sort of songs?"

"'*L'amore mio lontano*', for instance, do you know it? Or '*Di sera, l'amore si fa nero nero nero*'. Do you remember that?"

"Always songs about love?"

"So it seemed."

"Then she'd get up, she'd look at herself in the mirror, that one over there, and she'd say, 'Stefana, how do I look in this skirt?' I'd say to her 'It's fine, Miss Angela, it's lovely.' Actually she was so beautiful, she looked like a film star but it was as if she didn't know that. She was so full of fears, of doubts, she felt she was ugly and that no one liked her."

"Did she used to say that?"

"Yes, she did. She'd say, 'Stefana, what can I do about these swollen ankles?' but they weren't swollen at all, or 'Stefana, what can I do about these two wrinkles on my forehead, do they really make me look old?' 'I can't see any!' I used to say, but she'd be really worried."

Suddenly the family's attention is captured, assaulted by the television screen where a girl in red pants and green pompons suspended from her bra, is writing lines from a well-known song on a blackboard. "Ladies and gentlemen, whoever guesses this line wins three million, three million, three!" At the word "million", she wriggles her hips and the pompons on her bra start to swing jubilantly.

The family are thrown into turmoil all at once, trying to guess the missing words. As if to excuse herself, Stefana says to me "I know it's a scam, but three million would be useful!"

1 3

When I get back from work I am so tired that I haven't the least desire to eat. A few days ago I filled up the fridge and everything is still there wrapped up; the bunch of asparagus tied with blue elastic, the little polystyrene tray with four tomatoes of a rather unappetising colour, eggs inside the box of transparent plastic, the milk carton with a broken off corner. I had let myself be tempted by the supermarket which is open on Sunday.

I pick up the carton of milk and sniff it. It smells sour. I try to pour it into a cup but nothing comes out; the milk has curdled and transformed into a solid mass. I empty it down the sink.

I do not feel like cooking. I decide to make myself a cup of tea but what if it stops me from sleeping? A lime flower tisane would be best. I put the water on to boil, then I think I hear the telephone ringing. I go and see but I am mistaken, it is ringing in the apartment opposite. But who would be calling the home of a dead person?

It is four days since Marco telephoned from Angola. He has always rung me every day from wherever he might be. There is no sign of him on the answering machine either, only the voice of Adele Sòfia telling me she has some more information for my programme, and the voice of my mother who as usual is worried about me doing too much. Ever since my father's death from a heart attack, she keeps her eye on me. Her anxiety is that he died from overwork and that I might be following in his footsteps.

But why doesn't Marco telephone? I take a sheet of paper just as I do at the radio station and write down: Marco has not telephoned; possible reasons for this. 1) He's in a place where there aren't any phones. But there is always a public telephone or a post office where he could send me a telegram as he has done before on other occasions. 2) He has had an accident and is in hospital; but in that case he would have got someone to

phone me. 3) He has met another woman and does not want
to tell me about it. But if this were the case it would be like
him still to ring me. 4) He simply has not wanted to phone;
but then why was it that the last time I heard from him, he
seemed so affectionate, so tender and kept on saying "I love
you"? Is this another mystery to be solved?

I could dial the number of Sabrina, the girl who rang the
radio station wanting to talk about Angela Bari. But a prostitute
could still be out working. Or might she be sleeping? Or she
might not be on her own, she could even be with the man
she accused of "being behind" Angela Bari.

I realise I am walking round and round the telephone looking
for a pretext to ring someone up and listen to a voice. I am
eager for voices whether they are soft or loud, monotonous or
lively. I love them for their extraordinary capacity to become
embodied. I can fall in love with a voice before falling in love
with a person. Perhaps that is why I work on the radio, or is it
that such work enables me to give physical form to a voice and
listen to it with casual concentration?

Why hasn't Marco given me his phone number in Angola?
I've asked him for it several times but he always finds one excuse
after another not to give it to me. But why? It seems that right
now the world is presenting itself to me only in the form of
guesses and enigmatic riddles.

Meanwhile the bed is murmuring something to me; it has a
low choking voice and seems to be saying, "Give me your
bones", but I am not certain of this. Even the saucepan on the
stove has begun to talk, in fact to sing, just like Stefana said
Angela Bari did when she visited them. Both voices are joined
by the spinning top which I'm turning in front of me on the
table; it makes a rhythmical piping sound as if it were wanting
to hypnotise me.

At this time of night objects become provocative: they
chatter, sing and vociferate. Where did I find this word
"vociferate"? Yes, in a story by Matilde Serao; I had to adapt it
for broadcasting in a series entitled "Midnight Stories".

Matilde Serao says of a poverty stricken mother that she
vociferates all day long and uses the word to describe how

she taught in a class of impoverished and needy children. I used to think that the word "vociferate" meant a voice scattering words around, gossiping, "people say that . . .". But I like the way Matilde Serao uses it and one day I shall do that on the radio; as I say this to myself I smile at my pedantry over words. Speaking on the radio one either uses language in a rough and careless way, or one begins to analyse a word, to weigh it, to turn it around, repeating to oneself the history of its origin and use.

While I am thinking about the word "vociferate" a shadow comes close to the bed. I cannot open my eyes; could it still be my father? Without opening my lips I say, "Papa, what are you doing at this hour?" But he does not answer and I am no longer sure whether it is him or not; if only I could manage to open my eyes.

I wake up with a dry mouth; my heart is pounding. There are noises coming from Angela Bari's apartment. I get out of bed and as I put my feet on the carpet I realise that I had lain down fully dressed.

I go to the front door, I put my eye against the peep-hole but the passage is clear and empty, the door of the apartment opposite is shut and sealed with strips of paper stuck round the door. I go back to my bedroom. But the noise is still there, a series of small thuds like a bird that has got shut in and is hitting out against the windows and the walls. I think I must talk to Stefana about it; it could be a bat or a swallow that has come in through a window not properly shut. And then I realise that I am talking nonsense because the entire apartment has been sealed and nothing is open.

I remember how when I was a child a kindly nun at my boarding school convinced me that when people die their souls come out of their bodies like doves and fly up to the heavens beating their wings. And in my drowsy state I can hear Sister Esterina's voice saying, "It's the soul of Angela Bari that isn't at peace, the poor little dove. Who knows how much she's suffering because she can't find an open window she can fly through to where Christ awaits her . . . Go and free that poor little dove, if you don't you'll be guilty in the eyes of God; go quickly, run!"

I get up with an effort, my eyes half-open. I go out on to the roof terrace and without thinking what I am doing I climb over the plate glass that divides the two terraces. I force open the window and go into the dark room. But I don't find a dove, only a pair of blue tennis shoes with white laces rolled neatly round the top. I tell myself that here is an explanation of the mysterious noise. It was not the soul of Angela Bari, but the tennis shoes tip-tapping along the length of the walls and the door as they search for a way out.

The telephone rings; it makes me jump. I am still asleep, fully clothed; the shutters overlooking the terrace are open and are banging rhythmically.

"Is that you, Michela, what on earth are you up to? I've been waiting for you for over half an hour. I'm alone at the control desk. Mario hasn't turned up and the director is beside himself with rage." Tirinnanzi's mellifluous voice brings me back to all the shocks and stresses of an entirely new day.

But what is the time? It is already nine o'clock and I am still lying here half-asleep, dreaming of getting up.

"I'll come immediately," I say but Tirinnanzi has already rung off. I get out of bed, I slip on my shoes, I wash my face and go out.

14

"Can we meet at Tiburtina Station at half-past ten?"

"In the morning?"

"No, the evening, Is that all right?"

"Yes, fine."

This is the time and place Sabrina has given me on the phone. But why Tiburtina Station? I guess she must work around there.

"In what part of the station?" I ask.

"You can wait for me in the second-class waiting room."

So here I am driving along the Viale Regina Margherita, the Piazza Galeno, Via Morgagni, Piazza Salerno. I go on a little further to pass alongside the Verano cemetery where my father is buried. It is a long time since I went to visit him there and today I have not got the time, and anyway it is closed at night.

It was winter the last time I visited it and the days were short. At five in the afternoon in the fading daylight one could see the red lamps that had been lit in front of each burial recess. "A real display of red lights", I found myself thinking, but isn't it an obscene perversion to spy on a decomposing body lying just the other side of those thin walls? It only happens because of the remote possibility that one day the trumpets of the Last Judgment will sound the call and the dead will rise from their graves happy to walk towards the gardens of paradise.

Surely cremations are better, the way they do them in India? A litter carried by the relatives, the corpse swathed in white bandages, a pyre of scented wood, a quick blaze, the crackling of branches, coils of smoke rising to the sky. In a quarter of an hour it is all over; pious hands gather up the ashes and scatter them into the river Ganges.

When my father died, I suggested he should be cremated but all the family were against it. "You want to put him in an oven like the Jews were in Dachau?" said Aunt Gina to me. She was very shocked. "The Church says the body must remain whole until the Day of Judgment," she added with conviction. It counted for nothing that I had explained to her the process of decomposition once the heart has stopped.

At last I have reached the big piazza in front of the station. I look for a place to park and I find one immediately, beneath the fly-over. Luckily at this hour there are hardly any other cars around. But how am I going to recognise Sabrina? I have not the least idea what she looks like and I never even asked her what colour she would be wearing.

I go into the second-class waiting room, as instructed. Three passengers are there, waiting for the night train to Milan. On the other side a bloated and derelict looking tramp is asleep, her head leaning against the wall, her dirty bare feet stretched out along the top of a cardboard box. As I come in she wearily lifts her eyelids and fixes me with two shrewd, enquiring eyes. Her muscular arms, smeared with black, emerge out of the sleeves of a circus jacket strewn with sequins.

A short while later an even dirtier male tramp arrives carrying a full bottle of wine. "Look what I've found in the rubbish bin," he says giving a kick to the cardboard box. He radiates such a triumphant and jubilant expression that I am unable to keep back a sympathetic smile. He immediately offers me a drink from the bottle after having drunk some himself and cleaned the top with his sleeve. I refuse, saying that I don't drink, and I thank him but out of spite he spills the wine over my shoes.

I have the feeling that I am being watched. I look around me but I don't see anyone apart from the tramps and the three drowsy passengers waiting for the Milan train. There is no sign of the transport police. But behind the window of the ticket office there is a man in uniform counting up money. It is already half-past ten and there is no sign of Sabrina. What am I to do? Then, just as I am about to get up, I see a small, sturdy woman coming in. She is wearing a short, bright green skirt and she comes towards me. It must be her. She smiles at me and says "Are you Michela Canova?"

The tramp, staggering and swaying, offers the newcomer a drink but she gives him a withering look as if she knows him and is telling him not to show his usual familiarity.

"Let's go," she says and sets off purposefully along the platform. She walks quickly, dancing on her high red heels. Her reddish hair shines and her short, pleated skirt flaps round her knees at every step.

We cross the platform and then follow the railway track, in the dark, clambering over piles of steel girders, bits of iron, lengths of cement. If anybody saw me they would think me mad, yet I am not afraid. I am following her as if I were still in the dream I had last night, among the unseen, unremembered shadows of my boarding school.

All of a sudden I see her stop in front of an ochre hut. In front of it, beneath a roof trellis held up by iron posts, is a small

square of cement slabs; on it are some plastic chairs and a
small table lit by a dim bulb buzzing with flies and mosquitoes.

"My own private bar," says Sabrina as she sits down lifting
her little green skirt over her muscular, suntanned legs. She
notices that I am looking uncertainly at the red plastic seat
covered in dead flies and she quickly cleans it with the bottom
of her skirt. Then out of a basket she brings a bottle of beer
and two glasses. She fills them both and hands me one. "*Salute!*"
she says, gulping down the cold, frothy beer.

The evening is warm, from the trellis comes a faint smell of
vine leaves. She seems friendly; what more could I want?

Meanwhile I look at her. She is petite and dark with regular
features, small and wrinkled. There is something rather affected
about her tired smile but her manner is straightforward and
generous. As a girl she must have been beautiful, now it is as if
she has just come through a long, devastating illness: an
ingenuous and lively face on an agile body able both to defend
and attack.

"Why do you want to know about Angela?" she asks me
crossing her legs and dangling a sandal with a high red heel.

"Because she was my neighbour, I knew her."

"I said nothing to the police and I shall say nothing here."

"I'm not the police."

"I know that, looking at you. You're from the radio," she
laughs. "I know you and I know your fiancé." She has a throaty
laugh and gurgles like a child.

"My fiancé?" I say in amazement, but I guess she is having
me on. "Didn't you say that Angela was involved with your
man?"

"Yes, that's how it was."

"And what was his name?"

"Don't ask me for any names," and she makes a threatening
gesture, a threat that seems too much of a pretence to make
me feel afraid.

"You said Angela was a prostitute."

"That's true, but not on the street like me; she used luxury
hotels with men who paid her a lot of money."

"Did your boyfriend get her clients?"

"I don't know, maybe. If he knew I was talking to you, he'd kill me."

"So why did you agree to see me?"

"I hated that girl Angela, I wanted her dead, but then when she really was dead, I was very upset. Knowing her was like knowing a child, one couldn't dislike her. It didn't take much for us to phone each other behind Nando's back." She stops, looking scared and puts her hand over her mouth. "Look, I've said his name, forget it!"

"And Nando threatened her?"

"No, Nando liked her. He did whatever she said. A five star hotel, yes, I'll find it for you. Flowers in your room, yes, I'll see you get them. He gave her so many flowers, lots and lots. For her he spent as much as I earn on the streets – do you understand?"

"Could he have killed her?"

"Nando?" she starts to laugh with a throaty chuckle, hoarse, like a frog in the moonlight. "Nando is a gentleman, he wouldn't dirty his hands."

"But he lives off your selling yourself."

"No, lady, he lives off dreams, you don't know him, he's an odd sort . . . money doesn't interest him, he earns it and then throws it away . . ."

"Why don't you introduce me to him?"

"He's too canny, he wouldn't let himself get caught by a little nobody like you!"

"But I don't want to catch him, I just want to talk to him."

"He's not the talking kind, not him. He's never talked to me, he only ever talked to Angela, with her he never stopped talking."

"And where does this Nando live, supposing I went to see him?"

"I'm certainly not a spy, I'm not that. And anyway he's always on the move. He's got another girl he protects around Ponte Milvo, she's a nothing like me."

"Sabrina, would you mind if I recorded your voice for the radio?" I ask, getting out my little Sony.

"Do you like the name Sabrina? He gave it to me, it isn't

my real name but I shan't tell you that. And then won't my voice be heard on the radio?"

"I'm doing a programme on Angela Bari and other women who've died like she did. Could you say something about Angela, seeing you knew her?"

"What do you want to know? I've already told you she was like a child . . . an obstinate child saying 'I want this and I want that . . .' She was attractive to men, made them go on turning their heads round and round; the more they turned, the happier she was. They all fell for her because she was a darling. Not beautiful, even Nando used to say 'not a good looker, she doesn't even know how to move, but I can fancy her . . .' She knew what to do with men but not how to earn money, in that whole area she was really dumb, completely useless, she'd no idea of business."

"But then why did she go and sell herself?"

"For money, of course. For what other reason would we sell ourselves? They're all good at getting their hands on you, kissing you, chatting you up, and then of course leaving you pregnant. You need help to get what you are owed, you're doing a job, aren't you, and they should have to pay."

"Did you know the man Giulio Carlini?"

"I knew he took money and didn't give any back, one of those who likes to dress well, always in fancy blue suits and English shoes at three hundred thousand lire a pair, but where did he find the cash to buy all those fancy things?"

"And Angela liked him? Did she ever talk to you about him?"

"She didn't talk about him, I don't think so, anyway not with me."

"Who did she talk about with you?"

"About Nando."

"Was she in love with him?"

"I don't know. I've told you she was a bit odd. I didn't understand much about what she was thinking but she often used to talk about Nando as if she really felt something for him."

"What used she to say about him?"

"That he was beautiful . . . she said it just like that."

I look at her in astonishment. She picks up my surprise and laughs. If I shut my eyes it is as if I were back in the country round Ciociaria: it is the only place I have heard frogs the size of melons croaking like that.

"Do you remember if Angela ever told you she was afraid of Nando?"

"Angela was afraid of everything; she was always running away but trusted whomever she was with. Is it true she had a rich mother?"

"I think so."

"It's strange, I think Nando was really mad about her but it wasn't for that he gave up on me and another girl called Maria . . . in fact I know that he got going with a third, Alessia, who's very young, and on drugs. He has to have so much money because he goes through it, gives it all away. I've never known anybody as generous as he is; even if he'd get angry sometimes because I hadn't brought him enough, the next evening he'd be giving me a necklace."

"With the money you'd earned."

"Of course, with my money. But the other pimps don't give a lira, they won't spend anything on their protégées, but he does and he never has anything, where he lives is a real tip."

"Would you tell him I'd like to talk to him?"

"I'm not sure, he's a peculiar sort of guy, I don't know how he'd react but I think it'd be no rather than yes . . . but if he does say yes I'll ring you."

She gets up, finishes drinking her beer and goes off towards the lighted platform, passing an abandoned train. "Sabrina, wait," I say catching up with her along the lines. "Did Angela ever talk to you about other men?"

"No."

I realise she doesn't want to tell me any more. I am uncertain whether I should offer her some money, but don't want to offend her. At this moment I see her turn round and stare at me in a provocative way.

"I've given you information and now you're going to pay me."

"Yes, that's fine. How much?"

"Let's say five hundred thousand."

"Sabrina, I'm not a millionaire. I work for a private broad-casting company and I earn two million a month, that's all."

"Okay, I understand, then don't give me anything. I just spit on people like you."

"I've got two hundred thousand with me, do you want that?"

"What would I do with it? If I wanted, I could earn that in half an hour's work." She says this arrogantly, knowing I know it isn't true.

"Do you really earn two million a month, like my cousin Concetta who's a machine operator at Siemens?" she asks in a disconsolate voice. Then, with a gesture I hadn't anticipated, she unbuttons her blouse and from out of her bra pulls a white, plump breast.

"Have you ever seen such a beautiful youthful breast? I may be forty but my breasts are the same as when I was twenty. Do you want a loan, Michela Canova? I'm worried about you."

"Lovely," I say, as I look at her immaculate breast exposed in the darkness of the night; milk white against her brown sun-burned hand, it seems like part of the moon.

"Would you like to touch it?"

"Thanks, Sabrina, but I must really go now."

"Touch it like in a museum, that's what I used to say, And if you like I'll teach you a few tricks to get some money out of the bastards."

"Do you want to teach me the game too?"

"Why not? I taught it to Angela Bari who lived next door to you."

"Did you take her out with you on the street?"

"No way, I've told you she wasn't a girl for the street. But Nando told me to teach her two or three things about the game like an affectionate mother would."

"Did he really say 'mother'?"

"Yes, a mother. And do you know what I'm telling you? She was only ten years younger than me but as I got to know her, I came to see how she really was a daughter. She was good at learning, she took everything in . . . wearing that little white dress, and sky-blue tennis shoes she looked like she was only just out of a convent school."

"Did she often wear those sky-blue tennis shoes?"

"Yes, often, and she used to walk fast . . . she was tall, not small like me. Without heels I'm at ground level while she flew."

"Did she ever talk to you about a guy who wore boots with heels and a ring with a tiger's-eye on his little finger?"

"But that's Nando!"

I look at her, incredulous. So the student disguised as a con man was really him: the sly looking man who came with me in the lift up to the top floor without saying a word, lit a cigarette and threw the match on to the floor of the passage, and then went down by himself, was none other than Nando.

Sabrina puts a hand on my shoulder and says "Ciao, beautiful."

I watch her walking away with quick footsteps, scrambling over the cement railway sleepers. Her dark hair with its red reflections becomes a violet-coloured cloud, almost a halo, under the neon lights and the haze of the night.

15

I have brought together all the newspaper photographs that Tirinnanzi gave me and put them to one side.

There are so many photographs of women tortured, butchered, cut to pieces. It seems odd that he kept them; I wonder what he intended to do with them. A newspaper account which appeared eight months ago is underlined in red three times with lots of exclamation marks. A mother who killed her daughter with an iron bar and then buried her in the small back garden of their house. Tirinnanzi has written underneath the photograph of a woman with a haggard face, "Women are killers too."

I know what he is trying to tell me. "A human being has animal instincts and chromosomes that are specific to a tendency to criminal behaviour," as he explained to me only a few days ago, "to kill someone is part of human nature and it is only through taboos, religious prohibitions, magical rites, social conscience, that human beings become able to restrain this entirely natural instinct, whether they are men or women."

It is in order to counteract arguments like his that I have recorded the voice of Aurelia Ferro, who refers to history rather than to nature.

"Murder forms part of the social environment of men and not of women," she insists in a pleasant voice, "since in the training of men learning how to fight and to kill is a vital part of their education. Throughout the world, every boy as soon as he reaches the age of reason, is sent off in a group to prepare himself to kill or be killed. Isn't this so? In anticipation of war, either near at hand or far away, the state orders him to be trained to shoot, to stab, to throw bombs, to butcher, to mutilate . . . Luckily, women throughout history have been able to establish other functions for themselves, such as taking care of the home, preparing food, looking after the sick . . . So we can see how rape and murder are intrinsic to a patriarchal ideology which aims to subject and control the enemy's body. At the same time, what forms part of man's culture is the barely concealed thought that women are in some way part of the dangerous world of enemy freedom."

"But yesterday in the criminal court, a woman was found guilty of sexually abusing her three sons aged from six to fifteen," insists Tirinnanzi, who does not like discussions about historical differences between men and women.

"But what's so extraordinary is that it's been put in all the newspapers, it happens so rarely that everyone is talking about it!"

Adele Sòfia has also sent me a box of papers by car from the police headquarters. When Stefana saw the car stop in front of the entrance, she was frightened out of her wits.

"What if they've found the murderer in our block of apartments, and are coming here to arrest him?"

"Are you suspicious of anyone, Stefana?"

"I'm as much in the dark as everyone else, but sometimes

I've wondered about Diafani, the engineer who lives on the first floor . . . don't tell anyone, for heaven's sake, but Giovanni says he heard him coming back about ten o'clock on the night of the murder and he took the lift to go up to the first floor which he never does normally. Isn't that odd?"

"Why didn't you tell the police about it?"

"I did tell them . . . when they were asking me about the movements of all the tenants on that night, but they didn't even question me about it."

The engineer Diafani? I try to remember his face, the way he walks. Actually there is something heavy and gloomy about him, attributes that could well belong to someone potentially homicidal. But are they enough?

I ask Stefana if the engineer lives alone. "With his mother," she replies. Now I recall Signora Diafani's look which I can feel creeping down my spine every morning as I walk across the courtyard on my way to work. She stands motionless in front of her window with a bewildered expression on her face watching everyone who enters or leaves the building.

It is the first time I think of my apartment building as being a frightening and sinister beehive; it might have a murderous bee inside and no one would know anything about it. There is such a coming and going of people at all hours of the day and night; women with babies in their arms, youths in blue jeans and dark glasses, workmen in overalls, men in dark suits, women carrying shopping bags. Where they are going, what they are doing, what they are thinking, I can't imagine; it is altogether beyond me. Before Angela's death I had begun to recognise a few familiar faces and would greet them, and then make my way upstairs carrying the scent of the lime flowers with me. Nowadays I always turn round when I am half-way across the courtyard and look suspiciously at all the windows, some dark, some lit up, some with curtains and some without.

"Diana B, age 36, beaten, tied up, gagged and stabbed. Found by her father at 13 Via Panisperna in the evening when he returned from work. Mother died when she was a child; two brothers live abroad. Was separated from her husband a few months ago and has been living on her own in an apartment on the third floor. No evidence of theft or break-in; her clothes were in order in a cupboard, including two fur coats. Her former husband was in Milan for a few days on business. It seems she had no lovers. No one saw the murderer enter or leave the building.

"Debora C., age 19. Raped and strangled at home in Via Tagliamento. An only child, Debora attended the college for interpreters in Via Cassia. Father and mother were both out at work. She was wearing a tee-shirt with a Mickey Mouse design. The door had not been forced. No one noted anything suspicious.

"Lidia B., age 25. Was beaten to death and left near the tennis courts at Olgiata. The daughter of elderly parents who were separated, she lived on her own in the Trastevere district. On the evening of February 15th she had gone to visit her father at the Fatebenefratelli Hospital. Since then there had been no sign of her. Five days later her body was found hidden behind a rose bush. No useful evidence fron witnesses.

"Giulietta F., age 32. Raped, beaten up, died from blows from an unknown weapon. Her body, wrapped in an army blanket, was recovered from the boot of a stolen car. No father. Giulietta F. lived with her mother and her brother in an apartment on Via Zambarelli. Worked as a clerk in the electronic company Orbis. Assailants unknown.

"Giovanna M., age 39. Gagged with her own underclothes. Found abandoned behind the central dairy with cuts and bruises on her head. It was only after lengthy investigation that it became possible to identify the body since her handbag containing all her documents was missing. The body was recognised by her son aged twelve who lives with his grandmother. Giovanna worked as a prostitute in the district of Tor di Quinto. It is not known if she had a pimp. No suspects.

"Annamaria G., age 45. Stabbed to death in her house on Via Gemini. She lived alone and worked as a nurse at the Santo Spirito Hospital. The house had not been broken into. In a drawer an envelope was found containing her last salary payment: one million two thousand lire. Assailant unknown."

*

I look up from the pages, stunned. Inside my head I see them walking, all together, slim, spattered with blood, feet bare, not a sound. Is it possible that it all ends in this macabre way with a police report stacked away in a filing cabinet and a label with the dates of birth and death attached to a toe?

The memory of the city holds no traces of these crimes, no recollection even, no word, no stone bearing the inscription "Unknown Victim" as on the tombs of unknown soldiers. But the women are there and they will continue to walk up and down, seeking recognition.

Many of them have been welcoming to their attacker, most likely with a trusting smile. Their doors, in fact, have not been forced open, even if, like Angela Bari used to do, they locked them each evening with several keys. They were friendly, perhaps even cheerful, when they opened the door to the person who murdered them.

What can I do, faced with this crowd of women wailing, walking, smoking, laughing, and crying out loudly for justice? How do I accommodate them in my small office at Italia Viva? I would like to make a portrait of each one of them, record their voices, call a loving witness who remembers their gestures, the way they moved, their desires, their aims. But where to begin?

I am alone with my tape recorder and all the voices are pursuing me, forewarning me. They make a big uproar, the dead bodies of these murdered women and I don't know with whom to begin. What is it about the softness of a woman's body that provokes the fury of a man's fist? I think I shall have to talk to Adele Sòfia, perhaps she will be able to explain some of the patterns behind sexual crimes, for it is through repetition and habit that certain modes of behaviour fall into place.

16

As I come out of the gate, I see in front of me a huge inscription on the wall of the house opposite saying *Attenta a quello che fai!* – Be careful what you do! It's the use of the feminine in the word *attenta* that worries me. The previous sign was removed by Giovanni Mario who, like an industrious ant, cleans the space on all sides of the nest.

I turn down Via Santa Cecilia looking for my car. From a distance the cars all look the same, yet there are not that many small cherry-coloured Fiats around. I'm not mad about the colour; I got it through an advertisement in the listings paper, *Porta Portese*. At that time, my Vespa had been stolen. I have had no regrets; it takes me anywhere, slowly, with little petrol.

Finally at the corner of the Via Anicia and the small street of the Tabacchi, I see from afar the unmistakable colour of ripe cherries. It is parked beneath the leafy branches of a lime tree and small, yellow, sticky wers are scattered all over the bonnet. I had gone round looking for the only lime tree around so as to enjoy its scent.

As I start manoeuvring the car I see an elderly woman in front of a low brick wall. She is dressed in dark blue, hunched up, carrying a big parcel. Suddenly, as if summoned by a trumpet call, dozens of cats come out from everywhere, very young ones that have difficulty standing on their paws, large ones, grey or ginger, with long whiskers, strong paws and the look of ruffians. They are all thin, with dirty fur and bristly tails. They throw themselves on to the paper bags which the woman is opening on the pavement and they start to devour the food with hoarse, ferocious cries.

The woman sits on the little wall and watches them with a motherly look. From time to time she bends down to give a gentle push to a domineering cat that tries to snatch food away from a weaker one. By now the cats are in front of my wheels and I cannot move. I switch off the engine, get out of the car and sit down on the wall next to the cat feeder.

"They're hungry," she says without looking at me.

"Do you come here every day?"

"Not every day, but whenever I can. There used to be a girl who came for a time when I wasn't here. The cats would wait for her and when they saw her arrive in a little white coat and sky-blue tennis shoes, they'd come running from everywhere. Then she disappeared."

"What was the girl's name?"

"I don't know; every now and then we'd exchange a few words. How is the ginger one?' 'He's got a cough,' I'd say, 'the grey one went underneath a car, the white one has had eight kittens, the black one is dead, it got poisoned."

"Do you know where she lived?"

"In Via Santa Cecilia, I think, but I don't know what number."

"She was called Angela Bari, I'm sorry to tell you she's dead."

"She was so young . . . was it an accident?"

"She was murdered."

"Exactly what happens to the street cats, either they go under a car or they're killed."

I watch her get up to collect the empty paper bags and then set off down to the end of the street. On the ground a small sheet of greasy paper remains to be pounced on by some of the cats. Others settle down on the low wall to digest their meal under the shade of the lime tree. One has clambered on to the bonnet of my car and looks as if it is playing the cello, with one paw up in the air and its head bent down over its belly.

I look at my watch, I am twelve minutes late. I chase the cellist away with a gentle push and I start to move the car, trying not to crush some awkward cat.

At the radio station I find Tirinnanzi is very curt because he has been busy at the control desk all on his own. The technician has not turned up and the morning session with Professor Baldi has already started. There is no point in trying to explain about the hungry stray cats and Angela Bari buying kilos of mince to feed them in the little street of the Tabacchi; it wouldn't mean a thing to him. "I was thinking you'd run into a tree," he says as if he were rather wishing it had happened.

I take his place at the control desk. I listen through the headphones to Professor Baldi being lavish with good advice, his warm voice barely affected by early morning drowsiness. Eventually Mario Calzone arrives and sits down at the controls with a lighted cigarette between his lips, in spite of the notice on the wall which says in big letters, PROBITO FUMARE.

While I listen to Professor Baldi's voice rising and falling, I choose music for the intervals, separate the advertising tapes, and check up on the details of the morning broadcasts.

There are still ten more minutes of Baldi and then we move on to half an hour with a well-known chef; this morning it is the turn of the Frenchman Tibidault, who will be giving advice on *nouvelle cuisine*. Then it's the news, written and read by Tirinnanzi, followed by an expert on simple exercises. The broadcasting company relies on experts who are not paid very much. This is the policy of Cusumano, one of "big economies and big yields" as he describes it. Six of us work full time: three technicians, one secretary, two journalists and that's the lot.

At midday there will be a programme on legal problems. Merli, a lawyer, will be coming to the studio; he is a kindly man with hair dyed black that at times turns decidedly lilac.

He is the shyest and most awkward man I have ever come across. I cannot imagine him in court, and actually I do not believe he has much success. He takes on cases of the lowest sort, petty fraud, disputes between neighbours, unpaid bills. He advises clients who have little money and he often ends up not being paid at all. But he never ceases to be unfailingly kind and conscientious, and his clients take a liking to him even if he doesn't win their cases because they know they can count on his discretion and on his human sympathy.

He wears a wedding ring, but no one has ever seen his wife at the radio station. Occasionally I have heard him mention an absent son. Perhaps he went away with his mother.

Merli comes to the radio station on Mondays and Fridays to give advice on legal matters. He is not a cheerful sort of person, and he is also awkward and clumsy, but the way in which he raises his grey eyes with surprise and interest makes me feel happy. Suppose I talk to him about Angela Bari?

But today he is in a hurry. I notice that he is continually looking at his watch. He trips up several times while he is talking, until Mario Calzone smiles understandingly. Many people see him as a failure even though he does his work here well, with patience and understanding. He is liked by the listeners because he takes each case to heart and thinks and reflects on it without sparing himself and that is enough for the director.

"Michela, the director wants to see you."

I get up and go and knock on the boss's door, which looks as if it were made of sugar and chocolate like in the story of Hansel and Gretel; it's so shiny and brightly coloured. I knock. I enter. I find him seated at the big writing desk made of black glass. His beautiful butterfly hands are toying with a paper holder in the shape of a naked woman.

"Where have we got to in the research on crimes against women?"

"I'm still collecting material."

"You know that we shall be going on the air in a few weeks time?"

"I know that, but if I have to continue working on other programmes it really doesn't leave me enough time."

"My dear Michela, a good journalist is at everyone's beck and call . . . I remember my father writing articles while he was eating standing up, always interrupted by the telephone. And they were articles of the highest quality, I can assure you."

"Radio isn't like newspapers."

"All self-respecting journalists give of their best without sparing themselves whether it's for a newspaper or a radio broadcast. Have you seen Adele Sòfia?"

"I have seen her."

"Did she give you material?"

"A mass of papers."

"Have you been doing interviews?"

"Some, I've been thinking of putting the case of Angela Bari at the centre of the ones that are unresolved. She was killed by stab wounds about a month ago and so far the murderer hasn't been found."

"Who was this Bari?"

"A girl who was an actress, no, more of a model, perhaps even a prostitute but it isn't very clear."

"Good, good, but don't let's be too limited. We don't want

personal cases, what is required is information, trends. I want precise statistics that reflect the data. That's why I put you in touch with police commissioner Sòfia. The listener needs to have an overall view of these incidents. Is that clear, Michela? We don't want too much messing around, what's needed are events and dates, names and cases, do you understand?"

"Yes, yes, I'm working on all that."

"We need really good interviews with people who are familiar with the problem . . . a psychologist, a sociologist, a doctor, a priest. We can start off with Professor Baldi since we have him here."

"It might be better not to have Professor Baldi," I say, looking apprehensively at his hands, pale and agile, quite beautiful as they move restlessly and disquietingly in front of my face.

"Why not? Do you know how much he's paid for his advice? If we use him, we could be killing two birds with one stone."

"Professor Baldi already has his daily spot. We can't put him on everywhere. It would be ridiculous."

I know that what he most fears is ridicule. To be accused of corruption, intrigue, of being authoritarian, doesn't bother him; it is only the suspicion of ridicule that gets him beside himself. I realise that the dread of being ridiculed predominates over his fear of spending money,

"Okay. We'll get in other experts."

"In this field of work, experts are only in the way. And it's possible that listeners would prefer to hear stories rather than a lot of theories."

"Michela, you're being hard as nails. Do some of what you want, but I'm warning you; if it doesn't work, I shall have to take the programme away from you."

I nod my head, feeling I've won, but only by half. I have too little time to investigate more deeply and too much material to sort through. As usual I must do what I can, and make it work.

17

I ask Ludovica Bari for the phone number of Giulio Carlini in Genoa. I ring him. He answers quietly in an educated, rather affected voice. I ask him for an appointment and he replies saying he is very busy but, if I really insist, he will be in Florence on Friday on business and could meet me at the station.

Yet another meeting at a station, this is becoming quite compulsive! I haven't heard from Sabrina but I am expecting her to call me. I always hope to see Nando in the lift; he doesn't frighten me any more. But he has not shown himself.

Angela Bari's mother actually lives near Florence, at Fiesole, so why not "kill two birds with one stone", as the director would say. I get the telephone number from Ludovica but this time she doesn't seem too pleased as if she does not like the idea of me talking to her mother.

She gives it to me reluctantly, adding that it would be better if I didn't go, because her mother isn't well, and as a result of living alone has become rather unbalanced and moody, and also somewhat inclined to invent stories, to tell "a pack of lies". Ludovica actually puts it like this, in a confident tone of voice with a little embarrassed laugh.

So here I am on the way to Florence, with a small suitcase of grey canvas, my tape-recorder in a shoulder bag, papers, books, and a change of clothes. The director has given me the day off to do the interview, and I am happy to have twenty-four hours free of worrying about the control desk, Professor Baldi and the sound mixer.

As I go down the street I feel as if I were being followed. I keep turning round while I look out for a taxi. The latest writing on the wall opposite said *Peggio per te!* – all the worse for you! But Giovanni Mario has cleaned it off with whitewash.

"I've seen Diafani the engineer with a felt tip in his hand," Stefana whispers into my ear breathlessly. But I don't have the time to talk with her about it. I have promised that I will do so as soon as I get back.

In the train the air-conditioning is not working. It is hot, I am unable to read, my eyes are dazed by the landscape slipping past the window. The fields of grain are a beautiful straw yellow that makes me think of Van Gogh's paintings. The vines are starting to become thick and heavy with little bunches of grapes; peaches and pears are beginning to show between the dark leaves. Summer has reached its zenith. I can't help remembering some of the journeys I went on with my father when I was six or seven years old. Then there was no air-conditioning and the windows went up and down behind the bars in front of the glass. We always used to arrive late for the train, I don't know why. We would fly over the last hundred metres, our hearts in our mouths. Once I even fell down, my father didn't stop but raced on ahead pulling me along by my arm and grazing my knee.

We would leap into a carriage just as the train had begun to move, in danger of ending up underneath the wheels, while the guard was angrily blowing his whistle as he tried to stop us. But my father really enjoyed the risk, the race, clinging on at the last minute to the door of the train with his right arm, holding on to me with his left.

And that would not be the end; his taste for danger led him to play with his daughter like a cat with a mouse. "Where are you going, papa?" I would ask him as the train drew into some small station where I knew it would only stop for a minute.

"I'm going to get something to drink."

"Papa, there won't be time, please, please don't go." But he would shrug his shoulders as if to say "only silly little girls get frightened."

He would leap out at a run, looking very confident, and I would watch him striding into the station with big, cavorting footsteps. I'd clutch at the window feeling terrified, waiting for him to reappear, but the train would leave without him and tears would start to roll uncontrollably down my cheeks. I was petrified with horror. Then, after a few minutes, I'd see him coming down the corridor looking happy and pleased with himself, holding a small bottle of beer in his hand.

"Were you frightened? How silly of you, you must have more faith in your father, you know I'm always in time to catch the train as it moves off." And he'd laugh, pleased at having given me a fright and to have resolved my fear with a surprise worthy of a circus acrobat, but also of a father who was young and light-hearted.

Do my thoughts, like a wounded cat, always come back to dig up a mousehole belonging to the past?

I force myself to open the novel I have brought with me; it is by Patricia Highsmith. I am curious about her as a feminine misogynist and intrigued by her understanding of crime. What is it that drives the hidden demon, this fiercely ironic writer seems to be asking; is it the inescapable pain we carry sewn into our heart as if it were a secret pocket, or is it a loss of moral responsiveness? Is crime a disease, and how do we get ill?

18

The meeting place is the station waiting room. I find it crowded and oppressive. How will I recognise him? My worry is unfounded because as soon as I take a seat I see him in front of me, legs elegantly crossed, a smart light blue suit, reading a newspaper.

As I approach him he lifts his head up from the page and smiles at me confidently. Then he gets up, bowing stiffly in military fashion and kisses my hand.

"Michela Canova, I presume? Are you related to the sculptor?"

"No."

"I remember when I was a child, my grandfather took me to see Canova's bust of Paolina Borghese. It looked as if it were made of sugar, I'd have liked to eat it. At that time I didn't know that neo-classicism made use of these sugary effects so as to distance itself from the subject, creating far-off aesthetic

spaces just as it is giving the impression of reproducing reality
with an obsessive faithfulness."

"I'm also sorry that I have got nothing to do with the
sculptor. Where shall we sit?"

"In the bar, come, I'll lead the way. I like Florence station
because it's all on one level, like a big, open square that flows
into the centre of the city at both ends. There aren't any stairs,
underpasses, underground passages, or tunnels. It's a station
that's rather like a painting by Chirico, don't you think? What
can I get you, Michela?"

We push open a heavy glass door and go into the bar. We
sit down at a small table covered with a pink tablecloth. Before
sitting down, Giulio Carlini clears his chair of crumbs with an
elegant gesture. Then he leans over to me as if to say, "Here I
am at your disposal".

"May I record our conversation?"

"Yes, if you want to. You're Italia Viva, aren't you? I've never
even heard of it."

"It's a private radio station. Do you want to know how many
listeners we have? Of course it depends on the programmes,
but our lowest rating seems to be about ten thousand and the
highest two hundred thousand."

"And why are you doing a programme about Angela Bari?"

"It's not only about her, it's a documentary about crimes
against women which remain unsolved. That is what my
director has asked for, a series of forty spots on crimes in which
the victims are women and the killers are never found."

"I'm glad you're talking about Angela, she merits it. She was
exceptional for her sensitivity and her intelligence. I adored her,
although I never could rely on her completely . . . you see,
her personality was unbalanced; she could never bring herself
to think of the future . . . By nature she was generous and kind
like I said, and so lovable, yes, so very lovable, but at the same
time she was a difficult person, very difficult if I'd wanted to
keep my distance from her but I didn't want that . . . she had
the power to draw you in and overwhelm you with impossibly
erratic demands. She wanted to marry me, that's curious isn't it,
coming from a woman who'd had such a bitter and devastating

experience of marriage ... she asked me several times. . . .
Anyway why me? I asked her but she didn't answer. Did she
want to marry me because I gave her reassurance, I must have
given her something but who knows what it was? I'd like to
get married too, it's something I've always wanted but I haven't
yet found anyone on whom I could really rely, someone I
would like to be the mother of my children."

I watch him talking, astonished at the openness with which
he exposes himself; he gives himself away without a second
thought, at least that is how it seems. I encourage him to go
on but there is no need; he anticipates the questions I want to
ask him and responds to them with calm intensity.

"Angela was sincere, totally compliant and at everyone's disposal. She was also a woman of the night, mysterious and
contradictory. But where is the truth, you'll be asking. Well,
Michela Canova, I don't really believe in the existence of
truth ... we are made up of so many different strands, so many
layers of truth ... and Angela was aware in herself of the
arrogance of the sun and the timidity of the moon ... Truth,
as moralists understand it, is reduced to a tedious monotony,
stuff for fanatics and the builders of empires."

The waiter has come up to us, curious about my tape-
recorder; he is bending over us listening impertinently to our
conversation. I see Giulio Carlini lift his penetrating eyes and
look at the boy with annoyance.

"Bring me a Bloody Mary," he says arrogantly. And he catches
him out because the boy is embarrassed, not knowing what a
Bloody Mary is. Carlini enjoys his embarrassment; he doesn't
explain or insist, but limits himself to observing him as if he
were a little dog who can't understand his master's orders.
"What would you like?" he asks, turning to me.

"A glass of cold milk," I say and I see him making a grimace
of disgust. He probably hasn't drunk milk since his mother's
breast.

The young waiter goes off to ask for explanations at the cash
desk. Carlini laughs at the manoeuvre and I see he has stained
and broken teeth. Perhaps he is older than he looks. At some

times he gives the impression of being fifty, at others less than thirty.

The dark rings under his eyes suggest nights of insomnia, large quantities of alcohol, a secret pleasure in the letting go of himself.

"Can I ask you how Angela Bari seemed the last time you saw her?"

"Actually we met here in Florence four days before her death. I came to fetch her from the station and went with her to visit her mother at Fiesole. We all had lunch together, then I left her there while I went to see clients. At eight o'clock I went back and fetched her. We had dinner in a restaurant and at eleven I took her back to her mother's house. They asked me to stay the night but I preferred not to. I went to a hotel and the next day I took her to the station."

"And how was she?"

"Fine, she was happy, a bit worn out, too many sleepless nights. She took sleeping pills to get to sleep and stimulants to stay awake. But on that day she was relaxed, possibly a little dazed, I don't know if it was because of sleeping pills or alcohol. She was someone in a constant state of unreality . . . let's say that for her reality was unpleasant and she tried to block it out if she couldn't dominate it . . . but how can one blame her for that? Reality isn't welcome even for me, I'm always trying to find tricks to escape it, although perhaps in less desperate ways."

"Forgive the question, but did you love Angela Bari?"

"I most certainly loved her, I was deeply involved with her, even though I'm not the sort of person who lets go of themselves completely. Angela gave a lot of herself, she was both generous and changeable, but she didn't seem able to make concrete plans for the future, she lived inside a shining cloud . . . to my mind marriage is above all a projection of the here and now, setting up house, having children together . . . how could one think of having a son with a reckless little girl like Angela?"

"A reckless little girl . . . can you explain that better?"

"I don't know how to put it more clearly . . . above all, she was so unpredictable. For example one day she'd go on a diet and she'd only eat one apple, the next day she'd devour a kilo of spaghetti. First she'd want something and then she'd throw it away. At times she was unbearable, she would moan and groan, she suffered from all the ills of the world; at other times she'd be delightful, calm, smiling and serene. With her one never knew what to expect. She was always on the alert . . . let's say too that for me such continual provocation was like a craving for beneficent pain."

"Could you explain better what you mean by this idea of 'beneficent pain?'"

"I don't know if the listeners would understand me . . . I'm someone who feeds off contradictions, ambiguity. Don't get me wrong, I don't mean factual ambiguities, I don't have anything to hide . . . I run away from anything commonplace, you see, and pain keeps me company. However, no matter what, inside my head I keep a space for pain and I see it as something noble . . . the trouble is I'm not able to find the right words to clarify my own mental complexity. My thinking is better than my words which lag behind, plodding breathlessly . . ."

He stops as if waiting for me to contradict him. Meanwhile the young waiter arrives with the tomato juice and vodka. He puts the glass down on the table clumsily and next to it leaves a bowl filled with toasted nuts.

Carlini points to the tape-recorder as if to say let it take a break, it must be tired like me. I stop the tape, he smiles at me gratefully, drinks the Bloody Mary in one gulp and orders another.

Every movement he makes implies a hidden desire to seduce and I am undoubtedly allowing myself to be seduced.

19

"Would you think it indiscreet of me to ask you where you were on the night of the crime?"

"I was in Genoa at a restaurant with friends. They are all willing to come forward as witnesses. I've said this to the police."

"Do you live alone?"

"Yes, on my own."

"Did Angela ever come to your place in Genoa?"

"No, we usually met half-way, either here in Florence or in Bologna. She liked to move around and I was happy to follow her."

"What exactly is your work?"

"I buy and sell houses for a firm of estate agents."

"Do you do this in Rome?"

"Of course, the firm for which I work does business in all the major cities of Italy. Their main office is in Genoa but they operate in Bologna, Naples, Florence and Rome."

"Did you know the apartment in Via Santa Cecilia?"

"Of course, I went there whenever I was in Rome."

"Did Angela ever talk to you about anyone in the building who was looking for her or following her?"

"Angela was a mystery, although in an angelic way as her name says: she had whole areas of feeling that were totally unknown and I certainly didn't seek to pry into them. I can't stand nosy people. I fully realised she led a double life, but why torment oneself with trying to understand other people? One has to take them for what they are in all their existential grace . . . I myself am not free of ambiguity, perhaps you know that I have a woman with . . . with whom I've been in an intimate relationship for over twelve years."

I don't know whether he is saying this in order to be open with me, or out of a sincere desire to admit to a truth in which he says he does not believe.

"I'm not married, if that is what you are thinking . . . she has been a friend from my student days, she was close to me in my youth. Then she got married to a businessman but she wasn't happy. We met up again, I a bachelor, she married, and we became lovers, then left each other and then came together once more . . . she's called Angela too, isn't that strange, almost as if it were my fate to be locked between two women with the same sacred name, the echo of some supernatural force."

He laughs, showing his discoloured teeth; his eyes are a limpid, radiant blue. He has the look of a boy growing up reluctantly, ready to invent an imaginary picture of himself. I can understand how Angela fell in love with him.

"Obviously I ask myself why I never married the first Angela after she divorced her husband, which is what happened. But as I've told you, I've not yet found anyone with whom I would be happy to think of having children . . . 'Angela never asked me to marry her but she made use of a fiendish strategy: she made it impossible for me to be without her."

In the meantime the waiter has brought another Bloody Mary and Giulio Carlini is swallowing it in little sips. I still have my glass of milk which I have not touched. I am too involved with the effort of following what Carlini has been saying, and keeping the microphones at the right distance so they do not pick up the background noise.

"My life has been consumed between these two angels," Giulio Carlini continues while he swings one leg over the other. "On the one hand, my wife of the morning who knew how to take care of me, heal me; on the other my wife of the night who brought me the pain of continual provocation, the blind compulsion of desire. The beauty of Angela at night, you just can't imagine it . . . in the day you wouldn't notice her but at night she shone like those flowers that only bloom in the dark . . . the delicacy of her white arms, the softness of her breasts, of her long slender neck . . ."

He hides his head in his hands. Is he weeping? But he isn't, it is simply an expression of grief. His long sunburned hands press against his tired eyes and against his frowning forehead. Then they are slowly and gently drawn back.

"Have you any idea who might have killed her?"

"I can't think of anyone."

"Not even the least conjecture as to who it could be?"

"I haven't got the least idea . . . for me it has resolved a dilemma. I say this in all sincerity, but believe me it's so unutterably terrible that I used to hold her in my arms . . . and then such a cruel, brutal murder . . . Why, why?"

"About this dilemma, are you implying that through her death Angela has released you from a conflict that you weren't able to deal with?"

"If you are trying to insinuate that I had any interest in her death, you are mistaken, even if I've said something along those lines, to want to find a solution through violence is not how I am. I would rather a thousand times know she was alive so I could go on loving her, even if it were part of a dilemma." The look in his eyes is clear and his voice sounds sincere.

I have been unaware that he has ordered another Bloody Mary, probably with a flick of his fingers, and now he is drinking it in long gulps as if it were water.

"Now I have to go, I'm sorry but my train leaves in ten minutes. I'm so glad to have met you."

He insists on paying for the drinks in spite of my telling him that the station would pay. With a simple gesture he takes a hundred thousand lire note out of his pocket and gives it courteously to the waiter. He kisses my hand once again and catches up with the waiter at the cash desk. I watch him going off in his light blue suit, and I am left asking myself like he does, "But what is the truth?"

20

I telephone Augusta Elia, the mother of Angela Bari, to remind her of our appointment. She says she is ill, although she doesn't sound it. I insist, reminding her I have come all the way from Rome especially to see her. In the end she seems touched by this and says she will see me, but not until tomorrow.

What am I to do? The only solution is to stay overnight in Florence.

I telephone Cusumano and ask him if I can prolong my time in Florence by another day. For once he answers in a cheerful voice and says it will be all right. "Good luck with the work, Michela!" and he rings off. He does not even ask me to econ-omise, he knows that I won't waste his money.

I go to the Pensione Raffaello near the station. They give me a big, bare room on the third floor with shutters that don't shut properly, a high rickety bed, a wash-basin fixed against a yellowing wall, and nothing else.

I sit down on the bed which is covered by a bedspread spotted with rust-coloured marks and threadbare from frequent washing. The light is dim. I don't know what to do. I turn on my tape-recorder and listen once more to Giulio Carlini talking. I can imagine him in front of me in his light blue suit, his long legs crossed. Each time he puts one leg over the other, he adjusts the line of his trousers. It is very difficult to think of him with a knife in his hand.

His voice continues to run on seductively. In what he says there is such a desire to please. I am aware of the slow pace at which he weaves sentences as if they were tapestries he is putting up for sale, showing the rich density of the fabric, the beauty of the design, the brilliance of the weave.

And how he lingers over the final vowels and how he glides snake-like into the microphone almost as if he were trying to swallow it.

I am being invaded by other voices, nearer and more lively. I turn off the tape-recorder. The sound of angry quarrelling comes from the room next door. A man and a woman who have many things in common. I recognise this from the sloppy, rancorous tone of their voices; hers insistent and petulant, his contemptuous and bored.

My life seems to consist of nothing but strange voices which I try to decipher and analyse. Here too, as on the radio, I try and guess who is at the other end of the sound waves, the walls, the city, so that I can go on playing this enigmatic game.

I put the tape-recorder on again, turning up the volume a little. The squalid room of the Pensione Raffaello becomes invaded by the persuasive voice of Giulio Carlini, fragile but at the same time strong-willed. I wonder whether the seductive quality of his voice comes from the internal rhythm of the sentences that are so skilfully intertwined and magnified, or from the intelligent way he pauses between one word and the next.

One can step lightly inside the voice of Giulio Carlini, impelled by a feeling of curiosity, but at the same time there is something which makes me feel apprehensive. Could it be the almost imperceptible crack in the high notes bringing an unexpected stridency, or is it the slight ruffling in the texture of his voice which seems to conceal a trap or some sort of deception?

If this man has killed Angela Bari, he must have had a very deep-seated reason which he brooded over for a long time. He does not seem like a man who would be taken over by passion or provoked by sudden rage or given to ill-considered actions. If he did it, he would have prepared it with care, determined to make it the perfect crime.

The room in the Pensione Raffaello is too dismal to spend the evening alone in. I turn off the recorder. I hide it at the bottom of the cupboard and I go out carrying with me the big metal door key.

Outside the air is tepid. The birds are flying low. At this time of the evening there are so many birds in the city; perhaps they are swallows or perhaps not, they could be bats or pigeons or turtle doves. In the sunset Florence looks severe and impassive; I find it very beautiful.

As I walk I get mixed up with a group of Scandinavian tourists who are strolling along eating pizzas. They are wearing shorts and leather sandals, their noses and thighs are red with sunburn and on their faces they have the dreamy bewildered look that tourists have after a day of museums and monuments.

They all stop in front of a stall selling small marble reproductions of Michelangelo's David and ashtrays with a portrait of Dante. The two stallholders are laughing their heads off, perhaps at the tourist who has lost a shoe and now sits on the edge of a fountain massaging his foot.

The idea of eating alone depresses me but hunger propels me into the first trattoria I see. A waiter wearing a yellow kerchief round his neck puts me at a table in the corner. I bring out my pen and an exercise book while I wait for tomatoes stuffed with rice and a green salad, and at the top of the page I write the name: Angela Bari, died in Rome on June 24th at 22 Via Santa Cecilia between 10 p.m. and midnight.

Presumably she was alone in the apartment and opened the

door to her killer. She was probably expecting him; he was someone she trusted. But why did she take off her shoes to open the door to the person who murdered her? Or did she remove them after opening it?

I make a small drawing of the courtyard in Via Santa Cecilia with the two big lime trees dense with leaves, the fountain with rocks covered in fern, and the many windows opening on to the courtyard. Who knew Angela was there? Was someone watching her, someone who saw her and did not speak? Only Stefana and Giovanni Mario talk about her, of how she used to come and have coffee with them, about how she confided in Stefana telling her how ugly she felt. I think of the presents she brought Berengario, of the spinning top with its cascade of silvery notes.

I turn over the page and I start to make a list of the characters in the story: Angela's sister Ludovica with her lovely chestnut hair falling down her shoulders, who said of Angela that she never got it right, and of her mother that she told "a pack of lies". On the night of the murder Ludovica was at the cinema with Mario Torres.

Augusta Elia: married to Cesare Bari by whom she had Angela and Ludovica. When Angela was eight years old and Ludovica twelve, her husband died, leaving various properties. After only six months of mourning Augusta married Glauco Elia, an architect and sculptor. The marriage lasted fifteen years when he left her and went off with another woman. Since then she has suffered from terrible headaches and eczema on her hands. On the night of the murder she was at home in her house at Fiesole.

Giulio Carlini: from Genoa. He works for an estate agency and often travels on business. When in Rome he stayed with Angela. He suspects she led a double life about which he says he wasn't curious. He loved her but did not want to marry her. He has another woman also called Angela whom he knew at college and who has been married and divorced. On the night of the crime he was in Genoa dining with friends. Have the police verified his alibi?

Sabrina: a self-declared prostitute. She says that Angela used to sell herself but only to very rich men in luxury hotels. Sabrina says that her protector Nando has attacked her, but she refuses to admit that he could have killed Angela. And Sabrina? She had a reason for jealousy. Where was she on the night of the crime? On the street with a client. How could that be proved?

Nando: Sabrina's protector. He knew Angela and, according to Sabrina, made her a prostitute too. He was seen in the lift at 22 Via Santa Cecilia a few days after her death. It is difficult to understand what he was looking for. Where was he on the night of the crime?

Mario Torres: described as being quarrelsome and violent. But would this make him capable of killing his girlfriend's sister with a knife, and for what reason would he have done it?

Glauco Elia: the stepfather. I know little about him. It seems that for years he has not seen either his former wife or his stepdaughters. He got married again to a girl thirty years younger and lives near Velletri where he now dedicates himself to his sculpture.

When I raise my eyes from the exercise book, I realise that the other diners have all gone. The room is empty and my stuffed tomatoes are lying in a pool of pink oil. I decide to leave it there. I eat the salad quickly and ask for the bill.

21

The taxi is climbing. The ascent between walls of grey stone gets steeper and narrower. Here and there are glimpses of olive and peach trees. We are leaving the city with all its noise behind us as we clamber up among old and new villas, submerged in green, surrounded by flowers and glossy box trees.

The taxi stops in front of a black iron gate. "This looks like a prison!" exclaims the driver on seeing the double locks and the points which protrude menacingly on top of the iron railings. On a brass plate, in ornate lettering, is the name "Augusta Bari Elia". I ring. A click releases the bottom of the imposing gate which opens in front of me as if pushed by a ghostly hand; it moves slowly, with a strident creaking.

I enter and find myself walking up a small path of white gravel like the one in the courtyard of Via Santa Cecilia, except that this path seems as if it were made of tiny pebbles from a river bed, each one polished with a duster. Along the sides of the path are big tubs of lemon trees, well-raked lawns and flower beds of pansies and petunias.

When I look up I see a good-looking woman, slim and elegant. She stands at the top of a large stone staircase which opens out like a fan. As she watches me come up, she holds her hand across her forehead as if shielding herself from the sun. Only today there is no sun to be seen, the sky is clouded and the air is veiled. I am followed by a cloud of small midges; I can't escape from them.

The woman is dressed entirely in green, even her shoes and her gloves are of a bright emerald colour. But why is she wearing gloves? Is she about to go out? Then I remember Ludovica telling me about the eczema on her hands.

"Come in at once if you want to escape the midges," she says, laughing. She seems happy. She has a high-pitched voice, it sounds friendly and makes me feel at ease. On the telephone she was so cold and reticent. Now I am close to her I can see how the green enhances her pale complexion and reflects her large moss-green eyes. She is much better looking than in photographs; in a way she looks like Angela but with something firmer, more decisive.

Indoors the rooms are kept shaded with the curtains drawn and the shutters half-closed. There are flowers everywhere and fine lilac-coloured carpets, paintings of pale seascapes and woods inhabited by coloured birds. A small white dog comes and sniffs me, wagging its tail.

"Carlomagno, get down!" she orders and the dog lies down obediently.

We sit in a corner of the room scented with a stick of incense which sends spirals of bluish smoke up to the ceiling.

"Can I get you a cup of coffee?"

I follow with fascination her long hands with the green gloves

as they move nervously around. Close to, her face looks slightly
stiff and papery, only her lips are expressive and sensual, painted
a deep ox-blood red.

"How much sugar?"

"Do you mind if I put on the tape-recorder?"

"Go ahead, I'm prepared for the worst."

"Why the worst?"

"Oh, you're not the first journalist I've had here since
Angela's death. They ask meaningless questions, they play at
being detectives and they get nowhere."

"I'm doing a broadcast for Italia Viva on crimes against
women that remain unresolved."

"I know, that's fine. Begin, by all means."

"Do you have any idea who might have murdered your
daughter?"

"As I see it, one should leave the dead in peace. What value
is there in knowing what has happened when you can't come
back to life? Only people like Maria, Angela's old nurse, can
think that the souls of people who've been murdered go round
the world asking for revenge . . . A mint chocolate? . . . I don't
want to know who killed my daughter, it doesn't help, and the
idea of revenge fills me with horror."

I watch her as she unwraps a small chocolate with her green
gloved fingers. She puts it in her mouth and rolls the silver
paper into a ball without dirtying her gloves.

"Did you often see your daughter?"

"No, hardly ever. She used to say she loved me but she kept
well away . . . from time to time she'd turn up in Florence with
someone called Pallini, Gerlini . . ."

"Giulio Carlini?"

"Yes, that's who it was . . . the way I see it children think
only of getting free of their parents, in spite of not wanting to
lose them . . . 'please God, keep her alive, keep her alive because
I don't want to lose her!' But isn't this really a prayer for the
dead . . . What's the name of your radio station? Oh, yes. Italia
Viva . . . your director, Cusumano I think, telephoned me
here . . ."

So I have been preceded by an introductory phone call.

Or was he simply checking on me to see I hadn't stayed in Florence on my own account?

"He assured me I can listen to the recording before it goes on the air . . . a nice man who . . ." She has a tendency to leave sentences unfinished, in spite of giving the impression of being alert and determined. Her eyes wander over things and then become blank.

"Another coffee? For myself I hate the . . ." I watch her as she pours more coffee into a little cup, delicately curving her gloved fingers. They are silk gloves, light and smooth and they fit her hands perfectly.

"Sometimes Angela was very affectionate, too much so, you see I can't stand anything too emotional and then . . . I'd damp down her outbursts and she didn't forgive me for this. I do believe it's because . . . like she never forgave me for getting married again to Glauco . . . she was too bound up with her father. But when a husband leaves you on your own . . . you can understand how I . . . what should I have done, shut myself up in a convent for the rest of my life . . . children are . . . Are you married? Do you have children?"

"No."

"Do you have a man you're in love with?"

"Yes, but at present he's working in Angola."

"Men escape just as soon as they can . . . look what happened to me . . . he went off with a girl thirty years younger with whom he had . . ." Her conversation is repeatedly broken off like a thread stretched too tightly. She looks softer since talking about husbands; there is something reassuring when two women are confiding in each other.

"Is the man you're in love with good-looking?"

"Well, not quite like Giulio Carlini," I say and I laugh with embarrassment.

"So why haven't you got married?"

"He's got a wife."

"There is divorce."

"But he doesn't want that."

"I see, a question of numbers . . . I know so many men like

that . . . they never want to leave one woman for another but
only to add her to the pile . . . how old is he?"

"Please, can we talk about Angela. Could you tell me what
she was like as a little girl?"

"As a child she was timid, almost paralysed by shyness . . .
she couldn't even manage to . . . as she got older she was more
self-confident, but was always tortured by the shyness. She was
not a happy little girl, even when she was cheerful she was, she
was . . ."

"Is it true that she had to stay in a psychiatric clinic?"

"Who told you that?"

"Ludovica."

"What an idea! But it was really Ludovica who . . . it was
Ludovica who was in a clinic, not Angela."

"So it isn't true that after her husband left her she had to
have an abortion and then became severely depressed?"

"It was Ludovica who had an abortion, not Angela. And
Angela left her husband because he got together with her sister."

"I don't understand any more . . . didn't Ludovica also get
married?"

"Ludovica hasn't ever been married," she says decisively and
with her gloved fingers she chases a copper-coloured curl that
has slipped down over her cheek.

"And Mario Torres?"

"Oh him! That love affair has been dragging on for years . . .
she torments him and he's too kind."

A maid comes in to tell her she is wanted on the telephone.
She says to me, "Could you wait a moment, please?" and goes
out swaying on her beautiful long legs. I wonder if she takes
off her gloves to telephone.

22

She has been gone for more than a quarter of an hour
before she comes back into the room. And I had thought I
would go exploring round the house to look for Angela's

bedroom. Instead I have stayed sitting on the milk-white sofa in a daze, staring at a photograph of her as a child which is on top of the piano.

I feel sure that I know that child, but where have I seen her? And then, searching through my memory, I remember another exactly similar photograph of a child with a sad smile and a look of being lost. The same forehead, naked and as if in pain from some inexpressible thought, the same eyes looking out on the world with apprehension, the same mouth set into a crushed, propitiatory smile; the attitude of someone who asks to be forgiven for being born and who hopes, by surrendering to other people's wishes, to demolish the fearful mechanism of seduction and possession. Eventually I understand: that child is me in a photograph taken by my father when I was just about the same age.

"Excuse me if I've kept you waiting, but . . ." she begins and as usual leaves the sentence half-finished.

I turn on the tape-recorder and arrange the microphones on the small folding trestle.

"Do you know a small, pale young man who is always dressed in black and wears high-heeled ankle boots?"

"Ah, that's Nando," she says at once without any show of embarrassment.

"Do you know him?"

"He came here looking for Angela, he's a likeable person. We became friends."

"He came to see you here when he was looking for Angela? When did he come?"

"A few days before Angela . . . I invited him to dinner and he stayed. A pleasant person, helpful . . . he told me a whole lot of stories about seagulls . . . it seems that when he was a boy . . ."

"Did he say what he does for a living?"

"He's in the wholesale business, I believe that . . ."

"His business is women."

"No, no . . . he did tell me bad things were being said about him . . . he also told me about his travels, that he wants to buy a house in Spain . . . he has some land on Capri where his father was a well-known builder . . ."

"He didn't tell you that your daughter Angela sometimes prostituted herself?"

"What are you saying? Why should she have done that? Wasn't I giving her five million lire a month?"

"Ludovica said she hadn't any money."

"Look, since her time in the clinic Ludovica gets everything muddled . . . she doesn't always know what she says . . . she invents things, she rambles on, but I . . ."

"I was told that Angela sometimes went as a prostitute by someone who is also on the game."

"Absolute rubbish! All you journalists specialise in making a lot of noise out of the tallest stories so as to create a scandal by mixing truth and lies together." In the heat of her emotion she actually succeeds in finishing her sentence.

"Then you don't accept that Angela worked as a prostitute?"

"I totally refuse to accept it, not from any moral standpoint or out of maternal love, believe me. I don't accept it because firstly, she had money and one prostitutes oneself for money; and secondly, she was too shy and sensitive; and thirdly because she would have told me. Whenever she came here she'd lie down on the bed beside me and tell me everything about herself like a child and I . . . I'd only hope she wouldn't start crying because when she cried she had a strange smell of . . . like . . . silkworms."

"Silkworms?"

"When I was a child my father kept silkworms. We had mulberry trees in our garden. When I went into the room where the silkworms were I used to smell that smell of saliva mixed with worm-eaten wood and over-ripe grapes, I don't know . . . bunches of grapes used to hang from the ceiling and my daughter . . . when she cried she gave out the same smell, which made me feel slightly sick . . ."

"Is it true that Angela was afraid of her stepfather?"

"I suppose Ludovica must have told you this . . . that girl tells so many lies! I who . . . Angela and Glauco loved each other very much, they were always together, they used to go on motorcycle rides up in the mountains to swim, to ski, they were both very good at sport . . . Then when Angela reached thirteen she began to want to do her own things . . . she didn't want to be with him all the time like she used to, she didn't go to the sea with him any more. She grew more solitary, read a lot and listened to music, she'd stay for hours shut away in her room . . . but she wasn't afraid of him, that's ridiculous."

"I would like to talk to him. Could I have his telephone number?"

"Glauco's telephone number? If I have it, by all means but . . . he won't want to talk, not on the radio . . . he's an odd character, the kind of man who . . . Perhaps it's his amazing looks . . . Glauco was the best-looking man I've ever known . . . a subtle beauty, hard to define, not at all like a film star, but he certainly could get people to fall in love with him, so perhaps . . . with me he was very straight. When he became infatuated with a girl he told me and I . . . yes, I went to his wedding. I wore a long gold dress and everyone looked at me instead of the bride, not only the dress but because of my situation . . . they were waiting for me . . . but instead I was happy and I ate canapés and drank champagne. I was glad he'd found a girl as charming as Emilia . . . When they had a daughter he wanted to call her Augusta after me, and indeed I . . ."

The green hands are poised delicately on top of the box of chocolates. "Are you sure you don't want one?" she says and I understand how she needs my complicity before she can eat any more herself. I accept one to please her. I watch her discard the silver paper with her nimble green fingers like a gecko or an intelligent lizard.

"Do you not have any suspicion about who might have killed your daughter?"

"A madman . . . there are so many around; because of that I live barricaded in here, and then, even if I knew, what purpose would it serve? From what I know of the human soul, that man is already living in hell, so leave him where he is. In his heart he only wants to be found out, that's what I think . . . therefore the best punishment is to let him stay unidentified."

"How can you be certain it's a man?"

"Twenty knife wounds . . . can you imagine a woman with her sleeve rolled up? I can't . . . a strong, robust man . . . with a wandering tremulous soul. Do you remember Hadrian?"

And it is with surprise that I see her put another chocolate into her mouth, close her eyes, and quote Hadrian in a soft, assured voice: "*Animula vagula blandula*, that's Hadrian, isn't it? For me the soul of a murderer is the most fragile, most tenuous, most frail thing in existence . . . a mosquito like all those that live on stagnant water and die at the first breath of cold. I feel almost tender towards the soul of a murderer, don't you?"

"Can you tell me anything Angela did when she was a child?"

"What kind of thing?"

"Anything, so I can understand her better."

"Let's see . . . one day my daughter wrote in her diary that I was a queen . . ."

"Your daughter kept a diary?"

"Yes, as a teenager."

"And afterwards?"

"Afterwards I don't know, but maybe she did; she had a mania for putting everything down because she said she had a bad memory and lost things . . . Now I think about it, after her death they sent a packet of papers from Rome that I . . ."

"Would you let me have a look at those papers?"

"I would do, willingly, but I . . . I've burnt everything . . . and who knows . . .?"

She interrupts herself, thinking of something else. Now she frowns at the photograph of Angela when she was a child and it seems as if she is questioning her impatiently.

I am about to ask another question when she raises a green hand and tells me she is tired, has no more voice and can feel the onset of one of her terrible headaches.

23

I cut and reassemble the recorded tapes on the editing machine. I hear again the voice of Augusta Bari Elia, her unfinished sentences, the smacking sound of her tongue sucking chocolates. It is curious how distracted I was by her long green gloves and the dexterity of those lizard-like hands. Hearing her voice again in the studio, it sounds less cracked and uncertain, almost fluent in spite of all the interruptions, enlivened by a hidden, somewhat crazy determination.

Ludovica's voice, heard beside her mother's, seems awkward and artificial; the tones are sharp and expose sudden abysses of anxiety.

I rush along impetuously and listen to the voice of the lady with the cats talking about Angela, which I'd furtively recorded.

"The cats always waited for her, you should have seen how they waited . . . when they heard her footsteps on the pavement they pricked up their ears. And then she disappeared."

I am still lacking many voices; the voice of Nando, of Mario Torres, of Glauco Elia, the stepfather.

Meanwhile I dial Adele Sòfia's number to know if there is anything new. But while I am asking for her, I catch sight of her walking down the passage making straight for the director's office. I catch up with her and tell her I'd like to talk to her and she makes a sign by rotating her first finger as if to say "afterwards" and then she closes the door behind her. She hasn't even smiled at me; I wonder whether she is annoyed with me.

Later, while I'm having a coffee at the bar, I suddenly find her beside me. She is wearing silent, soft-heeled shoes and an ugly brigand's hat on her head. She orders an iced coffee and as she sips it she draws close to my ear in a conspiratorial manner.

"Cusumano is worried."

"What about?"

"He doesn't want Italia Viva to become a branch of the police headquarters."

"I'm only gathering information."

"I calmed him down. I'm sure you'll do a really good job."

"Any news of Angela Bari?"

"They've found a small bloodstain on the inside door of the lift."

"The lift that goes up to my apartment?"

"Yes, but it was so small it went unnoticed."

I think of all the times I have been in the lift, opening and closing the door without seeing that very small spot of blood.

"Could I have an interview with the examining magistrate to talk about the bloodstain?"

"Yes, if you want . . . no, I'm afraid you can't, only because he's in Milan on another case. But if you like, I can give you the phone number of my colleague Lipari. Call him and say I've given you his name. He's dealing with the Bari case . . . he's already talked to Cusumano, so he won't be at all surprised."

"Him as well?"

"You won't believe how your director looks after you . . . if it were not for him, you couldn't get around as easily as you do to interview all and sundry!"

"But why doesn't he tell me?"

"He likes to stay in the background, does Cusumano. I'd say nothing pleases him so much as secret intelligence. You, Michela, are the one who makes the recordings and assembles the voices but he wants to remain the hidden engine behind the whole enterprise."

"But he shouldn't go and talk to the person I'm going to interview before I do, it ruins everything!"

"Well, have you discovered who murdered Angela Bari?" she asks smiling slyly from inside the white china cup.

"I know absolutely nothing. The deeper I go into it, the less I understand. I'm totally in the dark."

"That's the difference, we're interested in who did it and you're interested in why."

"Sometimes the who can include the why."

"Have you understood who Angela Bari was?"

"Someone with so many different faces."

"Don't try to understand and explain too much. Things are always more complicated than one thinks . . . Trust in what the voices suggest . . . but isn't this Lipari? Wait while I introduce you."

"He's going to see Cusumano. It's him who's turning the radio station into a branch of the police headquarters, not me!"

"No, I think he's come to look for me."

At last I meet Lipari, a large young man, big and tall with massive hands and lifeless eyes. Hair grows thickly inside his ears and tufts emerge from the collar of his shirt and escape out of the ill–fitting sleeves of his jacket.

I ask him to sit down with me at the end of the bar. He looks at his watch and shakes his head as if to say he can't, but with a smile Adele Sòfia urges him to stay. He accepts, although obviously put out.

We sit in a corner of the small room, beside an ornamental ficus plant with yellowing leaves. I bring out my small Sony. Lipari looks at it with suspicion but acts as if nothing has happened.

"Can I ask you if you have found the knife that was used in the Bari murder case?"

"The knife used in the attack? No."

"Have you found any traces of blood in the apartment different from that of the murdered girl?"

"No, we only have blood samples from the victim."

"And the bloodstain found in the lift?"

"We haven't had it analysed yet."

"At what time was Angela murdered?"

"Between 22 and 24 hours on June 24th."

"Can you tell me in what state the body was found?"

"Naked, in a curled up position, the knees touching the chin."

"Where was it?"

"On the floor in the end room which looks out on to the terrace."

"And her clothes?"

"Neatly folded on a chair. One pair of silk trousers, khaki coloured, a white shirt, a pair of cotton socks, pink nylon pants and bra."

"And shoes?"

"There was a pair of blue tennis shoes by the front door, placed side by side as if she had removed them before the arrival of the killer."

"Had the door been forced?"

"There were no signs of the apartment having been broken

into. We must assume that the victim opened the door spontaneously to the killer."

"Do you have any suspects?"

"No, not for the moment."

I look at him while he lights a cigarette. He must be about thirty years old, but looks younger. His pedantic intelligence, controlled and severe, contrasts with all the simian hair that escapes from his neck and his wrists.

"Would you allow me to visit the apartment, Signor Lipari?"

"Yes, as long as my superior, police commissioner Sòfia, agrees to it."

24

The sultry weather hangs heavy in the courtyard; I am sweating in the shade of the lime trees. Stefana and Giovanni are talking to the postman. She is dressed in red and looks like a student just back from college; he is in overalls and is cleaning a shovel while he chats with the young postman.

Lipari leaves the blue and white police car in front of the main entrance. "Call me if someone needs to go out," he tells Giovanni. I have difficulty in keeping up with this tall young man.

The lift ascends at its usual slow pace. Lipari stands right in front of me and gazes diffidently at the ceiling. It looks as if this morning he has done some assiduous gardening to collect and push inside his collar the strands of hair that normally escape all over the place.

The lift stops at the top floor with a hiss and two small jolts. I observe the door of my apartment as if I were seeing it for the first time; it is dark, with the frame in lighter wood, the peep-hole like a round golden eye, two brass locks, one for the big key and one for the small one. How fragile it all seems!

Opposite is Angela Bari's door, identical to mine, except that it has three locks. But they did not help to keep out the killer whom she herself let in so trustingly. How many times have

I also opened my door with an impulsive welcome without first looking or checking!

Lipari takes a bunch of keys out of his pocket and tries one after the other in Angela Bari's door until he eventually finds the right one.

Now it is simply a matter of breaking the paper seals. On the stairs I hear the light footsteps and gasping breath of Stefana.

"I've come to see if you need anything," she says, genuinely wanting to be of help.

"No thanks," Lipari replies discourteously and he shuts the door in her face.

"It's Stefana, the concierge, she came up out of kindness," I say while he switches on the light. There is still a smell of disinfectant lingering in the air and something else I seem to recognise as the smell of rotten fruit. What might still be in the fridge?

"Can't we let Stefana in?"

Lipari looks at me with annoyance and straightens his back. "The examining magistrate has only given permission for you and me, and that is all."

Is he a person tied to a strong sense of duty and is this something I need to understand, or is there a hidden feeling of hostility? "The body was found here," he says, going in front of me into the end room which corresponds to my study.

On the floor there are still chalk marks of the body traced on the floor tiles.

"May I record what you are saying?"

He looks at me uneasily. He evidently does not know whether the regulations allow it. I realise I have to push rather harder. "Adele Sòfia told me I could," and I take the Sony out of my pocket.

"I have nothing to say," he tells me discouragingly.

"Could you repeat what you first told me?"

"What was that?"

"Where the body was found and how."

"As I said to the lady, orders were given to recover the corpse from this part of the room." The voice becomes toneless, the language official.

"How do you think the crime took place?"

"The reason for the attack is not known. However, it may be presumed that the victim was attacked from the rear."

"Where would Angela Bari have been when she was stabbed?"

"Presumably in the corner sector of the window."

"What do you mean by the corner sector?"

"It is probable that Angela Bari was looking out of the window with her attacker standing behind her."

"She obviously couldn't have had any suspicions or she wouldn't have turned her back."

"She might also have turned away out of fright . . . it is probable the attacker knew the victim, this much seems certain."

"Can you let me see where her clothes were put?"

"Here they are, they're still here," he says, indicating a chair hidden by the shadow of the open door. And it is as if I am seeing Angela's body come to life. Those khaki-coloured trousers, that white shirt so carefully folded. It is as if her hands are in front of me, pressing the material, lifting it up, folding it; there is something so touching about these simple articles of clothing that I remain there, wordless, staring at them. I remember a similar feeling when I went to visit Auschwitz; the ovens with their black mouths, the rusty iron bars, the huts where birds had made their nests, had not made much impression on me, only a feeling of unending distance. But when I saw a pair of striped trousers hanging in a glass case, the whole camp fell on top of me with all its horrors, its screams, its atrocious deaths, and my breath was caught in my throat.

"We must presume it was the victim herself who put them there," Lipari explains. "It is women who fold up clothes, it is unusual for a man to do that."

"Isn't it possible she was first stabbed and then undressed?"

"No, otherwise we would have evidence of her clothes being torn. But, as you can see, they are untorn and clean just as they were when she placed them here."

"Isn't it odd that a woman, having opened the door to her

attacker and let him in, takes off her clothes, and then goes to look out of the window while he is standing right behind her?"

"There are details which need to be clarified."

"From your point of view, is there anyone who might be under suspicion among those we already know?"

"We are not in possession of proof, and the evidence is scarce. Even Judge Boni is puzzled. Her fiancé, Giulio Carlini, has a firm alibi which we have checked, her former husband was in America, we have checked on him as well; her sister Ludovica was at the cinema with her fiancé, or so they are saying, and only the testimony of the cashier is lacking."

"And Nando?"

"We are not aware of this individual."

"He was a friend of Angela's."

"How do you know this?"

"I was told by Sabrina."

"Who is Sabrina?"

"A prostitute who is a friend of Nando's. Look, if we had been able to meet sooner, I would have told you about Nando and Sabrina and you could have got more information."

"Ours is an investigation, not a story to be broadcast on radio."

"According to Sabrina, Angela worked as a prostitute under Nando's protection."

"We have no evidence that Angela Bari was a prostitute."

"But Sabrina has."

"Now you can come with me and we will take down your evidence. Have you recorded anything?"

"This will be of great interest to the listeners," I say and he gives me a sideways look, uncertain whether to laugh or to be severe. Then he twists his mouth sideways and opts for a forced smile.

25

The sink has a crystal clear, petulant voice; whenever I turn on the taps after I have been away for the day, it emits a jubilant hiccup; it suffers from "a dryness of the faucets", as Lipari might say.

While I wash my stockings and bra in a small plastic bowl, I think of Angela Bari's rose-pink nylon underwear; her bra, hanging from the arm of the chair, her pants, so delicate and transparent, folded up and put on top of her shirt. Is it likely that a girl who was in love would fold her pants before actually making love? I wonder whether Angela washed her under-clothes in the sink with a bar of washing soap like I do?

At the moment the papers are creating a big uproar. I dry my hands and open one of them. Since I have been involved with unsolved crimes, I pay much more attention to the crime section of the newspapers.

"She was murdered in the park in front of her four-year-old son," I read in today's paper. It happened in London, on Wimbledon Common. A young mother who had taken her son out for a walk was knifed by an unknown man.

"Little Alex, the only witness, is unable to speak. Even the caring attitude of the social workers has not helped him, he stays imprisoned in silence.

"The killer made his escape and no one has any idea who he might be. How do you set about finding someone who is totally unknown to the woman he attacked and killed when she tried to defend herself against his attempts to rape her?

"The woman was assaulted in front of her son whose body was covered in bruises as if he too had been attacked while trying to defend his mother. The man stabbed the woman in the throat and then ran off. An hour later a passer-by noticed the child lying huddled on the ground with his arms round the body of his mother. Inspector Michael Wickenden from Scotland Yard stated, 'I have never seen such a brutal crime . . . this young woman was out walking with her son in one of the most beautiful and peaceful areas of London . . .' Later on he said that 'over the last few years crimes in London have increased by 11 percent. From March 1991 to April 1992 there were 184 murders, 1180 rapes, and 3000 sexual assaults. The majority of the perpetrators of these crimes go unconvicted.'"

I tear this out of the paper and put it into the green folder with other newspaper accounts and items of news to take with me to the broadcasting station. As I am putting the folder away, I hear a ring at the door. I go to open it, but look through the spyhole first. I see a head of hair with mauve reflections moving frantically from side to side. It is Sabrina. I open the door and she rushes in impetuously, shutting the door behind her as if she were scared of being followed.

"What is the matter?"

"They came and questioned him."

"Who?"

"Nando."

"And then?"

"He accused me of denouncing him to the police."

"Why should he be so worried if he didn't kill Angela Bari? And he doesn't live at your place either, so they can't even accuse him of procuring."

"He'll kill me, that man will kill me seeing as I don't work for him as much as I used to . . . I've lost ten kilos and men don't want me any more. They look me over, you know, and then they push off. What can you say . . . It's as if I make them sick."

She says this laughing gently at herself, with a charm that is the opposite of her heavy make-up and the showiness of her gaudy clothes.

"Are you frightened of Nando? What's his surname?"

"Any old excuse is good enough for him to leave me. And if he wants to get rid of me his friends will help him out because I know too much about all their deals."

She lights a cigarette, her small suntanned hands are shaking. The gold lighter slips through her fingers and ends up on the floor; she picks it up showing her thin muscular legs. She puffs the smoke out angrily through her nose and mouth as if she were defying the gods. Fear has made her seem even wilder, her neck muscles are tense and rigid, her hair is shining and streaked with red: it curls like snakes.

"He's called Nando Pepi, but what'll happen now? I've really got myself into a fix, that guy'll kill me."

She notices the cigarette ash is falling on to the floor and looks around for an ashtray: she can't see one so she puts the ash into her cupped hand.

"It'll burn you," I say as I look for a small majolica vase that is usually there.

"No matter, I'm used to it, cars don't always have ashtrays," she says. "Some clients get livid if cigarette ash gets on to the floor. One bloke, after telling me how he'd just come back from his wife's funeral, saw me letting a bit of ash fall on to the car mat and he pushed me out swearing at me. 'It's only out of respect for your dead wife that I'm not reporting you,' I said to him."

She laughs, showing her small white teeth. "Ever since I was a child I've been able to pick up red-hot coals, my fingers don't feel it much. I've got hard skin even if I don't work with a pick and a shovel . . . it's because of having to take a trick's soul into my hand . . ."

"Soul?"

"How else can you call it? They're so attached to it, they're so crazy about it. If you don't look at it they're frightened they'll lose it . . . I like the ones with a delicate gentle soul, a little bit excitable that swells up as soon as you touch it. Others have what looks like a toad, they put it in your hand and wait for you to say 'That's great, congratulations!' . . . but I'd say it certainly doesn't count that much . . . The ones I like best are the older souls with experience, they're polite, they're discreet and they don't ever dream of doing it by forcing themselves on you."

I watch her with amusement while she tells me about the virility of souls, her face taking on an absorbed, happy expression that doesn't seem part of her. She is glad to be able to amuse me and in her voice I notice a theatrical subtlety I have not been aware of before.

She lights another cigarette; she has jettisoned the last one out of the window with an acrobatic throw. She seems all of a sudden to have forgotten the reason for her visit. She makes a little bow. "I greet the good soul like this!" she says with a little lascivious laugh.

Then in the same way as she came to life, she shuts down. She squashes the barely smoked cigarette beneath the sole of her shoe and puts it in her pocket; she passes a hand through her hair and says she has to go.

"Aren't you afraid of Nando any more?"

"I know how to deal with him but you should be giving him a wide berth. I don't want any trouble with the police."

"I didn't go looking for him, he just turned up here. Since then I haven't seen him."

"If you do see him, don't tell him I've been here."

"You say Nando would be capable of killing you, so do you think he could have killed Angela Bari?"

"Nando? No, he might easily kill me, but not Angela, not her, he'd too much respect for her, he loved her, he'd never lose his cool with her. No, I don't think so."

26

I am back in the Tyrolean sitting room with the carved wooden hearts and the green and white majolica stove. Adele Sòfia sits facing me, her legs stretched out on the floor. She looks tired. She is wearing silk stockings that squeeze the flesh under her knees. She looks intently at me, as she always does, opening wide her soft hazel eyes. She is a woman who doesn't seem to know what hypocrisy is; she tends to say exactly whatever she is thinking, but she is never prejudicial, not even against the sort of criminals she has to prosecute. Yet in her shrewd look and ironic smile, there is a basic reticence: for all one knows this could be her way of distancing herself from all the horrors.

The small dental brace glitters giving her a pouting and

slightly cruel appearance. She explains to me how the blood-stain, found on the door of the lift, has been treated with sophisticated techniques which can analyse the structure of human plasma.

"Each person has a genetic make-up that is delineated on the print-out according to recognisable categories." Then, patiently, like a mother, she explains to me the function of DNA analysis. "There is something curious about the very small spot of blood we found in the lift; it appears that the DNA blueprint of Angela Bari is mixed with another DNA that is not hers. I believe that for the first time we've got hold of precise evidence relating to the suspect."

"So all that's needed is to examine some blood samples and then it is possible to identify the murderer?"

"Michela, you are forcing me to work on a case that isn't really mine. Between your director, Signor Cusumano, and yourself . . ."

"Have you talked to him again?"

Once more the director has been forestalling me, controlling me, directing me from a distance. He pretends to leave me free and then he follows every move I make. And I know already how he will drastically cut all my interviews.

I can see his pale butterfly hands fluttering in front of my nose, rising up to screen and to reproach, hovering with dancing movements over the explosive material I bring him, confining me within the magic circle of his will.

"Your director is an intelligent man," says Adele Sòfia. "He confronts me with a whole lot of questions and they aren't the usual commonplace ones. It really seems as if his main interest is in crimes against women, a sign that he's taken your series to heart, and you should be glad of that."

"Yes, I am glad."

"However, the way he's always phoning me has awakened the suspicion of my superiors. They are beginning to think the programme might turn into some sort of documentary on the police, or so they're saying. They think Lipari won't be up to it, so they have asked me to assist in the enquiry. They really pushed me, I'm actually involved in another case that could be much more useful to me . . . but what can I do? Obviously I can see it as a mystery and it's my job to find a solution . . . Do you remember Oedipus? 'If anyone amongst you knows who killed Laius, son of Labdákou, let him now tell the truth.' "

"What has Oedipus got to do with it?"

"Oedipus was looking for an external solution to the misfortune he himself had brought upon his own city through his own flesh, his own history."

"I don't understand."

"It's a warning not to let our attention get distracted by signals coming from the enemy. Often we don't know how to find solutions because they are right in front of us."

"Do you have any ideas?"

"You know what Goethe said, 'The most difficult thing in the world is to see with one's own eyes what is beneath one's nose.' "

"Are you saying that the solution to the Bari case is right here and we aren't seeing it?"

"It's possible."

"What does Judge Boni say?"

"He doesn't seem very interested in the case. Actually that could be to our advantage; it leaves us freer. He's suspicious because the press has got so involved. He's very capable but rather reserved, and he's distrustful of being dragged into the limelight by the media."

"Lipari doesn't seem to me to be very thorough: he didn't know about the existence of Sabrina, even though she had phoned the radio station to give information about Angela Bari. He accuses me of treating it all as a story for radio."

"I've made inquiries about Sabrina, otherwise Carmelina Di Giovanni; she is a compulsive liar. It isn't the first time she's got us going down the wrong track, she's a brilliant story-teller, even her man says that about her."

"Nando Pepi?"

"Yes, he's somebody who knows what he's about. For a pimp, he is quite out of the ordinary. He has none of the traditional characteristics, he doesn't hoard money, doesn't ill-treat his girls and he falls in love. Indeed he's altogether strange. He's educated, and he has a certain virile charm."

"It sounds as if you've fallen for him yourself!"

"He denies absolutely that Angela Bari was ever a prostitute. He met her with friends and took her out twice to a restaurant; that is all."

"And if he were lying?"

"The woman Di Giovanni has retracted everything she said and admits to having lied. She says she invented everything to make herself more interesting for the radio."

"Why don't you believe Sabrina might have been telling the truth?"

"We've been verifying it."

This caution is a sign of her need to oppose me.

"Does verification mean proof?"

Adele Sòfia looks at me impatiently. I am sure she's thinking how tiresome I am being. But then her natural good humour supervenes and she smiles, making her dental brace sparkle.

"It must seem odd that I'm wearing a brace at my age," she says as if able to read my thoughts. But she doesn't look offended, only amused and as if under an obligation to respond in her usual careful and precise manner. "It isn't only children who have to wear braces to straighten their teeth, sometimes adults have to as well if their teeth are too far apart. It's only for another few months."

"The brace doesn't worry me at all, I was only thinking how it makes you look quite childlike."

"I'm not really aware of it now, but to begin with it was intolerable. I felt I had an armed mouth, like a shark."

Strange she could think that. I have never looked on her as a fish, more like a bear. I tell her this and she laughs.

"I think Sabrina is telling the truth," I persist.

"We got information from all the luxury hotels in Rome but no one had ever seen Angela Bari."

"Even if they'd seen her, they mightn't have said so."

"That's true. However, without proof, we only have words. Why would Angela Bari, with a monthly income of five million, have worked as a prostitute?"

"Ludovica says Angela didn't have any money."

"Signora Augusta Elia showed me cheque stubs."

"Did you see them all for every year?"

"No, not all."

"From what Ludovica says, her mother only gave her daughter money from time to time, not every month."

"In that family one never knows who is telling the truth. I've already summoned Augusta again to police headquarters, she's coming the day after tomorrow."

"Have you talked to the stepfather?"

"Yes, he came forward as a witness without being asked. He brought a card from the hospital stating he was there at the birth of his daughter on the evening Angela was murdered. We have the evidence of the nurses, and in any case he and Angela hadn't seen each other for years."

"Who told you that?"

"The mother and also her daughter Ludovica."

"They said quite different things to me."

"My dear Michela, I'll question them both again."

I understand I am being dismissed. I watch her getting up on to her feet with dignity. Everything about her gives a feeling of calm, patience and mental vigour. It does not seem as if crimes make her want to run away as they do me; she moves with perfect equilibrium among the butchered corpses, the slaughtered bodies, without any hint of evasion or repugnance, with a cold passion for the "theorems of proof" that animated her.

She comes to the door with me, telling me about a recipe she is going to make for me when we next meet and might have a little more time to "chatter away without the intrusion of work".

"It's made with macaroni, olives, yellow peaches and squid, I'm just waiting for all the ingredients . . . ah, here comes Marta."

Marta Girardengo appears with a shopping bag in front of the entrance door.

"You're back already?"

"Luckily there weren't many people. I didn't have to queue."

"Did you get the yellow peaches and the squid?"

"Yes, I did."

"And the olives?"

"Black olives from Puglia."

"So Michela, seeing we have everything, why don't you come to supper with us this evening?"

"This evening I can't, I've got an appointment."

"Well then, tomorrow evening?"

"Fine, thanks."

"And maybe I'll have talked to Ludovica Bari by then. And with Judge Boni. We must carry on with blood examinations to find out whether there are any coincidences, as soon as the judge gives the green light. And who knows whether the case mightn't be solved sooner then you think? Seeing that Angela Bari opened the door to her killer means that the list of suspects can't be that long."

27

Actually I have no appointment for this evening but I want to stay at home and wait for Marco's call. I don't know why I think he might be going to ring me this evening; a presentiment perhaps, or only a longing.

I lie down on the divan with a book in my hand. When I am alone I don't cook, I have a glass of milk and a slice of bread, I peel an apple, or I eat a couple of apricots.

But this evening I am unable to follow the words on the page, my thoughts keep reverting to Angela Bari. Right now she is part of the mystery to be resolved as Adele Sòfia would say, and perhaps this mystery touches me more than I was able to foresee.

I have put Pergolesi on the record player and I am thinking how this evening the music disturbs me, suggesting so many perspectives; so ethereal and so magnificent, but too remote.

In the silence of the evening I hear the shrill sound of the front door bell. I get up and without thinking go to the telephone, but rather than a voice calling me, there is a body standing at the door. I go towards it on tiptoe, I can feel my heart racing beneath my blouse. Who can it be at this hour? And how have they managed to open the main gate without buzzing the interphone? I decide to pretend to be out but how to make this credible when the lights are on and the *Stabat Mater* resounds through the apartment?

I put my eye to the spyhole. I see Stefana's beautiful dark head and I breathe a sigh of relief. I open the door to let her in.

"Excuse me for coming so late, I've really wanted to talk to you but I've been busy all day, up and down stairs, taking turns with my husband in the porter's lodge, looking after Berengario, and simply haven't had a moment. Now the porter's lodge is closed, my husband is sitting in front of the television and my mother-in-law is knitting, so I said to myself I'm going up to the top floor to talk to Signorina Canova."

"Sit yourself down, Stefana, I was reading and . . ."

Stefana sits down on the divan and looks at me with her big clear eyes in which the white seems to have taken up all of the black.

"What's been happening, Stefana?"

"You remember when my mother-in-law said she'd seen that small man, the one with the high-heeled ankle boots? I'd actually never seen him, but yesterday when I was cleaning the stairs, there he was. Suddenly I saw him beside me like a ghost. I don't know how he managed to be so silent with those heels . . . he was moving like a cat . . . I said 'Excuse me, where are you going?' and he gave me a little smile and went on up the stairs. I didn't have the courage to be more insistent, I don't know why but he frightened me . . . there, that's what I wanted to tell you!"

"Thank you, Stefana. Why do you think this man keeps on coming here?"

"I don't understand it at all myself but it frightens me. In the papers they say he was a friend of Angela Bari but I'd never seen him here before."

I watch her while her two big capable hands that I've often

admired go up to her forehead in an unconsciously compelling gesture, as if she were trying to grab hold of a secret thought.

"I wanted to tell you to keep the windows that overlook the balcony closed, I don't trust that man!"

"Is the door that opens on to the communal terraces firmly shut?"

"Yes, I saw to that a short while ago . . . I've got the key, here it is and there aren't any spare ones. But I wanted to ask you, Michela, have they analysed the blood they found in the lift?"

"Yes, it appears they've found it to be a mixture of Angela Bari's blood and the blood of her killer. Now they're going to analyse everyone's blood."

"Who is everyone?"

"All her family, her fiancé, her stepfather, her sister. Do you remember Giulio Carlini, did he often come to see Angela?"

"Was he that tall, handsome man always dressed in blue? Yes, I remember him, he always came with a tiny suitcase, he'd go across the courtyard looking very reflective. He never noticed the flowers or the lime trees or the fountain, he saw nothing. He was always pleasant to me if distant. He used to stay for a day, a night and then he'd be off."

"Did you ever see her stepfather, Glauco Elia?"

"What did he look like?"

I show her a photograph I found in a newspaper. Meanwhile I turn on the Sony without asking; I don't want her to become reticent and shy as happens to most people. I am becoming a secret stealer of voices.

Stefana looks at the photo for a long time and seems uncertain. She presses her chin with her finger until it starts to turn white.

"I don't think I've ever seen him."

"He says he's never been here but Ludovica says he has."

"It's possible. Maybe I did see him once."

"When was that?"

"It could have been three months ago, or even four, I'm not sure."

"And if we asked your mother-in-law? She seems to me to

be a good observer. She looks people in the face and makes a note of them. She's really got something of the detective in her."

"Let's go."

"She won't be asleep?"

"Not yet. She doesn't go to bed till her television programme is over, until then she knits, she's never still."

28

Signora Maria Maimone is sitting on a sofa bed patterned with red flowers. She is wearing slippers and knitting; her eyes move up and down from the television screen to the wool. "Mother, here is Signorina Canova from the top floor apartment. She wants to ask you something."

Giovanni Mario gets up to greet me and turns down the television so we can talk in peace. Maria Maimone gives me a weary look, yet last time she had seemed so lively; perhaps she is feeling sleepy.

"Go on, then," she says sharply and dauntingly.

"Do you by any chance remember seeing a tall, thin gentleman, slightly bald, good-looking and in his fifties? He was Angela Bari's stepfather."

"I remember everything," she says and I understand how she enjoys showing off her memory.

"Your daughter-in-law has told me you remember almost everyone who goes through the courtyard. Do you remember this gentleman?"

I show her the newspaper photograph which she snatches from me with great rapidity.

"A tall man, rather bald, who looks like Saint Joseph. Yes, I remember him."

"When did you see him here?"

"I don't know."

"What a pity, I was counting on your memory."

She gives me a quick look, unsure whether to snap up my

compliment or ignore it. Then she decides to allow herself this small expression of vanity. She gives me to understand that she is not stupid, that she knows I am praising her and that she is doing it because she has decided to play the game rather than from any feeling of trust.

"My mother-in-law remembers everything, she really does," Stefana says in encouragement and the woman looks her up and down with a mixture of satisfaction and repugnance.

"So then?"

"Then," and she looks like an actress who is relishing the attention of her audience, measuring out the time with masterly skill. "I saw him . . . I saw him . . . let us say between the 28th and the 30th of May."

I hope she doesn't notice the small Sony I am holding in my hand almost completely hidden by my sleeve, but from one of her looks I realise she has clearly seen it and that in the presence of so far-reaching an ear, she will force herself to remember accurately. "I saw him on the 29th of May, I do remember now. I was closing the entrance door as he arrived and said good evening to me. He had a parcel in his hand."

"Are you sure he was on his way to the top floor, to Angela Bari's apartment?"

"I didn't ask him where he was going, I counted the floors the lift went up to and it went up to the top and came back empty."

"What a pity Mamma wasn't here when Signora Bari died, because she would have remembered everything."

"When did you go back to Calabria, Signora Maimone?"

"On the 30th of May."

"And when did you return here?"

"Mother comes and goes. She doesn't like being here that much, she'd rather be in San Basilio where she has a house and the meat business. But if the little boy isn't well or there are workmen to supervise I telephone her and she comes," explains Giovanni sounding kindly and apologetic. "Since her husband died," he goes on to say, "her second husband of course, her first husband was my father who died when I was a year old, Mamma has been alone and I think that . . ."

"What on earth are you talking about, it's of no interest to her," she interrupts him sharply, "and now I'm off to bed because it's late."

She makes it clear that she isn't going to say another word. She casts a last look at the tape-recorder, twists her mouth into an enigmatic smile and sets about transforming the chair into a bed for the night.

I say good-night to Stefana and Giovanni and go back to my apartment. Almost as soon as I've closed the door I hear footsteps coming up the stairs. I bar the door and turn out the light. The footsteps come closer, up towards the top floor. I stay silent, immobile, my back pinned against the wall.

I hear the footsteps stop in front of my door. I do not even dare to turn round to look through the spyhole, I am so afraid of anyone knowing I am here. A moment later the footsteps sound further away, but only a little. Now the person is in front of the door of Angela Bari's apartment. Finally I move away from the wall and, trying not to make the least sound, put my eye to the spyhole.

In the passage with his back to me I see a man fiddling with the sealed door. I hold my breath, I see he keeps turning round as if he were listening. Even though the light in the passage is dim, I immediately recognise Nando Pepi. From a movement of his hand and from the way it glints I also recognise the tiger's-eye ring.

Now the door opposite is open and he has the keys in his hand. He looks round again cautiously and then he goes into the apartment closing the door softly behind him.

I ought to telephone the police headquarters at once but I dare not move. I keep very quiet, leaning against the door, waiting for him to come out. Until I see him go away, I certainly cannot go to bed.

But time passes and he doesn't come out. Suppose that he has clambered over the glass partition that divides the two terraces? I keep telling myself the window is shut, yes, I certainly shut it, so he can't come in like a ghost. Yet a doubt remains. With the utmost caution, I go into the bedroom where fortunately the window is closed. I go to the study and there too, on Stefana's recommendation, everything is bolted and barred. In the kitchen, however, the window is open and it too opens on to the balcony. I am sweating and my hands are trembling. As I close the shutters, I have the impression of seeing a shadow on the terrace. At last I have closed everything and if he tries to break a window I can escape through the door. But just at that moment I hear noises coming from the passage. Barefooted I rush on tiptoe to look through the spyhole. And there he is, carefully closing Angela Bari's door. He has something in his hands. Is it a box? He lifts his pale face towards me and I have the definite impression that he has seen me, even though I know he would not be able to do so through the tiny rounded glass.

His expressionless face ripples into a sad, forced smile, as if in greeting. I force myself to stay put; let's hope he takes the lift, I keep on repeating, let's hope he takes the lift, and then I can check up on him. If he walks downstairs, I will never be sure if he has really gone all the way down; he could walk down a few stairs and come back. I might have to stay here on the look-out all night long.

He isn't taking the lift. He can hide better on the stairs and he is starting to walk slowly down them. Fortunately his heels make a dull, definite clunk, and I can follow them down to the ground floor.

After I had talked to Sabrina and got his name, I no longer felt afraid of him, but now he terrifies me because he has been so close and I do not what he is up to or what is in his mind.

I dial the number of Adele Sòfia. I don't care that it's two o'clock in the morning, she must be interested in whoever comes at night with keys to open the door of Angela Bari's apartment. "I'm sorry to wake you up but I wanted to tell you I saw Nando Pepi in the passage a short time ago. He unlocked the door of Angela Bari's apartment and went in, and after a quarter of an hour, he came out carrying a parcel in his hand."

I hear incomprehensible gurgling sounds and then an "Ah, yes!"

"I'm very sorry to phone you at this time but . . ."

"Nando Pepi, it was really him?"

"Yes, I'm certain."

"Are you sure he used the keys to open the door?"

"Yes, I saw him."

"I'll send someone round at once to see . . . only I don't know who I can find at this hour. Good-night Michela, we'll be in touch tomorrow."

I get into bed and turn out the light. At half-past eight tomorrow I have to be at the radio station. But I cannot get to sleep, my ears are on the alert to pick up the least sound from the stairs. Only at first light do I fall asleep, exhausted, with that melancholy smile in front of my eyes.

29

As I go out into the passage, I see two policemen outside Angela Bari's apartment examining the broken seals. Behind them is a locksmith waiting to replace the locks.

I run out in haste so as not to be late. Should I take my little Fiat or should I not? If I go by bus, heaven knows when I'll be there, and it is just the same when I go on foot. Since I am in a hurry I decide to go by car.

I drive through the Piazza dei Ponziani, I take the Via Titta Scarpetta; in the distance I see the lady with the cats busy feeding her animals. I stop alongside the pavement. She lifts up her head in surprise and greets me with a wave. Her hand is smeared with rice and gravy.

When I arrive Tirinnanzi is swearing and cursing because for the hundredth time this year he is alone at the control desk.

"And where is Mario?"

"I don't know where he's gone and hidden himself . . . I should be at my desk sorting out the news and instead I have to be here struggling with Professor Baldi."

"It isn't half-past eight yet," I say.

"It will be in seven minutes," he replies dryly.

I take his place at the controls and wait for the technician. I read the title for today's topic which is: "The temptation of crime", no doubt a last minute idea from Cusumano, who is circling like a vulture round my series. He could have told me he had changed the topic, I don't know whether he has warned Professor Baldi; it would be best to send him a fax.

Mario Calzone arrives in a strawberry-coloured shirt and white gym shoes. His eyes are swollen but otherwise he is in a good mood. Now I can go and get myself a coffee.

While I wait for the dark liquid to spurt out into the plastic cup, I hear the director talking in a loud voice on the phone. "Don't be such a pain in the arse!" He is really shouting and I can't but be amazed; it is so rare for him to raise his voice and very unusual for him to be using such a coarse expression.

"I know I owe the post of director to you but I still don't have to be under your thumb . . . no, no . . . but what has that got to do with it? Who has been in touch with you? . . . So it was the chief of police, was it? And what did he want? . . . No, I'm telling you once and for all, I've decided to cover unpunished crimes and I'm not giving up. Is that clear? I don't give a damn if you think it's going to damage the image of the police . . ."

So they are talking about my programmes. I wonder why he is so worked up about it. It is possible they are trying to censor him in the same way as he does me. Tirannanzi once spoke to me very bluntly about the way our radio station functions.

"You're such a little innocent, you think it'll be free just because it's privately owned. Where do you imagine the money comes from?" I can still hear his voice whispering in my ear. "Who do you think finances it all in exchange for publicity that'll win votes and other favours. Our director does a deal with one foot in politics and the other in journalism. If he didn't keep that foot well supported with plenty of backing, do you believe he'd have made the career he has, young as he is? Yes, of course he's ambitious. He's a prison guard, that's what he is . . . he's here to make sure we don't venture outside and that we don't go trampling in some protected area."

The technician signals to me through the glass screen that he is taking his place at the little table. I sit down in front of the microphones, I put on the headphones, I thread the wrist pin, I check the volume control and the tunes.

"He's coming on line," Mario warns me through his gum.

I raise the volume. This morning Professor Baldi seems to be in good humour; he greets me in a confident tone. "Good morning to Michela Canova, the pillar of studio A at Italia Viva! So, my dear Michela, what is the theme for discussion with the listeners this morning?" he asks absent-mindedly. He obviously has not looked at the fax I sent him a short while ago.

"The temptation of crime," I reply.

"Not bad, eh; who thought of that? I bet it was our inimitable director Ettore Cusumano. Bravo!" He says this knowing how the director frequently listens in at the start of a transmission, especially in the morning.

"The first phone call, are you taking it?" the technician asks through the headphones. I nod "yes" with my head and he puts me on air.

"Hullo, can I talk to you?" A young voice, it is unclear whether it belongs to a girl or to a boy for the voice is breaking.

Even Professor Baldi must have realised this but does not want to appear thrown off balance and in a fatherly voice asks, "Who are you?"

"My name is Gabriele," says the voice, "and I'm seventeen."

"Do you know what today's theme is?"

"Yes, I've phoned because of it."

"Are you telling me that at seventeen you feel tempted to commit a crime?"

"It's my father, I hate him, I keep feeling I'd like to kill him."

"My dear Gabriele, that is quite natural; at your age one wants to distance oneself from what one is closest to, from what has power over us. At your age, on a metaphorical level you understand, I too wanted to kill my father."

"Do you know what my father does when we're all playing cards, my mother, him and me? He cheats!"

"All parents cheat a little in order to please their children."

"No, he cheats to win."

"Do you often play cards as a family?"

"And do you know what he does when we're having a meal? He has two bottles of wine, one of good quality for himself and one of lousy quality for us. He says bad wine is bad for him. But what about us? If my mother wasn't like a child and incapable of living on her own, I'd have killed him already."

"I imagine you get on perfectly well with this child mother of yours?"

"Oh yes, when my father isn't there, she puts on her lipstick and we go off to the cinema together."

"My dear Gabriele, have you ever read *Oedipus*, the play by Sophocles?"

"Yes, I've read it, I've read it, I'm not that stupid, I know all about Greek tragedy."

"You are wanting to kill your father and get off with your mother, it's a classic. Think about it and you'll understand that yours is a common situation."

The professor is in a hurry and instinctively he is putting down what the boy has been saying. Or perhaps the discussion is embarrassing him.

"Gabriele may not have finished," I intervene, seeking to prolong the discussion, and indeed Gabriele does want to go on.

"Do you know what my father does at night? He goes to the lavatory and he never lifts up the toilet seat; he's always leaving drops of urine on it. In the morning I go there, I sit down and I get all wet. I've told him, 'Lift the seat, it won't cost you anything, all men wipe the seat after doing a pee.' And do you know what he says to me? 'I've got a good aim.' I say, 'No, it's a bad aim, papa, if I'm forever getting soaked!' For that I could kill him."

"My dear Gabriele, have you ever thought of getting a room away from home where you could live on your own? This situation of everyone living together can be an unhappy one . . . it's you who has to go away in the end, you know that. But instead children stay at home, full of despair and hatred, made ill by resentment, but they stay, they go on staying until total exhaustion sets in and then there's a catastrophe." He talks heatedly, as if taken over by his own personal preoccupations, and having apparently forgotten all about the boy. I find myself wondering whether the professor has a grown-up son. He has never told me about one.

"But where's the money coming from, Professor?" The far-away voice of the boy can be heard protesting, "My father has a pension, my mother lives off him and I live off both of them."

"My dear Gabriele, you must try to understand your father, not only judge him. You have to understand his age, his poverty, his tiredness. You are young, he is old; let him live his last years in peace, you will not regret it . . . Be tolerant of him like a strong person is able to be, don't make yourself wretched through an anger that is hurting both you and him." At this point the sermon is brought to an end and the boy who has become resigned to patiently listening, realises this.

From some small explosions coming down the microphone I gather that Professor Baldi is in the middle of one of his acrobatic feats of making coffee and talking at the same time.

I imagine him in his dressing gown with his feet in slippers. He lights the stove, leans over the espresso machine and then once again takes hold of the microphone which he has been keeping wedged between his shoulder and his ear as if it were a violin. He does it skilfully though, so the listener is not aware. Only I, with my trained ear, can recognise from the slight changes in tone how his voice becomes a little distant from the microphone and then comes back with a rush of sound.

A little later, while he is talking to a woman who is telling him about the way she is tempted to kill her son who is a heroin addict, I can hear the coffee machine puffing and hissing.

The conversation continues calmly and fluently; the woman comes over spellbound as if by a boa constrictor. His strategy is more one of hypnosis than reasoned discussion, so as to "touch the heart of the listener with the tip of the tongue", as he once described it to me facetiously over the telephone.

To help him I join in the discussion with the exasperated mother; giving him time to swallow a biscuit. I encourage the woman to talk and she, half crying, tells of how her son has been transformed into a thief, and of how he takes anything valuable of hers and goes to sell it, and of how, when she protests, he threatens her with a bread knife.

When the broadcast is over, driven by sudden hunger, I go down to the bar below the radio station. As I gulp down a cappuccino I see the director come in; he suddenly rushes to the cash desk to pay for me. I try to stop him because I do not like feeling indebted to him, but he doesn't leave me time to bring out my purse.

Such unexpected generosity must compensate for months of delay in paying my salary. While it is true it is not him who pays it, I have never seen him take our side with management.

"So how is it going, the work on crimes against women, all these crimes which go unpunished?"

"Do you want to see the material?" I ask, arming myself with good will.

"No, I trust you, Canova. I know you work well and conscientiously."

Meanwhile he has ordered a cream cake which he grabs impatiently out of the waiter's hands. He squashes it between his teeth, making the cream spurt out all over his clean shirt. With a gesture of anger he asks for talcum powder, meanwhile cleaning himself with the paper tablecloth. He appears to have entirely forgotten about me, there is no point in waiting for him. I say goodbye and go back up.

The computer is waiting for me with the titles of the soap instalments and outlines of the broadcasts that need to be edited. But my mind stays empty and inert. In front of me something is swaying to and fro in the air. Surely it can't be the same spider I put gently outside the window two days ago. When I arrived early in the morning, I found threads woven between the lampstand and the jar that has all the pens and pencils shoved into it.

The web swayed in a draught of air every time the door was opened. With my finger I took one end of the web with the spider hanging from it and placed it gently outside the window.

Two days after I carried out this manoeuvre it is back again; unless it is another spider exactly like the first, a son perhaps? I take hold of a pencil that has the threads of the web wrapped round it and look closely at the little spider; it has a minute, light-coloured body with slender legs which when they are retracted, form a ball almost like a turd. I open the window and let it slide down along the wall towards the plants on the balcony below. I close the window and go back to the computer.

"A woman found strangled and left abandoned on a refuse site." Someone had cut off her hand before leaving her there, dead and completely stripped. An act of revenge? There have been many suspects but they have found nothing and the investigation has been dropped.

A little girl of eight years old has disappeared. The person most active in the search for her, the most upset by her disappearance is her father. The child is found strangled underneath the floor of the house. The mother accuses the father of having raped and strangled her, he accuses his wife of having killed her out of jealousy. No proof is found and neither parent is charged with the murder. The case is filed away in the archives in spite of the discovery that the girl had actually been raped.

I shift my eyes from the computer screen to the jar full of pencils. I am amazed; a little spider with a small light-coloured body is imperturbably weaving a web that joins the edge of the computer to the point of a felt tip pen that sticks out of the jar.

I get up to go and get a glass of water from the cloakroom. As I pass in front of the mirror I see a pale face covered in tears. I touch my cheek with my hand, I have been crying without being aware of it. I can't distance myself from the image of that tortured little girl. Tears well up from the bottom of my heart which I thought detachment and logic had made impervious.

30

The dish of macaroni with peaches and squid impinges on my scattered thoughts. I think that the way Adele Sòfia concentrates on her cooking demonstrates a sensuous intelligence which will always win over her guests.

I eat slowly and lazily, savouring this mixture of sweet and bitter, of tender and coarse.

"*Canaderli* and macaroni are from two different, separate worlds, one from the north, green and wooded, the other from the south, more like a desert. The story of my life," she says, chewing slowly and looking at me intently. "I am myself half from Bolzano and half from Syracuse, part Mediterranean and part Alpine."

I raise my eyes from my plate to look at Adele Sòfia's hands. Working hard as usual, they move quickly and deftly between a dish and the white tablecloth, between the toasted bread and the glass jug of red wine; with those fingers that are so familiar with the tactile quality of food, she clasps handcuffs on to the wrists of murderers. A mixture of softness and hardness, of nurture and punishment – the attributes of a mother.

Meanwhile Marta Girardengo is relating a dream she had last night of a woman with a lion's head who is laughing and weeping at the same time.

"Was she sad-looking with long whiskers?"

"No, not whiskers, but a strange face, cat-like."

"Without realising it, you were possibly thinking of Sikmeth, the Egyptian goddess of plague and healing."

"Plague and healing?"

"Sikmeth is both, she feeds off corpses, she is ferocious and cruel but at the same time she can cure any illness with a touch of her winged fingers," explains Adele Sòfia while she goes on eating calmly. "At night she knows how to inflict unendurable pain and in the morning she becomes someone whom everyone would like to meet."

"But how can I dream of a goddess I've never even heard of?" says Marta Girardengo, a little put out that someone else should have appropriated her dream.

Whereas Adele Sòfia is extroverted, direct, and has a cool, rational mind, Marta Girardengo is introverted, shadowy, and modest: while one is matronly, ungainly, clumsy and motherly, the other is agile, feline, daughterly. Adele wears her hair tied behind her neck, Marta has it long and curling down to her shoulders. Yet in spite of their differences, one feels that they have a profound companionship, a long and complex friendship.

While we are having dessert, I make up my mind to describe what happened last night, But Adele Sòfia anticipates me by asking about Pepi.

"The mistake occurred because whoever was in charge of the case didn't have the locks changed," she says, "the seals are only strips of paper stuck to the doors, it's easy to break them. The lock should have been changed but no one remembered about it. On the other hand it is hard to envisage someone having the effrontery to return at night to an apartment after it has been sealed. But the fact he had the key will be held as evidence against him, it will be an incontestable proof . . . however you will have to give evidence that you saw Pepi go into Angela Bari's apartment with the keys."

She sees I am not happy about this and forestalls my protest.

"It has nothing to do with being a spy, Michela, it's about telling the truth."

"Supposing he isn't the murderer and I didn't want to cause him any harm?"

"The DNA will be proof of this; meanwhile the fact remains that he did break the seals, that he got into the apartment with the key, which indicates a familiarity that was not suspected earlier. These are not only indications, my dear Michela, they begin to be proof and therefore to carry some weight."

"Have you interrogated him?"

"Yes, once. Now he can't be found – which further aggravates his situation."

"How do you mean, he can't be found, if last night he was on my landing?"

"He isn't at home, nor at Carmelina di Giovanni's place."

"I wanted to tell you that Signora Maimone, the porter's mother, says she saw Angela Bari's stepfather going up to see her three weeks or so before the crime took place. He said he hadn't seen her for years."

"We've also spoken with Signora Maimone but she is not a reliable witness."

"Why not?"

"Do you know what they call her in her village? They call her 'the saint'! Years ago she made quite a stir because she claimed to have seen the Madonna. Some people listened to her but then it was discovered she had set up a business in replicas of saints . . ."

"But she's got a butcher's shop."

"Only since her second husband died, not before. Canova, you need to be wary of people who are somewhat quaint, they are the ones that lead us down the wrong path . . ."

As she talks she puts a large spoonful of strawberry ice-cream on my plate, and places a long pointed biscuit on top of it as if it were a flag.

Perhaps she is right; if Maria Maimone is prone to having visions, her evidence will only be disregarded. What judge would take her seriously?

We move into the Tyrolean sitting room. On a shelf a huge bunch of yellow roses towers above us; a little faded, they give out a dense, cloying scent.

"So what happens next?" I ask, feeling discouraged.

"I've already said that Signor Elia does not come into it, and Judge Boni is also convinced of this after having questioned him. We have a letter from the hospital and the evidence of two nurses that he was present when his young wife was giving birth on the evening of June 24th. All in all, at the moment we have few concrete facts. The most compromising evidence relates to Nando Pepi. He is in possession of the keys to the Bari apartment and he has been back at night to get something, possibly the knife since it has not been found. This is enough to incriminate him. And I think Judge Boni will be charging him, we only need an analysis of his blood to confirm it all . . . to me his guilt seems obvious."

"Almost too obvious . . . but why would a murderer come back so rashly to the place where he killed his victim?"

"Legend has it that the perpetrator always returns to the scene of the crime," she says jokingly, making the braces on her teeth glitter. "They have a morbid fascination with the place where their rage has exploded. Every violent crime also involves a loss of self, or so they say . . . and the murderer goes back to the place where he has thrown away part of himself in order to find it again, or perhaps even to contemplate the extent of his loss, something that gives rise to a dizzy state of exaltation."

"Do you mind if I put the tape-recorder on?"

"Go ahead, but are you never separated from this diabolical contraption?"

"If you knew the quality of this machine, you would love it as much as I do."

"I don't really love machines, they give me a headache. I use a car very little, I either go on foot or by bicycle. Do you know when they first saw me arriving at the police headquarters on my rickety bicycle, they nearly arrested me?"

"She expected to go into the big courtyard, where all the big shots keep their luxury cars, on her old bicycle with a shopping basket!" Marta Girardengo is speaking and I notice that she has a restrained throaty voice: a voice that shuts out any internal echoes and is kept tightly under control even when there is no need. Now she is laughing, and her laugh, instead of releasing her voice, makes it sound more arid and more tightly swallowed, as if it were a considerable effort.

"My tape-recorder is like a blackbird I once knew; one that had a prodigious memory and repeated everything it heard in a shrill voice of complete mimicry. It didn't understand, yet all the same something of itself was there."

"And like a blackbird you carry it around perched on one shoulder!"

"Police Commissioner, can we go back to the murderer? Could you say something about him?"

"What can I say? It is likely we are dealing with a man who is strong and robust, presumably quite young, about Pepi's age. The examination of the stab wounds shows them to have all been made at the same angle indicating a hand with a firm, tough wrist. The stabs were made with determination, without hesitation, one could say they were from a man in full control of himself. There was nothing casual or erratic in the way he acted. One can surmise a given plan of action, and a straight-forward emotion brooded over for a long time."

"It could be that Angela didn't open the door to her killer but that he opened it with keys she'd given him or that he'd got hold of. As I remember it, the keys were found on the inside keyhole, so how could Nando have inserted them?"

"He could have had the keys and could have her open the door to him and if she were waiting for him, nothing would be more probable."

"There's still the mystery of the carefully folded clothes. Isn't there something quite controlled and routine in this folding of clothes on a chair as if it were an old habit between two people who'd known each other for years?"

"That's true, there's so much sadness in the clothes being folded with so much care, like saying goodbye."

"Or as if she wanted, in the ritual of love, to defer the moment of embrace."

"Who says they had not been lovers for many years?"

"Sabrina maintains they'd only known each other for a few months."

"I've already told you that Di Giovanni is not a credible witness. She has given evidence and then retracted it, she has contradicted herself a thousand times, she is totally unreliable."

"To begin with you didn't believe her, only after the seals were broken and that night-time visit, you realised she might possibly be telling the truth."

"Partial truths are not valid when it comes to the law."

"And the shoes? Why had Angela left her shoes by the entrance door?"

"It's understandable in summer . . . she could have taken them off after coming into the apartment."

"That's one thing to clarify with Ludovica; was her sister in the habit of going barefoot?"

"This has been done. It seems she did, but perhaps also she didn't. It is difficult to get sense from that woman. I think she is mentally unbalanced."

So they are under pressure to solve the case of Angela Bari. Adele Sòfia takes note of my surprise and smiles contentedly.

The braces on her teeth have an uncanny way of never entirely disappearing even when her mouth is shut, like the cat in *Alice in Wonderland* which stays hovering in the branches with a phosphorescent smile, always blinking mysteriously.

"So what did Ludovica Bari say?"

"I didn't conduct the interrogation. Judge Boni did and I have the recording. She says that as sisters they were very different, she was active and well organised, always studying, while her sister was fragile and untidy, incapable of getting on with her studies and later on, with a job. She was first a model, then an actress, but not in a very professional way. From what Ludovica says she was in really bad films that didn't give her any satisfaction. She had very little money. Ludovica always says that, contradicting her mother who maintains she sent her a cheque for five million every month. Her mother paid for the apartment in Via Santa Cecilia after she had lost two apartments inherited from her father; her car was a present from her stepfather years ago. It was second-hand but it turned out she didn't use it, she kept it in a garage. The fiancé, Giulio Carlini, seems to have intended to marry her as soon as he was free of another woman, called Angela Neri with whom he's had a long relationship . . . Carlini, by the way, does not seem to me to be entirely straightforward, he's contradicted himself on several occasions. We have checked up on his alibis through the police headquarters in Genoa, but out of the four friends he mentioned, only one has confirmed it, the others seem to be away. But isn't it a bit of a coincidence, say I, all three away at the same time? Is this really likely?"

"Have you carried out an analysis of his blood?"

"Not yet, we're waiting for the judge's permission . . . if only we could get some blood from Pepi. We shall be keeping an eye on Di Giovanni to find out if she goes to see him but it's possible that the two are in league. It won't be easy, they're both accustomed to lying low. Pepi has been arrested for theft and for aiding and abetting. He's been in prison and served several short sentences which means we have his fingerprints for identification."

"Did you find his prints in Angela's apartment?"

"No, he's quite astute, he knows what to do not to leave traces."

"But would an astute person be so unwise as to go in the middle of the night to the apartment of a woman he's murdered and risk being seen?"

"Even murderers have their contradictions," she says with a sniff.

Then she gets up to go and get some index cards which she puts down on the table in front of me, shifting the dirty plates and crumbs of bread.

"Here it is . . . Pepi, Ferdinando, born at Rovigo on December 13th 1960. His mother came from Venice and was a prostitute. Father unknown. Spent his childhood with grand-parents in a village near Rovigo. After stealing from a market he was sent to an institution for young offenders. There he studied successfully and took higher examinations. From 1982 he is again in Rovigo, married to a woman by the name of Nina Corda. After two years of marriage this woman died in childbirth and he started drinking. A few months later he was reported to the police in Rome, arrested for drunken behaviour and then released. In 1984 he was denounced for aiding and abetting. That is all. Since then he has been in no trouble with the law. His legal domicile is in Rome at 41 Via delle Camelie. It appears he is regular over paying his rent and the shared expenses of joint ownership. We carried out a search but found nothing of interest except for an envelope containing photographs of Angela Bari; they are conventional photographs which she would have had made to send out to agents. An empty apartment, no furniture, no sign of food in the kitchen. It is possible he lives elsewhere."

"And Sabrina's place?"

"That has also been searched, without anything of import-ance being found. Except for very high phone bills as if someone were making international calls. We asked for specific dates and we've discovered that she's been in communication with someone in Angola. We are trying to find out who is the receiver of these calls."

"In Angola?"

"Do you know someone there?"

"Oh, Marco works there."

"Marco who?"

"Marco Calò, my . . . my . . ." – Ludovica's words come to my mind – "partner is too official, comrade too political, lover too sinful", "the journalist with whom . . . with whom . . ."

"Your man," she says brutally.

"Yes."

"Give me his number so we can call him."

"It's usually him who calls me . . . he hasn't given me his number."

"That's not good. It's always a bad sign when a man says 'I'll call you' and won't leave his number."

"The fact is he's always moving around so it's a lot easier for him to call me." I am trying to defend him as if I knew already that he is the person Sabrina telephones.

"Ah, we'll get it from the telephone exchange . . . But right now it's probable we don't need to do any more research . . . Pepi is under strong suspicion and I think it likely he's the culprit."

"Why would he have wanted to kill Angela?"

"Probably because she wouldn't come to heel, something that wasn't part of her character. Pimps must command fear, otherwise the girls they protect disobey, and that means less cash."

"Then you do believe Sabrina, you think Angela was a prostitute who provided him with money?"

"I don't know . . . it's a hypothesis."

"Seeing him that night on the landing, I didn't have the impression of a murderer who was coming back to 'the place of crime' as you were describing, but of a small fox who defies the night to show his tail is longer and thicker than that of the others."

"If he went to get hold of the weapon used in the crime as I think he did, he has got what he needed, and we will never find it."

The tape-recorder is making strange noises like a mouse, as

if to let me know the tape has nearly run out, but the conversation doesn't show any sign of ending.

"Tomorrow morning I have to be up early, I must go."

"If there is anything new do call me, even if it's in the middle of the night, I shan't hold it against you!"

I rewind the tape and put the microphone away in its cover. Marta Girardengo comes to the door with me while Adele Sòfia is noisily washing up the dishes in the kitchen.

31

Coming into my apartment I find under the door an envelope addressed to "Michela Canova. Personal". I open it and take out a sheet of white paper folded into four. Typewritten in the middle of the page is the message: "Be careful, Nando is after you. Danger! Sabrina."

What does this sybilline sentence mean? What does Nando want from me and why is there danger? Should I telephone Adele Sòfia? No, it would be better to hear first from Sabrina what it is she is trying to tell me. I dial her number, she answers in a voice thick with sleep.

"What is it?"

"It's me, Michela Canova."

"At this time of night?"

"It's only eleven, not that late!"

"Yes, sorry, but I haven't slept for two nights."

"I'm sorry to bother you, but I found this letter with your signature. What does it mean that Nando is after me? And why is there danger?"

"I don't know anything about it."

"How can you say 'I don't know anything about it' when the letter is from you, signed Sabrina? Didn't you leave it?"

"Oh, that letter, Nando gave it to me for you."

"So Nando signs himself Sabrina?"

"I don't know, he gave me a sealed envelope. He said 'Take

it to her', and I did. Now I'm standing here falling asleep on my feet. What's the time?"

"The letter says: 'Be careful, Nando is after you. Danger!' It's signed Sabrina. Is it a threat or what?"

"He's crazy! I really don't understand. He wants to see you but I don't know why. He wants to talk to you but I don't know what it's about. I don't understand him . . ."

There is an insolence that exasperates me, a desire to dramatise at any cost. And willing or unwilling I am being dragged into her drama.

"Where is Nando?"

"How should I know?" I hear her giggling as if the drama were being watched by someone else I can't see. Suppose it is Nando who is there with her?

"Let me speak to Nando. Sabrina, I want to talk to him."

"There's nobody else here," she says and slams the phone down.

All I can do is to go to sleep. After having checked that all the windows are properly closed and above all the glass door which gives on to the terrace.

I go calmly to bed with the certainty that Nando is at Sabrina's and won't come to disturb me. I pick up a novel by Conrad but before I am able to read more than two lines, the phone rings. Should I answer it or not? It could be Marco ringing from Angola. I answer it. It is him.

"I've been wanting to talk to you so much, Michela."

"Do you really mean that, after having left me for a week without a word from you?"

"Telephoning from here is really difficult. I'm away all day. I had to change my hotel because it was too expensive and here there isn't a telephone in the room."

His voice sounds far-away and hesitant. I don't want to waste time getting at him, I let him talk.

"I've been thinking about you a lot, Michela, I long to see you so much that I'd be ready to leave everything to be with you."

"Is that really true, Marco?"

"Michela, do you still love me?"

"I'm longing to see you too. When do you get back?"

"I don't know, possibly next week." And then as if to change the subject, "I've been so afraid you might have forgotten me."

An almost entreating voice, very sweet. I understand he has reversed our roles; actually it is he who is afraid of forgetting me, and he turns his anxiety upside down and projects his feelings on to me.

"Have you fallen in love, Marco?" I ask him, attempting to put on a light, jokey tone of voice.

"Why do you want to spoil everything? I've been saying I love you."

"I'm sorry but I'm very tired. I'm doing a programme on crimes against women and I've run into a crime that happened right here, next door to me, in the apartment opposite."

"We haven't got time to talk about your work." I am aware of him slipping away as if he feared any discussion that was not about his nostalgic feeling of love.

"Do you remember Angela Bari who took the apartment opposite me? You saw her sometimes in the lift and you used to say you found her very beautiful, do you remember? She was killed with twenty knife wounds."

"I think I've read something about it here in an old Italian newspaper. So have they found the murderer?"

"No, and for this reason . . ." Suddenly I remember he was still in Rome when the crime took place, so he must have read about it in the papers here and not in Angola since he only went there three days after Angela was murdered.

"I love you, Michela, I want you."

"Can't you say more definitely when you'll be back? Isn't the peace conference over yet?"

"Yes, it's over, but now there's a meeting of the heads of state from Francophone Africa."

That is true, I have read about this meeting in the newspapers. But is it really necessary for an Italian paper to maintain a special correspondent in such a far-away place for a meeting that has nothing to do with Europe? Perhaps it is; why do I not believe him?

"And when does this meeting of heads of state finish?"

"I don't know, I think in ten days."

Since when do meetings between heads of state last for ten days? Haven't they got other things to do? But I do not contradict him; his forced cheerfulness makes me feel I have to accept the pretence; outside it lies a minefield.

I know the extraordinary talent for duplicity he has, the handsome Marco with his starry eyes. If I don't play his game, I risk losing him, I know that. So out of love, out of cowardice, out of tenderness, I force myself to believe him, but I know the game is becoming ever more risky and treacherous.

32

As soon as I sit down in front of the computer I raise my eyes to look at the jar with the pens in it. The spider is still there, minute and impudent; it has started to remake its transparent web with miraculous patience. I am not sure if it is always the same spider or whether there are two or more brothers who take turns in sharing an obstinate persistence.

It is probably at night that it does most of the work, spinning saliva to draw diamond-shaped patterns and triangles in space. By day the spider rests, hanging from a long, pendulous thread that glints in the sunlight. I blow gently, and watch the geometric rose quiver and dance without breaking the thread. "One can't help liking spiders." It is my mother's voice talking in my ear. Why used I to hate that voice so much that I changed mine and made it separate and unrecognisable from any family association? It was the voice of everyday common sense, inhabited by dark shadowy fears that I refused even to guess at, a voice that was not only educated but also controlled. It needed years of working on the radio for me to learn how to make the artificial patterns of daily speech sound natural.

"You've got to sound reassuring, the listeners have to be reassured," Cusumano would say. Reassured about what? Is it to flatter the listeners, perhaps?

"No, no. Caress them, my dear Michela. Your voice should caress them."

"But vocal caresses aren't spontaneous, they end up sounding mannered and artificial."

"Look at Tamara Verde, she has a caressing voice," our director says admiringly, and I understand that for him all female voices have to be caressing, while men's voices must be assertive and confident.

"What a prostitution our work is!" Carla Meti used to say. She was a woman I worked with on the radio for a year who had to leave when she got lung cancer which reduced her to a skeleton in the space of a few months. Yet she went on smoking, and her voice, made hoarse by cigarettes, sounded sad and dreamy and was much appreciated by listeners.

The telephone interrupts my thoughts. I stretch my hand out pick it up. It is Adele Sòfia. She tells me they have arrested Carmelina Di Giovanni, aka Sabrina.

"Why?"

"She wasn't cooperating, she was messing up the evidence. You too, Michela, you haven't behaved all that well. We know you talked to Di Giovanni yesterday evening but you've said nothing about it. You have received threats and concealed them; what sort of game are you playing?"

"It wasn't Carmelina Sabrina who sent the threats."

"Can you bring us the letter in question?"

"Of course, I was going to do that today, anyway."

"Ferdinando Pepi is being sought for murder. Whoever is involved in hiding him, or in concealing information that could lead to his arrest, becomes guilty of aiding and abetting. Only the result of the DNA test can provide us with absolute certainty; meanwhile he is the prime suspect in the murder of Angela Bari . . . we're on the right track, Michela!"

Adele Sòfia makes much use of idiomatic expressions, and this makes her quite unusual given all the technical jargon used in the police force. It is only when she becomes hostile that she resorts to the militaristic language of the police. I realise from her saying "we're on the right track" that she isn't too annoyed with me. All the same she has arranged for my telephone to be tapped. She must have heard Marco's telephone call, and what has any of it got to do with him? How does he come into it? I am already defending him. And suppose they wanted to do a blood test on him as well? But why should they? He only saw Angela two or three times in the lift, as I did. Although, come to think of it, they smiled as if they knew one another, with a certain amount of embarrassment. She had very slowly extended a hand which he had taken in a furtive grasp.

"I had the impression that Nando Pepi was with Sabrina when I talked to her on the phone," I say so as not be seen to be holding anything back.

"We thought so as well."

Her use of "we" rather than "I" puts a distance between us. We are no longer the police commissioner Adele Sòfia and the radio journalist Michela Canova, but the police and me, citizen under suspicion.

I am just on the point of asking her why they did not go immediately to arrest him, seeing that they had monitored the telephone call, when she, as usual, anticipates me.

"Maybe you don't know what happens when a telephone is being tapped. The voices are recorded on tapes which only reach the investigator after some hours, let's say half a day. I only had the tapes late in the morning and by the time we got there he had already disappeared. That is why we arrested Di Giovanni."

Meanwhile I have put on my tape-recorder and connected it to the telephone. This time I am not asking for permission. I will use subterfuge to record her voice just as she recorded mine. Is it possible that from being friends, we are now becoming enemies? "There were cigarette ends all over the place," she continues, "Camels, a brand that Carmelina Di Giovanni doesn't smoke. Anyway hers have traces of lipstick on them. She only smokes half the cigarette, while he smokes them down to the filter and puts them out with anger, crushing and twisting them against the ashtray."

"And from the cigarette end you could tell he'd been there?"

"Yes, also from fingerprints. You remember we had Pepi's

fingerprints. There were lots of them . . . if you had telephoned yesterday evening we'd have him in our hands."

Is she aware I am recording her voice? She sounds very formal and didactic. Perhaps I am imagining it, because she too is used to recording voices by stealth, sometimes simply from a love of stealing.

"Then I'll expect you," she says to me and I feel she wants to re-establish our friendship.

I go to get permission from the director, who frets and fumes and eventually gives his consent although not before he has himself checked with Adele Sòfia on the phone. Luckily the technicians are here today. I see Tirinnanzi who waves to me while he reads the news over the microphone. I also meet Merli the lawyer who gives me a friendly bow and stops as if to say something. I would really like to talk to him but this time I am in too much of a rush. I tell him this and he nods his head in agreement. He has a candid smile that puts me in a good frame of mind.

"When are you back on the radio?"

"On Monday."

"Till Monday, then," I say, knowing I won't be here because Monday is my day off. But of course I could be here, after all, because when things are very hectic, I have to give up my day off.

33

Tonight I have once again woken up with the feeling that someone has come into my room. I stretch a sweaty hand in search of the light switch but do not find it. Meanwhile the shadow glides towards my bed and it does not help to remember that I locked the door before coming to bed.

At last, in the dim light filtering in from the street I recognise the kindly, lifeless smile of my father.

"Oh, it's you, papa . . . you gave me such a fright!"

"I only wanted to watch you sleeping."

"And instead you've woken me up."

"Forgive me, do you forgive me?"

"Of course I do, don't worry . . . but why don't you let me get back to sleep?"

"Michela, do you remember that time we went down to the river? Do you remember?"

"What river, papa?"

"The Arno, don't you remember? I made you get on my motor bike and you sat astride in front of me. I went like the wind, it took your breath away. You smelled so good, of sweaty hair, crushed strawberries, freshly ironed cotton."

"I don't remember a thing."

"Then we got off along the river bank, outside the town. We got off and found ourselves surrounded by giant reeds and white rocks. Don't you remember?"

"No, I don't."

"You didn't have a bathing costume, nor did I, we had gone on a last minute impulse. We sunbathed there among the brambles. Don't you remember?"

"No, I don't."

"Then you said let's go for our swim in our underwear. I was so afraid, fear gripped me when I saw you pulled out by the current . . . I swam like mad to reach you."

"I wasn't afraid."

"At that moment the current was so swift . . . I thought you'd get drowned."

"You seized hold of my arm and you only just managed to save me from drowning."

"No, by the hair, I grabbed your hair. I remember it clearly. And you swallowed such a lot of water."

"No, I had only gone a little way out."

"You were trembling like a leaf."

"Are you saying you saved my life, papa? Is this what you are trying to say?"

"I think I did, Michela, I really think so. You were only seven and you couldn't swim very well. If I hadn't got hold of you by the hair you would have drowned."

"By my arm."

"By the hair, I remember it very well."

"But for days and days I had two big bruises on that arm."

"You were trembling and coughing and spitting up water . . . I held you so close to me . . . I would have given my life for you."

"Don't exaggerate, papa."

At that moment the alarm clock rings and I wake up. I decide that today I will really go on foot to the radio station. If I hurry I can be on time. I wash quickly, grab a biscuit and a pear and set off.

I stop in the Via Titta Scarpetta to greet the cat lady who has set down a big bag full of pasta and sauce. Her legs are disfigured with veins and lumps. All the neighbourhood cats are crowding round her.

There is no one in the office building yet, only the watchman who says with a yawn, "Good morning, Signora Canova. Did you sleep all right? Here we are all half-dead from the heat."

I watch the spider for a long time. It is spinning its web between the lampstand and the jar with the pens. I marvel at its determination; it makes me think of those peasants who live beneath the craters of volcanoes that are still erupting. In spite of the likelihood of their homes being destroyed every other year, they remain forever clinging to those inhospitable mountain sides with dark rocks, rebuilding their wretched huts on exactly the same spot where the lava has destroyed the previous ones.

I line up the new index cards next to the old ones. They are getting more and more appalling; each time I read them I am overcome by a painful and dismal feeling of impotence.

"Giorgina R., age 7. Was raped, strangled and abandoned on the shore of the River Ombrone. Her shoes were found at a distance of two hundred metres. Case unresolved."

The photograph slides between my fingers. It is a snapshot in black and white. It shows a pathetic little body, two dark downcast eyes, a strained half-smile, bare legs emerging from a small light skirt lifted up by the wind.

"Natalina A., age 12. The body was recovered from Lake Sant'Antonio, her head split by a stone, her lungs full of water.

The father committed suicide from grief. The mother ended up in a mental hospital."

Another photograph, also in black and white, taken at school. A plump little girl smiling cheerfully at the photographer who is probably her father.

"Angiolina F., age 8. Was raped and stabbed with a knife. Her body was found thrown into the refuse dump at San Michele. Case unresolved."

The third photograph; a little girl with a porcine face, not at all pretty but with an expression of confident happiness. Would she have looked with those eyes at the man who raped her? At the bottom, in very small letters, the additional information that she was disabled.

I fish about among the reels of interviews searching for some comment that I might add to the index cards and which I could introduce into the programme as Cusumano has suggested. But I find the common sense views of Professor Baldi rather too banal. I am also finding the complicated expressions of a child psychologist called Favi too full of technical jargon.

At last here are two voices engaged in a dialogue. I had almost forgotten this short debate in the studio. One voice belongs to Aurelia Ferro, a pleasant woman suffering from a liver complaint and with rings under her eyes which encroach upon her cheeks. The other voice is that of a well-known journalist.

"Some recent news items in the press suggest we are living with the idea of terrorism," says Aurelia Ferro, "of political terrorism. On the other hand, no political power has ever been able to maintain its dominance without some form of terror, and it seems that historically the patriarchal world has always made use of fear and violence to keep female sexuality under control . . . in some countries the clitoris is cut off . . . in others the cut is symbolic, less drastic because invisible but equally violent. Do you know what the Hite report says? It shows that in America two out of three women never experience orgasm during sexual intercourse. Isn't this also a way of cutting off the clitoris? And it isn't that these women don't have the capacity, for they can quickly pleasure themselves through masturbation . . . doesn't this contradiction tell you something?"

She has a husky voice with an unusual rhythm as if it were limping; she is short of breath at the end of every sentence, when her tone falls and then with an effort rises up again in a spiralling movement.

"The killers are ill, mad," says the journalist whose smooth voice belies his indignation. "Signora Ferro, you can't use the deaths of a few women to establish your theories on sexual racism throughout history."

"Certainly they are ill, and those who commit these crimes are mad," she continues calmly, "but they are the product of a system passed down the centuries and through a common social culture. Women haven't invented the hatred against them, men have absorbed it at school, in books, in church, in sport . . . and if men's illness takes the form of aggression against women, it is an illness which is telling us something about the culture of a country and its people during a particular historical period."

"But we can't identify ourselves with them, not even from a distance, with the vile beings who attack poor innocent children."

Signora Ferro follows on, unyielding and exuberant.

"Once upon a time they used to sacrifice goats and heifers, now they sacrifice children."

"To whom are they making these sacrifices?" he goes on with his voice rising.

"To the demands of the Lord of Heaven," she retorts. Now she is talking imaginatively and will not be understood, "to that Lord of Heaven who has nests of nightingales singing good-morning in the labyrinth of his beard . . . he is a loving father, but he is also savage and primitive and from time to time has to be appeased by the sacrifice of small, innocent hearts."

"You have a brutal and inhuman view of the relationship between men and women," he says, almost shouting.

"It is not I who am brutal but the masculine hand that falls on the heads of these children claiming its dream of sexual supremacy."

I put another reel on the tape deck; an assertive and grating masculine voice, that of Professor Papi.

"In the excitation of the male sexual organ there is something sudden and violent that originates in nature ... as in the ignition of an internal combustion engine ... rape is part of man's instinct for survival."

"And if instead it were seen as the spurious product of a history in which the domination of the other sex is seen as essential to the preservation of the species?" Another voice, that of the philosopher Giardini with his handsome leonine head and free and easy way of speaking.

"Man maintains an innate and profoundly irrational aggression which leads him to violent sexual possession," says Papi, "but since communal living needs peace and calm, such instincts are repressed through education in the name of family solidarity. However, this instinct does not disappear but hibernates in the depth of the human soul ... and only during certain occasions of collective excitement, masculine excitement, suddenly emerges so unexpectedly that whoever is overtaken by it cannot resist, especially if they are culturally unprepared to judge and reflect on their own actions."

"So do you think, professor, that rape is to some extent natural and inevitable?"

"Not inevitable, in fact it can definitely be controlled; it is sufficient to learn to live with the more obscure regions of the unconscious mind which experience in dreams the pleasure of the hunt, the ambush, the chase and the capture."

"So what will happen to the idea of sexuality linked to love, to respect for the other?"

"I would say that rape has little to do with love or even with sex. Rape arises from the desire to humiliate and degrade the female body. But it can also happen with a male body, look at what the strong do to the weak in prison ... the trouble is that there are still wars in the world and it is seen as the right of a soldier to rape, kill and humiliate an enemy body. In the past the right to rape in war was sanctioned by a supreme authority and sealed with the blood of the enemy. And even Jupiter had those appetites; do you remember the chase of beautiful goddesses? Nor did he disdain beautiful human beings whom he impregnated and then abandoned after having satisfied himself, often against their will. Is that not rape? But it was seen as licit and part of a divine right . . . and often a man in the closeness of his family feels himself to be a predatory little Jupiter to whom everything is due . . ."

I turn off the sound, I am satiated with explanatory voices attempting to teach and convince. I pick up the index cards. Where shall I begin, in 1942, 1946, 1977, 1980, 1992? Hundreds of little girls tortured, tormented, strangled, raped and hacked to pieces.

Perhaps I will begin with one of the last. In 1991, in a small village in the mountains of central Italy, a little girl aged five was found dead with her head split open, her clothes torn and spattered with blood. Someone says they saw her walking hand in hand with her uncle, a strong, tall young man with short blond hair. The uncle blamed his nephew, the brother of the dead child, claiming he had raped her and then hit her on the head with a stone. The family maintains the girl died by accident after falling on to a hard rock although the doctors who examined her maintained she could not have fallen in this way by chance. In their opinion she was hit savagely several times. In the end the uncle was sentenced because hair and blood from the child were found on a pullover he had thrown on to the roof of the stable after coming back from the wood. In prison the uncle continued to accuse the nephew and at home the nephew continued to blame his uncle.

The telephone rings. It is Adele Sòfia. Her voice sounds flat and gloomy. I feel she is going to tell me something disastrous. Then she says all in one breath, "Carmelina Di Giovanni has killed herself in prison."

"Carmelina?"

"Yes, she hung herself from the window with her dressing gown cord. Don't tell anyone, the press mustn't know about it."

"So what now?"

"Now it becomes even more urgent to find Ferdinando Pepi."

"It wasn't much use putting her in prison."

"We did what we thought was right. She wasn't sufficiently watched, I'd agree, but who would have thought it . . . she had no reason to . . . she would have been released in a few days."

I think of Sabrina's voice with its roughness of dialect, real warm-heartedness, total lack of self-esteem.

Now she too has gone. Who knows if she had shoes on her feet? They make so little noise, these dead women as they depart. Angela Bari took off her shoes and probably Sabrina did too; so did the child found on the shore of the River Ombrone. I remember having read of a Japanese girl who killed herself in the sleeping car of a train going from Rome to Palermo. In the morning they found her in her berth, her arms across her chest, her bare feet placed gently together. She had poisoned herself and her shoes were lying beside the door, placed side by side with the laces undone.

34

We are all three gathered together in the white and yellow chapel of the prison, Adele Sòfia, Sergio Lipari and myself. No one from Sabrina's family has been seen; her old mother died a few months ago at home in her village. They say that her father has been living for years in Argentina with another woman. She was the only daughter and from what I have heard, her cousins did not want to undertake a long journey to come to the funeral of a prostitute who has committed suicide.

A cheap wooden coffin, no incense, flowers or undertakers. They have wrapped her in a green sheet all naked, with the wounds of the autopsy on her body. They did not even have the time or the will to put clothes on her.

While she was still laid out in the mortuary along with another three bodies, Adele asked me if I wanted to see her. I said "yes" and she lifted up the plastic sheet. I was expecting something horrifying; instead, in front of me was a beautiful, relaxed face, rippling into the beginning of a smile. That face which in life had always seemed angry, in death appeared peaceful, almost as if it were happy, getting ready to leave for the best of journeys.

Round her neck was a blue circlet, the colour of the night, like the blue velvet ribbons worn by elegant ladies in 18th-century pictures.

I had left the basket of little roses I had brought for her in front of the iron door. Feeling ashamed because whatever I do seems to make me a subject of criticism and reprimand, I go and pick up the basket and put it beside the coffin.

A young priest arrives in a hurry, notices Adele Sòfia and me talking, blesses the coffin with rapid gestures and adds a few pious words. But his voice sounds dry and indifferent; what if Almighty God is offended because this woman has taken her own life instead of waiting until something else carries her off?

"Suicides should not be blessed," the priest explains to us, "but we are still benevolent and accommodating; we want to hope that this poor dead body will go to expiate its sins in not too unhappy a place."

Meanwhile the funeral mass begins. As I turn round I see a small group of nuns robed in black. They all keep their eyes fixed on the head of the young priest . . . Who knows how he has come to this prison church; he does not look very happy.

The service runs quickly. Adele Sòfia fans herself with a newspaper folded into four. The young priest bends his head to say goodbye to us and goes out with a rustling of his flowing cassock. An attendant in a brown apron closes the coffin lid, and with an electric screwdriver pushes glittering screws into the four corners, making them turn like spinning tops.

"Now to the cemetery!" says Adele Sòfia, making a place for me beside her in the dark car. Behind is Lipari; today he is dressed all in brown. Bristly black hairs escape from his tight collar and white cuffs.

"We've found Pepi," says Adele triumphantly.

"Where?"

"We intercepted a telephone call. He has an appointment arranged for this afternoon."

"Who with?"

"With someone called Maria at the Foro Italica."

"Is he really the murderer?"

"Before this can be confirmed we have to examine his blood. But the motivation is there, the keys will carry weight in any supposition of guilt."

"And if the blood test is negative?"

"The first thing to do is to take him in and do the test, with his consent, of course. Then we can talk further."

"And if it wasn't him?"

"That would be a problem."

The car is a sweltering box that proceeds through the traffic in fits and starts, using its siren. Through the windows the view outside appears broken up, as if it had become dispersed into a twisted mass of little rivulets.

At the cemetery I am the first to get out, the undertakers are already there with the lorry from the prison. They have stopped in front of a rough and dirty cement wall which contains the burial recesses. In each recess a corpse, a name inscribed in the cement and beside it a glass-sized container suspended from an iron ring with artificial flowers and a burning light. No digging of the earth, no gravestones, plants, fresh flowers; here the dead are buried one above the other and are remembered with bunches of plastic flowers.

The coffin, being made of crude, badly sawn wood, is difficult to get into the recess. The youngest undertaker pushes it with his hands and with his shoulder, but the coffin stays jammed. Then he climbs on to the roof of the lorry and shoves it with two hard kicks. Another undertaker in a dark blue apron wedges the slab that closes the recess. The youngest one covers it with fresh cement spread on with a trowel, while he chews gum.

It is done. The only fresh flowers are mine, the small white roses I bought this morning from a stall near the radio station. They make a strange impression next to so many artificial flowers.

Adele Sòfia signals to me to get back in the car with them but I say I want to walk. The idea of being shut again inside this glass box overwhelms me. I see Sergio Lipari shutting the door very firmly as if to say, "So much the worse for you!"

I wander slowly among the tombs. This is the new cemetery in Via Flaminia, not the old Verano cemetery full of pines and palm trees where my father is buried: here there are no wild cats or monumental tombs. Isn't it better to be cremated than to end up in one of these recesses?

I stop to look at a memorial inscription with the photograph of a little girl inside a porcelain frame. "Mirella Fritti, taken from her mother's arms by a terrible and untimely death. Amen." What did she die of? The date is July 8th 1992, so she died quite recently, but why a terrible death? Would one write this of a long illness? Perhaps she was murdered, strangled, cut to pieces? I am unable to think of anything else.

I walk a few steps further looking for the small path which leads to the way out when I see a man standing upright against the trunk of a cypress tree and staring at me. I give a start; it is Nando Pepi with his boots, his black jacket, his radical student look, and his ring with the tiger's-eye.

I look quickly around me, searching for a way of escape, but the cemetery has suddenly become empty. I don't see any undertakers, or fond relatives, or guardians, or wandering passers-by, nothing at all, only the sun blazing down on the cement recesses, on the artificial flowers, and on me standing motionless, turned to stone.

35

We are alone in the middle of the cemetery, underneath the burning sun. There is something grotesque in my frozen, questioning look, and in the way he eyes me stealthily from a distance.

I try to collect my thoughts so that they are not spinning round in circles like a swarm of restless gnats. It is one of those sweltering hot days: the caretakers have disappeared to have lunch under cover of some shade and the relatives have gone home to cook the midday meal. It is not surprising that the cemetery should be empty now but I need to reflect calmly on where the entrance is, since I could no doubt shout for help.

My gaze rests on the back of a cicada on a branch above Nando's head. He is very close, I say to myself, nearer than I had thought. I can distinguish the cicada perfectly; it has little brown spots on its back and its shrill buzzing hits my ear insistently. I reflect on how curious it is that my mind is wandering while my body is paralysed, incapable of movement. I am surprised at the silence around us, a perfect, harmonious silence, reminding me of another similar silence I experienced many years ago during a trip with my father into the mountains, a silence without interruption or blurring, absolute and total. I was seven years old or maybe less, and it was then I realised for the first time in my life with lightness and certainty that the world was not dependent on me, that its beauty was outside my eyes and would go on being admired as a thing in itself, independent and complete.

All this comes to my mind as I gaze fearfully at Nando Pepi's face; I stay there motionless, telling myself that my legs will be ready to run, my throat ready to scream at the first move he makes, yet I do not know whether I would actually be able to do either.

He also stays there without moving, like a statue. He seems to be waiting for the right moment to decide what to do. He appears to be listening, as if a sign might come to him from those cement tombs or from one of the rugged tree trunks, or even from the spotted back of the cicada that is above his head.

After what seems to me a very long wait, he finally opens his mouth, and at this moment I lose all my fear; my instinct tells me that by choosing words he excludes action, or at least delays it. I feel so much gratitude for the existence of words, what joy to hear the exquisite sound of a voice! Once again, I am being invited to enter into the artificial and controlled world of dialogue available to whoever can use words. "Angela has left this for you," he says in a quiet tone, which is light and soothing compared to the tension that has grown between us.

I watch him remove a small parcel wrapped in blue paper from his pocket; it is fastened with an elastic band.

"Is this for me?" I ask incredulously.

"I risked being arrested to get hold of it, but I knew where it was and I found it."

"Did you kill Angela?" I ask impetuously. I had not wanted to ask this question at all, but it jumps off my tongue quite naturally as if I knew that the answer could only be a truthful one.

"I did not kill her."

"I thought you hadn't."

"So you believe me?"

"I had doubts but I thought you didn't."

"Carmelina loved me; those imbeciles killed her but I will see she is avenged."

I tell myself he's descending to melodrama, putting on a heroic voice that's not his own. Is he too being theatrical?

"It would be better to give yourself up," I tell him, "they only want to do a blood test and you would be cleared because they already have a sample of the murderer's blood."

"I wouldn't ever think of giving myself up. I'm leaving in half an hour. I only wanted to give you this, and then goodbye!"

"What do you mean by 'goodbye'? You won't be going away, the police are waiting for you at your meeting with Maria. Aren't you going to it?"

"Maria has betrayed me, I'm having nothing more to do with her, the stupid bitch."

"Have you any idea who could have killed Angela Bari?"

"I wouldn't know."

"Angela gave you this . . . this packet for me?"

"Yes, it's for you . . . who loves voices, she said."

"Why did you leave me that letter the other day in which you said you'd be looking out for me and that there was danger?"

"It was Carmelina who wrote that letter, not me. She wanted you to stop following me."

"But she told me you were looking for me!"

"She wanted to frighten you, and she did, didn't she?" he smirks, lighting a cigarette.

"Was it true that Angela worked as a prostitute?"

"No, I never asked her to do that."

"But Sabrina told me . . ."

"Sabrina didn't always have her head screwed on . . . she was jealous."

"And how did you get hold of the keys of the apartment?"

"Angela was generous; one day she lent them to me and I had another set made, but I never made use of them while she was alive."

"If you disappear no one will ever find out who the murderer is. The police will think it's you and will go on looking for you and then they'll never find the right person."

"Let them sort it out, I couldn't give a fuck . . . here, take it and clear off!"

"I'll have to say I've seen you, I can't not say that."

"Say it if you like. They won't get hold of me, I'll see to that."

He doesn't hand me the parcel as I expected, but throws it on the ground beside my shoes. I bend down to pick it up keeping my eyes fixed on him. When I see his hand go to his pocket I think: "He's going to shoot me!"

He only wanted to take out a packet of cigarettes. They are Camels, I see him turning the packet over between his hands; the yellow camel in a white field is turned up and down.

If he refuses to let them do an analysis of his blood, it will mean he is guilty, that is "the logic of deduction", as Adele Sòfia would say. Yet I feel drawn to believe him when he says he didn't kill her, I do not know why.

I grasp hold of the parcel and get up. He is walking slowly towards the area most distant from the gate, leaving the path between the newly planted cypress trees and climbing over the stones.

I hurry to the gate. At the entrance lodge I see two of the

caretakers talking away to each other and eating big slices of bread and mortadella. I can clearly see the pink meat with its small white cubes pushing out from between the pieces of bread.

For a moment I think of telling them about Pepi but then I decide not to. I go out into the burning hot piazza, I look at the apartment, oblong parcel I am holding tightly in my hand. I understand; it reminds me of a burial recess. The red elastic band springs off easily. I unwrap the paper and find I am holding a sixty minute cassette, a small cache of hidden voices, precariously protected from an unknown oblivion.

Where did Angela Bari keep it hidden, so that the police never found it in spite of their repeated searches? Or perhaps they took no notice of it. It looks just like any other cassette. I slip it into my bag and go over to the taxi rank.

36

"Dedicated to my neighbour in the next door apartment whose voice I hear every morning on the radio."

It seems strange that whereas for me Angela Bari was someone I did not really know at all, she knew and watched me to the point of dedicating a cassette to me. Incredulous, I begin to listen; the voice is soft, sounding a little embarrassed but animated by an upsurge of joyfulness.

"Once upon a time there was a king who had a daughter . . ." But this is a fairy story, it really is. Angela Bari is bringing me a fairy story, telling it in an amateurish way, using the microphone she has at home. I run the tape on . . . I stop it, I listen, I run it on again. "The daughter says to her father . . ." I go on ahead, I listen again. "Then the father changed his daughter into a donkey."

At a first superficial listening the whole cassette seems a simple story. It is no more than a collection of fairy tales, either written by her or possibly copied from a book. All of them tell of a king and a queen, of disobedient children, dragons, bewitched fauns and lowering skies.

Is it likely that Nando would risk being arrested in order to go and recover a tape of fairy tales, putting himself under suspicion by using the keys to get into Angela's apartment?

However it could prove that Angela did not think she was in any danger. It could prove she had not felt either threatened or blackmailed, otherwise would she not have sent only fairy stories to someone she valued; she would surely have sent some more coherent message. It seems likely that Angela only wanted her neighbour to read the stories because she worked in broadcasting, perhaps with the idea of having them included in a children's programme.

So far I have only been listening to their content; they are fairy tales, that is certain, but what is their message?

Even though I have never much liked fairy stories since childhood, I get down to listening to them patiently.

The only obvious feature is that all the stories are about a king and a daughter; whenever there is a mother she soon magically disappears. The child is transformed into a fox, a wasp, and even into a cabbage, although she finally becomes human again as a reward for some sacrifice.

The king is portrayed as an unpredictable tyrant, sometimes he piles presents on his daughter, sometimes tortures her, keeps her a prisoner, or shuts her inside a tower without doors or windows.

There are about twenty stories, told with much charm, without conceit, and without any artfulness or pedantry. As I run the tape, her voice seems to get deeper and more desperate. Towards the end the stories grow more savage. The king is enraged and cuts off his daughter's head. In another story, he cuts off her hands and cooks them with rosemary, after giving her two beautiful rings of emeralds and rubies.

Angela's father died when she was eight years old. Could these stories represent a longing for that lost father? But these stories portray the father as far from benevolent; on the contrary he is threatening, tyrannical and cruel.

I must go and talk to Angela's stepfather, the sculptor Glauco

Elia. His voice is absent from my research. I must ask him what he thinks of Angela, about her death and about these stories.

Meanwhile the tape goes on running and Angela's voice continues, patient and undaunted, to tell of fathers and daughters who love each other and wound each other. In another story the father breaks his daughter's legs to force her to stay at home. To keep her company and to keep a watch on her, he sends her a little owl which roosts every night at the head of her bed, scrutinising her with its "timeless eyes of gold".

But the little girl finds a way of deceiving her father; she teaches the owl to imitate her voice and then, tying her legs to planks of wood, she escapes, leaving the little owl in her place where it will reassure the mistrustful father.

I think I should see Angela's mother once more. But I am certain the director will not let me go to Florence again. Suppose I talk to Ludovica instead?

37

I find Ludovica less anxious and nervous than when I last saw her. She moves with ease through the shaded rooms of the big house; her long chestnut hair is loose around her shoulders, and on her wrists she is wearing a dozen bracelets of coloured glass that jingle against each other with a cheerful tinkling sound.

Once again I am in the sitting room with the Chinese carpets, the gilded door handles, the chandeliers with glass pendants, the sofas covered in chintz.

"Would you like a soft drink?" It occurs to me that last time too she began in a similar way. I watch her stretch her thin arms, covered this time by full sleeves, towards the small glass table. They are gestures I have already seen her make and which she repeats with an effortless grace.

Her smiles have something deathly sweet about them; I think this is because of her false teeth which make her look older then she is. I observe her hands which are long and tapered and perfectly white without any mark or scar, a sign that reveals their unfamiliarity with domestic work, as if for thirty years they have been only been in contact with linens, silks and scented lace.

I arrange the tape-recorder on a table; she looks at it with suspicion; it seems as if for her the machine implies hostility and bias. Her neck muscles grow tense, and curls of hair slip down over her eyes. "I'll turn it off if you like," I say to reassure her.

She makes a grimace as if to say, "You could have spared me this discourtesy." But I am not intending to be polite and well-mannered and the tape-recorder is a valuable witness since I don't always trust my memory. She does not insist, perhaps because she is trying to appear well-mannered, and I turn on the tape.

"Did you know that Carmelina Di Giovanni has killed herself?"

"Who is Carmelina Di Giovanni?"

"It was you who first told me about Nando, do you remember?"

"I don't know who he is."

I can see she is shutting herself off by adopting an attitude of dignified refusal. What can I do to regain her trust?

"Carmelina Di Giovanni, also called Sabrina, knew your sister Angela. She revealed this one day on the radio during a phone-in, adding that she knew Angela was a prostitute. Carmelina's protector, Nando, definitely denies this. But you must know him, because you told me so on the phone."

"I think there must have been some misunderstanding, I don't know anyone of that name."

"Nando Pepi is being looked for by the police for your sister's murder and this has been reported in the press. You must be aware that the examining magistrate Judge Boni has the results of an analysis of the murderer's blood, so it is essential for Pepi to allow himself to be tested."

"I don't read the papers."

"But I recorded what you said on tape. Would you like to hear it?"

"I really don't want to be bothered. I can't bear to think about Angela's death."

"Do you not want to know who killed her?"

"Yes, of course I want to know, but anyone who was involved with my sister scares me . . . There are things in her life which upset me and which I'd prefer not to know about."

"Your mother told me she gave her five million lire a month but you said Angela didn't have any money. Whom should I believe?"

"My mother is lying. Yes, she probably gave her a few million when she was ill and without a place of her own, but nothing after that. If she'd asked me, I would certainly have given her money. But Angela was very proud, and didn't like asking for anything either from me or from our mother."

"Did you see your sister often?"

"Not very much, but that wasn't my fault. I would like to have seen her more often, but it was she who ran away and she wasn't easy to pin down. When I invited her, she'd say she was too busy. I felt pity towards her."

"Pity?"

"Yes, I always felt pity for her from when she was little . . . she was always late for school and I'd see her running all the way with a heavy satchel hanging from her thin, hunched shoulders, or I'd see her sitting on the pavement smoking cigarette ends next to one of the most violent local boys . . . I'd get a pain here in my stomach, but there wasn't anything I could do. It seemed to be the way she was going, forever getting into trouble. I once hit her really hard because she came back home blind drunk at three in the morning. But I didn't tell my mother or my stepfather and she kept it to herself."

"And your mother never intervened?"

"My mother was a very beautiful woman and everyone fell in love with her. She spent most of her time pushing away admirers. She was probably too young to be a mother, she was still a child herself and her mother was also a great beauty who didn't spend much time looking after her daughter. Who knows why daughters so often repeat detail for detail the story of their mother, even when they don't want to, even when they are

mercilessly critical . . . in the end, that's what happens . . . They
fall into exactly the same predicaments as their mothers did and
that includes illnesses, children, running away, hopeless love
affairs, abortions, attempted suicide and so on . . ."

Ludovica gets heated, she raises her arm without realising
that the sleeve has slipped back to her elbow revealing big
purple bruises. She sees my astonished look and modestly covers
up her arm.

"Yesterday I fell down the stairs," she says as if to explain it.
Her expression becomes vague but also more vibrant. There is
something she is wanting me to know, but what is it?

"Have you seen your mother recently?" I ask in order to
keep the conversation going.

"I went to see her last week at Fiesole. But she wasn't well
at all, shut away in her room with one of those terrible headaches and her hands covered in eczema. I stayed with her for a
little while and then I escaped. Glauco was there as well."

"Glauco Elia?"

"Yes, him."

"But they both say they haven't seen each other in years."

"They see each other from time to time, it's always him who
comes to see her, I think he's still in love with my mother."
She gives a bitter laugh and twists her hands. Then she suddenly
bursts into tears. She signals to me to turn off the tape-recorder
and I do so.

"I'm terribly sorry, is there anything I can do?"

"I don't want to talk about Angela, I don't want to talk about
my mother, please don't ask me any more about them."

"Only one more question; now that it's over a month since
the death of your sister Angela, have you any idea who could
have wanted to kill her?" Meanwhile I turn the tape-recorder
on again and she starts once more to cry but heartlessly I leave
it on. I don't know why, but I get the impression that her
weeping marks a transition to a new subject of conversation
that is difficult to begin.

From the way she sighs when I make a move to go away, I
understand that there is something confused and unpleasant
underlying her tears.

She suddenly stops crying, stands up, and starts to walk up and down the room swinging her silk dress with its long wide sleeves. Her bracelets tinkle at each step, she looks like a captive princess straight from *A Thousand and One Nights*. I know she is about to tell me something very serious but just as she is opening her mouth to speak, the door opens silently and on the threshold stands a handsome, smiling man.

"This is Michela Canova from Radio Italia Viva," she explains nonchalantly, "and this is Mario Torres."

The man holds out his hand. His handshake is hard and decisive, in an overdone way. In contrast his smile is soft and slightly artificial.

"Can I ask you a few questions for the radio, Signor Torres?"

I can see appearing on his face the same expression as appears on that of anyone I approach for an interview; a moment of vanity followed by blind dismay, "What can I say, how can I get out of it?"

He must be quite courageous because he accepts immediately, in spite of Ludovica who is squeezing his arm to get him to refuse.

But he sits down on the sofa, serious and apologetic as if to say "I am ready, here I am, I'm not afraid of anything."

Ludovica is left with having to find another glass. I go back and sit in the same place as I was in before, next to the window with my tape-recorder in front of me.

"You knew Angela Bari," I begin, starting off rather vaguely.

"Not that well . . . she was rather a stand-offish girl."

"How did you see her?"

"She wasn't a real beauty, never mind what they say . . . yes, she had something of Marilyn Monroe without the platinum blonde hair. It was her way of offering herself . . . not that Marilyn Monroe was a real beauty; she was small with short arms and legs and then frankly, Marilyn was very fragile and neurotic, never knowing what she wanted. At one moment she'd throw herself into the arms of a political figure, at another, into those of a truck driver. As for beauty, well, Angela was more than average looking."

"I wasn't asking you about Angela's beauty."

"But being beautiful was part of her character," he insists, "if she hadn't been beautiful she wouldn't have led the life she did . . . except that in that gentle smile there was a desperate quality which was quite trying for those close to her. One would be wanting to protect her, guide her, but if you began to say something she'd oppose you and she could become really quite exasperating."

"Did you try to guide her?"

"No, for Christ's sake. The life she led was her own business . . . but there are things one can see instinctively . . . Her extreme fragility, that was the most disconcerting thing about her, she turned it into a terrible weapon."

"Have you any idea who might have killed her?"

"If I had, I'd have turned them over to the police . . . no. I've got no idea . . . I didn't get the impression she had enemies . . . but I really didn't know her well, I didn't see her that much."

"Do you know of Nando Pepi?"

"Yes, Ludovica has told me about him; a good for nothing who lives through blackmail."

"Do you think it could have been him who killed Angela as the papers are suggesting?"

"I don't know, but yes, it could have been him."

At this point, Ludovica starts crying again. He leaps up, hugs her, caresses her hair, holds her close to him, planting little kisses on her neck. I realise it is time to leave.

"If you think of anything else, call me on this number," I say. Mario Torres takes the card I hand him, gives me a jovial smile and accompanies me to the door.

I leave them bonded together, as if they wanted to demonstrate a solidarity which I did not in any way have cause to question.

38

I tell Adele Sòfia of my encounter with Ferdinando Pepi. I tell her about the cassette which she immediately appropriates.

"Do you understand what a risk you took in staying at the cemetery on your own?"

"If he'd wanted to do me any harm, it would have been the right moment; there was no one around and you were all looking for him somewhere else."

"You're probably more useful to him alive than dead."

"What use would I be?"

"To give people a good impression of him. Aren't you involved in the relationship between the public and criminals?"

"Actually I am preparing a programme for radio on crimes against women which remain unsolved."

"At this moment you represent the so-called fourth estate." She says this laughing and the little brace on her teeth glints, "a journalist, in the eyes of a criminal, has a lot of power; you can make him famous, you can make him appear less squalid than he is, you can contribute directly to his transformation into a hero, even if infamous. Occasional delinquents are afraid of the media because they've got everything to lose if they're on the front page, but not a habitual criminal; on the contrary, he can't hope for anything better."

"Where do you think he's gone?"

"Pepi? I don't know, but we'll get him. We have been in contact with Interpol. We have his fingerprints, identification data, all the evidence. We'll definitely be able to make an arrest in spite of his protection by journalists and radio announcers!" She gives a little laugh without malice.

"What do you have to say about the tape with the fairy tales?"

"Angela Bari was a child and she had the dreams of a child; I think she was hoping for these little tales to be heard on the radio or even to have a book published. She wasn't very original, just one of the fifty million Italians who want to write. When I have the time, I also write . . ."

For her it is just one more absurdity. She laughs, slapping her hands on her thighs. It would not actually surprise me if she wrote quite well. Her mind is a well-tended garden, cleared of invasive weeds, where small flowers with firm, tenacious roots grow.

After having talked to me, I see her going through the door of the director's office. I don't know why those two have so much to talk about. I have the disagreable impression that they are plotting something behind my back.

I go back to the table where the light-coloured little spider is weaving a small web that stretches delicately from the pencils to the coat hook behind me. This time the spider has been more daring, I watch it going up and down with alacrity, sliding along the web to coincide with the moment when it unwinds the thread from its mouth, like Tarzan hanging from the creeping plants of a tropical forest.

Tirinnanzi comes in with a cup of coffee for me. He sits down on the table, and with a quick movement rips the web and sends the poor spider off with its legs in the air. Then it spins round and round on the floor searching for its lost equilibrium.

"I think they're plotting to take your work away from you," he says casually, swinging his foot.

"How do you know that?"

"I heard them talking, the director and that woman from the police headquarters. They named two well-known journalists."

"And what about me?"

"You are too much your own boss, Michela. If I were you, I'd make copies of all the voices and then, if the worst happens, you can blackmail them by saying 'leave the programme to me, or else I'll take it to another radio station.' You have done all the work and you have rights."

"I'll talk to Cusumano."

"Don't say I know anything or that I've told you anything . . ."

"You don't have to worry."

"If you so much as mention my name, that'll be the end between us!"

"Of course not; I'm not that stupid. I'll find a way, I'm not very pleased at the idea of having two months' work taken away from me."

"A man forewarned is a man forearmed."

"A woman forewarned, at worst . . ."

"Don't give up, Michela, make trouble for them, make them recognise your worth."

"I'm no good at blackmail, you know that; I feel guilty, I make excuses and then they eat me up."

"You can't get it right, Michela."

Once again I hear those words which link me with Angela. Meanwhile Tirinnanzi gets down from the table and goes away, waving to me with open fingers and a sly look that wrinkles his nose comically.

What if I talk to the lawyer Merli? He is someone I can trust. I don't know why as I hardly know him. But I have not seen him for days. What has happened to him?

I ask Lorenza the office secretary if she knows his home telephone number. She gives me a wink and disappears. She comes back with the number. "I got it from Cusumano's diary, don't tell him!"

Lorenza is large and fat but moves like a dragon-fly. She looks after Cusumano as if he were a son but at the same time judges him with some irony. She is always ready to help anyone who asks for a favour; at the radio station she does everything from typing to emptying ashtrays, from answering the phone to preparing drinks. Sometimes in the morning I have found her sweeping the floor even if in theory there is a cleaning woman.

I telephone the lawyer Merli. He answers the phone in a hoarse, plaintive voice.

"How are you?"

"Ah Michela, it's you, thanks for phoning. I'm not feeling very good, I'm in bed with a temperature."

"What's happened to you?"

"A bronchitis which I can't get rid of."

"Can I come and see you?"

"But I'm in bed," and I can hear the panic at the other end of the line. "I'm on my own and everything is so untidy," he says quickly.

"That doesn't matter. Do you want me to bring anything? I could call at the chemist."

"No thanks, really not." Then it seems he has another thought and with his voice rather hoarse he adds, "If you really want to do me a favour, you could buy me some milk."

"Nothing else?"

"No thanks, no . . . well, if it really wouldn't be too much trouble I'd ask you to get me some medicines at the chemist."

"Tell me what it is you want and I'll be with you in half an hour."

39

A house in the Prati district, a courtyard the size of a pocket handkerchief with shabby flower beds and three tall palm trees, dusty and impoverished.

"Lawyer Merli?" I ask the porter who is lounging in a chair with his sleeves rolled up and a cigarette end between his lips.

"To tell you the truth it's days since I last saw him."

"He's been ill."

"He's always ill. One day he'll kick the bucket and nobody'll notice. It's the fifth floor, number 25."

I walk up the stairs and arrive out of breath. I ring the doorbell. He comes to open it wrapped in a faded silk dressing gown, his white hair pressed flat against one cheek, a haggard and unhappy look on his face.

He gives me a sweet smile and sees me in. I hand him the medicines, the milk and also a packet of biscuits. From the way he quickly opens them and starts eating, I realise he has been at home without food since he became ill.

"Do you have no one to look after you, Signor Merli?"

"Not at the moment, well, really I haven't got anybody."

"Then do get back into bed, you're looking very pale. I'm going to get a glass."

"No, no, please leave it," he mumbles, but I see how he is barely able to stand up and I insist on his going back to bed.

I go into the kitchen and get a clean glass, I pour milk into it, I put the biscuits into a bowl and take both to him on an oval tray.

"Why didn't you phone the station? We would have been able to come and look after you."

"I didn't want to be a nuisance."

He gets back into bed and pulls the sheet up to his chin. His striped cotton pyjamas are buttoned at the wrists and at his thin neck. With his hair untinted he looks suddenly old. Yet he can't be more than fifty. His features are youthful, he has no wrinkles on his face, his hands are strong and agile.

"Signor Merli, I need to talk to you."

He looks up at me with grey eyes; they have a kindly expression. His lips are drawn back in a contented smile.

"I was afraid you might have come out of pity," he says.

"Have you ever heard of a woman called Angela Bari who was stabbed to death just under two months ago?"

"Yes, I've read about it in the papers. Have they found the murderer yet?"

"No, they haven't, and that's why I've come to see you. Angela was my neighbour. When I came back from a course in Marseilles, I found her door open, the floor awash with disinfectant and her shoes together just by the entrance door. The porter told me she had been stabbed to death. I tried to think what I knew about her and I was forced to admit that I knew absolutely nothing. As far as I was concerned she had been a stranger, but she knew of me because of the radio, she had aspirations to do that kind of work. At the same time our director, Ettore Cusumano, had asked me to prepare a series of programmes about crimes against women that go unpunished. My research into such crimes has got mixed up with research into the murder of Angela Bari."

I can see from his eyes that he is following me with affec-tionate attention, concentrating his mind on the details I am telling him bit by bit about Angela, Carmelina, Ludovica, Nando, Augusta, Giulio Carlini, all the characters involved in this mysterious affair, so many of which have been in my thoughts over the past two months.

During this time he has eaten up all the biscuits. I go and fetch another glass of milk which he gulps down.

"Shall I go and buy you something more substantial to eat?" I ask.

"No, please don't, I'm right inside your story and I don't want you to interrupt it," he says with such sincere involvement that I want to embrace him. How was it I didn't think of talking to him before? Although he is a civil rather than a criminal lawyer, he gives me confidence because he knows the law and is willing to explain it.

By the time I have finished telling him the whole story, it is dark in the bedroom; we hadn't thought about switching on the light, and through the square of the window I can see one of the three forlorn palm trees.

"Do you think Pepi is guilty?"

"From what you have told me it doesn't appear so, but the necessary evidence for a prosecution is there. If it's true, as Carmelina said, that Angela sometimes worked as a prostitute, if it's true that he 'protected' her, if it's true that Angela was wanting to escape from his control, if it's true that the porter's mother saw him a few days after the crime and if it's true that he has the keys of the Bari apartment, I would say it is very likely that . . ."

"Nando Pepi says Angela wasn't ever a prostitute. It's really hard to decide which of the two is lying, but would a murderer risk being discovered simply in order to get hold of a cassette of fairy stories?"

"The stories were thought of and recorded before the crime took place and there isn't any particular reason to think they have a significant bearing on it. You haven't mentioned it but Angela would have noticed how you were her opposite: hard-working, disciplined, self-reliant, doing work you enjoyed and which earns you a living without having to use your body – and I'm not talking about prostitution. In today's world of

1 6 7   v o i c e s

images many women are expected to provide an image of physical attractiveness and as a result they keep quiet about their intelligence and their capacity for rational thought. Angela would have wanted to imitate you and in order to do this she sent you a sample tape to give you an idea of her powers of creation. I find this tender and touching."

"But why do all these stories describe such an unhappy and cruel relationship between fathers and daughters?"

"Angela Bari lost her father when she was eight years old, as you've told me, so the relationship remained unfulfilled, and she had to use her imagination to fill an empty void. The cruelty is in his premature death and in the violent severing of a relationship of affection and respect."

"That's just what Adele Sòfia says."

"It's logical, Michela."

He asserts this with gentleness, running his fingers through his dishevelled hair.

"Do you know that white hair really suits you? Now that you're less pale, the white hair frames your face and gives light to it."

"I've always tinted my hair, ever since I was twenty-five. It was my wife who showed me how to do it. Then she went off, taking my son away with her and I carried on doing it, half through habit and half through vanity. How can I show myself with my hair suddenly gone white to people who've always been accustomed to seeing me with black hair?"

"It's a good white and a pleasure to look at. And it's so thick, wouldn't it be worse to lose one's hair than to have it change colour?"

"Now you've said this, I'll take my courage in both hands and you'll all see me at the broadcasting station as I really am!"

"In a word, Signor Merli, what do you think I should do?"

"Go ahead with your research, but don't get too stuck into the Bari case. See it as one of the unsolved cases and probably fated to remain so. Besides, if the case does get resolved, it will only be through the tenacity and passion which you put into it, and I think that all such enigmas are only solved through passion rather than through skill . . . but then of course you won't be able to use it for your programme because it won't any longer be an unpunished crime!"

He has a quiet and ironical way of drawing out a thread of reasoning which I find soothing. Two white moustaches of milk remain at the corners of his well defined mouth, making him look even more vulnerable.

"Now I'm going off to buy you some fruit and some bread, you can't go on starving yourself."

"But you won't be able to buy anything now, Michela, it's past eight o'clock."

He makes a funny gesture by pointing his finger at a clock that isn't there. He strikes his forefinger first twice and then three times against his bare wrist, and gives me a mischievous smile.

"Do you want me to call a doctor?" I say in a firm tone of voice.

"No thanks, I'm better now, the fever has almost gone and to get back my strength all I need is rest."

"Then I'll look in tomorrow morning before going to the radio station and I'll bring you something to eat."

I see him looking happy with my suggestion. He must be really lonely if he has no friend or relation to look after him when he is feeling ill.

40

I did not have the courage to take the tape-recorder with me when I went to see the lawyer Merli, and now I am sorry. His kind and understanding words would help me today when I feel persecuted by doubt.

It must have been Marco's telephone call last night that has poisoned my thoughts. He told me he loved me but that we would not be able to see each other any more. "But why?" I kept on asking him and he, almost in tears, told me he had "lost his head".

"Have you fallen in love?" No, no, he insisted, he hadn't

fallen in love, he had only "lost his head". And not over a woman, but in himself and for himself.

I do not even know whether or not I dreamed the telephone call. I suddenly saw a series of polished, dangling heads. "This is what the Gauls used to do," I remember my history teacher telling me, as he sat on the window-sill in his blue jeans and pink shirt. He described the most horrifying details. "And do you know what they did with the heads? They threaded them on a rope as if they were pearls, and hung them round the necks of their horses and then they went like that through their lands. And to stop the heads rotting, they would grease them with oil of cedarwood. That is what Diodorus Siculus tells us."

Seated in the back row, I imagined looking outside the school window, and seeing the greasy, sweating horses of the Gauls appearing through the morning mist laden with their burden of human heads.

If Marco says he loves me, he really means what he says, even if he has "lost his head". He must still have another head, I tell myself in my sleep holding on to the telephone, an ambiguous and indecipherable object.

My history teacher was called Monumento, an odd name which we were always repeating: what Professor Monumento has said, what Professor Monumento has done ... He was a man with the ability to make himself heard. He used to say laughing, "I am your monument". He liked to tell us about the dark sides of history that are missed out in history books, he enjoyed regaling us with gossip about the Greeks and the Romans; the bloodier the more he enjoyed it. Certainly with him history was never a boring subject.

"Hecate had three heads, one in the shape of a dog. But Janus, how many heads did Janus have, Michela?"

"Two, I think."

"Well done, Janus had two heads, one looking in front and one looking behind. And who tells the stories about the heads of Janus?"

I feel bewildered, I wander through the apartment not knowing what to do. Today is my day off but what time is it? Six o'clock in the morning. I am sleepy but can't get to sleep,

I am hungry but can't eat. I decide to make myself a cup of tea but even the idea of carrying out ordinary actions like turning on the stove, fills me with repugnance. Supposing I too were endowed with two heads, one for kissing and one for reflecting?

I wander into the bathroom and I see my head, insipid and uncombed. What would it feel like to lose my head, especially if it was the only one I had?

After all, I could be like Chinese women, I could stay in my room with its blue carpet, waiting for the bare feet of my lord and master to walk upon it, following the ancient custom of sharing affection: would it be once a week or once a month?

Bewildered, I look in the mirror at my head so miraculously joined to my body, when I hear the door bell ring. Who can it be at this hour? Suppose it was Nando Pepi again? In spite of everything, this man frightens me. I creep towards the door on tiptoe. I put my eye to the spyhole and see Ludovica Bari walking up and down smoking a cigarette. Her head is enveloped in a strange violet-coloured turban. I open the door and she slips in as if she were being followed.

"What has happened?"

"I'm terribly sorry, it's still so early but I didn't know what to do or where to go."

Looking agitated she pulls off the turban and shows me a bleeding wound in the middle of her sticky hair.

"How on earth did that happen?"

"It was him."

"Him? Who?"

"Him, Mario."

"But he seems to be so loving."

"He is, most of the time he is, but when he's been drinking he loses his head."

"Him as well?" I can't help saying this. She looks at me in surprise and continues, "When he's angry, he hits me all over. The bruises you saw the other day on my arm . . . it was he who did it . . . Last night he came back at two in the morning. I asked him where he'd been, and he replied 'Get to bed, you bitch!' Then I realised he'd been drinking, I screamed that I couldn't stand any more, I'd go and live on my own. He threw himself at me shouting, throwing me on to the floor and hitting me. Look here." She lifts her blouse and shows me a bruise on her bottom rib. "I kept on saying 'I'm going, this time I'm really going', and he got hold of a bottle and split my head open. It isn't bleeding any more because I've put ice on it, but look at the wound!"

"You shouldn't be here, you should have gone to casualty."

"But how could I? He took the house key and swallowed it. Then he threw himself on the bed."

"And how did you get here?"

"I waited till he was asleep and then I crept out through the bathroom window and down by the back stairs. I didn't have any money for a taxi."

"We should report him."

"If he knew we'd done that he'd kill me. I'm frightened, Michela, I'm really frightened. Could I lie low here for a few days?"

"First you've got to report him, from the hospital you go to for treatment."

"I can't go out, what if he's been following me?"

"If he'd been following you, he'd be here by now,"

"I'm frightened, Michela, I'm so frightened. What on earth can I do?"

"I'm going to telephone Adele Sòfia, she'll think of something."

"No, please don't do that, don't phone anybody," she begs me. Meanwhile the wound has started to bleed again.

"Wait while I go and get some ice and some disinfectant. Come into the kitchen. Would you like a coffee?"

"If the police find out he beats me up, they'll think he could have murdered Angela. You know I had to tell a lie to get an alibi for him, he wasn't with me that evening, I don't know where he was."

"Do you think he could have murdered Angela and if so, why?"

"No, I don't believe that he'd have done that, anyway he wouldn't have wished a life sentence."

"Did Mario and Angela know each other well?"

"I think they saw each other secretly. He was very fascinated by her. But no, no, it couldn't have been him, he's a man who values his own comfort too much."

Meanwhile I have dabbed her wound with disinfectant, taken some ice cubes from the freezer, wrapped them in a cloth and pressed them against her head.

"What about some coffee?" I am trying to counteract her state of confusion by simple reasoning. "Mario doesn't have to be afraid of anything, he won't be charged even if he did give a false alibi because what counts is the blood test. At the most they'll have him for assault. But you have to report it to the police."

"No one will believe me, no one . . . he's an engineer and he's highly thought of," she says mechanically, "an engineer who is so highly thought of.

"You know sometimes he can be so gentle, so affectionate and tender. He likes playing with my hair . . . he makes me sit on his knee and says 'wait while I braid your hair' and he'll spend half an hour plaiting it, pulling it and combing through it. Then we'll make love and he keeps on saying how he loves me. Friends think he adores me and when he's with them he's cheerful and relaxed, always laughing and joking. But when he comes home he gets all gloomy and since Angela's death he's started drinking again. Years ago he was treated for alcoholism and he stopped drinking completely. But now he comes to bed with a bottle and while I read, he drinks. To begin with he only did it to get to sleep, but he says sleep won't come and so he drinks like this straight out of the bottle. Eventually he falls asleep with his mouth wide open and snores like a caged lion. If I didn't wake him up he'd go on sleeping till the next evening."

"Since when has he been covering you in bruises?"

"Two months ago, when Angela died. After the funeral he came home dead drunk, he couldn't even talk and he looked at me with raging eyes. 'What's the matter?' I asked him and he said 'Go and peck somewhere else, you old hen.' 'But what have I done to you?' I didn't understand, I thought he had it in for me about something when in fact it wasn't against me but against himself, that's what he told me. The first times it happened he would be so horrible to me that one evening I asked 'If I'm a hen why do you go on staying with me?' and he hit me so hard it made my lip bleed. The next day when he asked my forgiveness, he was so scared. He looked after me so tenderly, you can't imagine it. Every few minutes he'd be asking me 'Are you better? Have you forgiven me?' And how could I not forgive him? 'Shall we go to the sea?' he asked, and we spent a wonderful day on the water laughing and joking. And you should see how he makes love when he is feeling guilty and wants to be forgiven, with so much gentleness and so much passion!

"Three weeks ago he started to hit me and kick me because I'd said to him, 'So what?' I can't even remember what I was referring to, but he was mortally offended by those words and went on repeating them. And that time he also wanted to apologise and said how when he drinks he loses his head, it's not his fault, he doesn't realise what he's doing. 'But I love you, I love you so much,' he said and again I believed him. I can't not believe him, he's always been so good to me.

"He stayed calm for two weeks, didn't touch the bottle and even managed to sleep at night. One evening he told me how when he was little his mother would pretend to be dead and he was so terrified that he'd begin to shake all over. Once his mother said to him, 'When I die give me a little hit so I'll wake up,' and he used to do that and he'd hit her more and more violently and his mother screamed but he wasn't able to stop . . . Is this why he hits me? Because he's afraid I might die like his mother?"

"Maybe but the report has to be made."

"Yesterday evening he came back late, all surly, and I immediately realised he'd been drinking, but I never imagined he'd crack a bottle over my head. Now I've made the decision, I'm leaving. I don't want to see him any more. I don't know if I'll report him to the police but I don't want to be with him any longer. It's all over."

I persuade her to lie down. Then I put on my shoes. It is now after eight o'clock. I tell her I am going to talk to Adele

Sòfia and that she is not to worry. I will only be asking her advice and I'll soon be back.

She looks at me, her eyes damp with tears. Exhausted, she makes a gesture of agreement. She turns her back and curls up on the bed and all at once falls into a heavy sleep.

41

"Everything happens to you," Adele Sòfia tells me.

"Won't it be necessary to get a blood sample from him?"

"Yes, we must do that. We were on the point of doing it anyway: we're going to examine the blood of everyone implicated in the case, but we're waiting for Judge Boni's consent and the lawyers are making a fuss. It isn't that easy."

"When I met him he seemed quite a sensitive, caring sort of person. I did an interview with him and noticed nothing."

"Clothes don't make the man. Why didn't Ludovica come to report him? You should have brought her."

"She doesn't want to accuse him."

"The usual thing: they get beaten up and then they protect them and cover up for them."

"He's affectionate, every time he hits her he begs to be forgiven."

"It's a classic case, you wouldn't believe the number of women I've come across like her. You should have sent her packing instead of letting her stay. Michela, do you really want to get even deeper into all of this than you already are? Send her along to us, I'll find her a place near here with the nuns where he won't be able to get at her. They're very nice, they won't ask her anything. Or we can send her back to her mother at Fiesole. But don't keep her with you."

"At the moment she's asleep in my bed."

"You should have sent her away immediately."

"She was injured and covered in bruises."

"All the more reason. You should have taken her to casualty.

To lodge any accusation written testimony from the hospital is needed. On the other hand a report is registered automatically."

"I've told her all that. But the injury is there, it won't heal that quickly, the bruises are very visible."

"Go back home and convince her. Then I'll bring the car over and we'll take her to casualty."

"Fine."

So I rush back home as fast as I can, but I find the door open and I realise immediately that Ludovica has gone. There is no sign of her either in the bedroom or anywhere else in the apartment. She has gone without leaving a note, nothing.

I go outside and start walking towards the Tiber. In the Via Titta Scarpetta I encounter the cat lady.

"Is it pasta with tomato sauce today?"

"Yes, the restaurant gives me some in exchange for an hour's dish-washing."

I look at her nonplussed; sometimes heroism is like a caricature of the sublime.

"Would you like the Pope to make you a saint?"

She laughs, waves to me with a hand covered in tomato sauce while tiny kittens crawl up her legs stretching out their mangy necks.

The day is hot. In some places the surface of the pavement is soft and shoes leave an imprint on it as if it were sealing wax. Cars glitter under the summer sun. I walk fast to reach the river where the plane trees give shade to the few passers-by.

I go past a telephone kiosk. I stop, turn back, go inside and call Adele Sòfia.

"We have them both here," she says, sounding really pleased.

"I had imagined that might be the case."

"When we arrived they were making love. I told them the examining magistrate had arranged for a blood sample to be taken to check on the DNA and that this had been agreed with the lawyers. They came meek and mild to the laboratory. Now the doctor is dealing with them. I haven't betrayed your confidence, you don't have to worry. In any case they seem quite happy and contented. We'll be sending them home in half an hour. I've arranged for Torres to be put under police observation. We shall be keeping a watch on him, I can't do more . . . I could be mistaken but he seems to be a pleasant, well-educated sort of person. Are you sure Ludovica hasn't made it all up?"

"You mean she could have injured herself?"

"She wouldn't be the first, some women are capable of anything."

"You speak as if you weren't a woman yourself!"

"I mean a certain category of woman where the habit of self-deception is such that . . . I remember a girl who used to squeeze a belt round her neck so she had a big black bruise, then she would blame her mother for having tried to strangle her . . . But then I'm rather suspicious when faced with these domestic melodramas . . . besides, your Ludovica seems to me to be a rather distraught person."

"She could have good reasons, couldn't she?"

"Torres seems to be in love with her. His eyes never leave her, he was very concerned she should be well treated. The doctor on duty sutured the wound on her head, it needed five stitches!"

"Did you ask her how she got it?"

"It was our first question, of course. She told me she had hit her head against the corner of the wardrobe door. Could this be a true version do you think? She gives the impression of someone who might invent anything to attract attention . . . she is somewhat disturbed, don't you think? But I find him quite calm and rational. She has an immature personality like Angela Bari which might explain it all. Perhaps the two sisters were quite alike, or more than Ludovica wants to have us believe."

I am about to walk further on, when I realise I have completely forgotten the lawyer Merli. I dial his number. He answers in a weak, listless voice.

"I was expecting you," he says. I know. I explain what has happened. He listens with sympathetic attention. He is not someone who makes reproaches, but he is coughing painfully in a way that arouses all my feelings of guilt.

"What is your opinion, Signor Merli? Adele Sòfia is

convinced Ludovica isn't telling the truth and that she is quite disturbed."

"If she rushed headlong to your house in the middle of the night with an injured head saying she wanted to leave her man forever, and then went back later on to make love with him, it suggests she is a bit unbalanced . . . however I don't believe anyone would make a wound needing five stitches simply to attract attention . . . a scratch, yes, a bruise but a gash like that . . . and then hasn't he already been arrested before for getting into a brawl . . . isn't he known to be rather free with his fists?"

"Adele Sòfia had a rather good impression of Torres whom she describes as being cooperative and rational. But if Ludovica's injury happened as she described it to me and as I believe, then he must posses an astonishing capacity for self-deception. Wouldn't someone like that be capable of murder?"

"Don't run on too fast, Michela. One needs to look at what his motives could be. No one kills without motivation."

"Let's say he had a secret relationship with Angela while he was with Ludovica and that she was forcing him to choose between her and her sister, and he was unable to decide . . ." but I realise I am telling Marco's story.

"As a motive that is too weak, Michela."

"All the same, Adele Sòfia has had a blood sample taken from him in the presence of the lawyer. If it is him, we'll soon know."

"That may not be sufficient . . . in such cases proof from a blood sample is only circumstantial evidence."

"The deeper one goes, the more complicated I'm finding it."

"Are you coming to see me, Michela?"

"Yes, I'm coming. What would you like me to bring you?"

"Nothing, nothing . . . but if it isn't too much trouble I'd ask you for some fresh milk and a small yoghurt, perhaps some biscuits, the ones you brought last time were so good."

He is alone and he is in need of company, I say to myself, ready to rush to help him. At the same time I feel we are slipping into the most commonplace drama with him in the role of the abandoned, unhappy invalid and me in that of a Florence Nightingale, a part I don't like very much. I tell him this and he gives an embarrassed laugh. Suppose I don't go to see him? It feels so good here leaning against the low wall along the Tiber, underneath the flowering plane trees, my eyes gazing at the slow-moving waters which today are a murky emerald green. I could still walk for a bit longer and then take the tram to the Tamara De Lempicka exhibition at the French Academy. But I already know that I shall go and see Merli with milk, biscuits, yoghurt, the newspapers, fresh flowers and eggs.

42

Merli and I have been sitting on his bed playing cards. He is wrapped in a pair of threadbare pyjamas, his shining white hair forms a crown around his smooth forehead. He spreads out his long hands to cut the pack of cards, he brings it up to his nose as if to smell it. Then he divides the cards, shuffles them and deals them with rapt attention like a child.

"I've always got a lot of enjoyment from playing cards," he says, "above all for the mathematical pleasure they provide; the numbers that become a gamble, the challenge, the little intuitions that all of a sudden stop and go into reverse, causing the wheel of fate to turn. And then those double kings and queens, the barely glimpsed mysterious presences that only live above the breast. Is anything more seductive than a Queen of Spades? It's no surprise that Pushkin made it the centre of one of his finest stories.

"One of the girls at my school," he continues, "was nick-named the Queen of Hearts, not because she was in any way wanton, but because she was large and well built and wore her hair cut short. From her chest down she was clumsy-looking, but her breasts looked as if they had been carved out of a single piece of wood, always covered by a brightly coloured, close-fitting blouse making her an image of the Queen of Hearts."

After having played and won, Merli asks me to tell him about

Angela Bari. I try to remember how she had seemed to me before I listened to the opinions of all the many witnesses of her life. I have to admit that her image is crumbling inside my memory, in spite of my obstinate attempt to clutch at what happened to her. I am not even sure any more that I ever actually met her. I no longer remember her face or her voice, yet she is there in my thoughts almost like a double of myself.

"Was she really beautiful enough to upset the chemical composition of the male brain?" Merli asks with an ironical look.

"Yes, she was beautiful but everyone saw her in a different way. For Giulio Carlini she had a fragile beauty that was crying out for protection, for Mario Torres she wasn't particularly beautiful but there was beauty inherent in her character. Her sister Ludovica talks about the beauty she paraded almost as if she were wanting to destroy herself."

"But when you met her in the lift, how did you see her?"

"Very luminous and light as if she might soar into flight from one moment to the next. It wasn't that she lacked solidity, she knew how to rest her feet on the ground, she had a decisive walk, but like some kinds of bird, which appear awkward when they're walking or swimming, as if they were waiting to open their wings to leave behind the encumbrance of the earth, so Angela seemed to be uncomfortable wearing shoes."

"It's not by chance she was called Angela . . . what was she like as a child?"

"From what Ludovica says she was delicate and awkward; 'not being able to get things right' is how she describes her. She always got to school late, studied without being able to learn, a child the teachers treated with impatience and other children sneered at."

"While Ludovica herself . . ."

"She always got good marks and was often elected head pupil."

"And Angela hated her for this?"

"No, on the contrary according to Ludovica, Angela was incapable of envy, she was proud of her elder sister even if by the end she was trying to run away from her."

"And the mother?"

"Her mother was always occupied keeping admirers at bay. Ludovica remembers this with considerable ill-feeling, whereas she has nostalgic memories of her father who died when she was only twelve. Only six months after his death her mother married again and her second husband, Glauco Elia, seems to have done everything he could to win over his two stepdaughters. But he didn't have much success. He seems to have had little influence. Ludovica married a man older than herself who was later killed in a car accident. Then she found this Mario Torres who is an engineer, good-looking with nice manners. But when he drinks, he gets violent. All this has been denied by the mother, Signora Augusta Elia, who insists that Ludovica was never married, that Angela separated from her husband because her sister started to get involved with him, and that it wasn't Angela who had an abortion but Ludovica, as a result of which she had to spend some time in a psychiatric clinic. In fact everything gets turned upside down and I haven't a clue which of them is telling the truth."

"And the father?"

"I don't know much about him, it seems he was affectionate but rather severe. He was a doctor who didn't know how to take care of himself. Glauco Elia, the stepfather, stayed with Augusta and her daughters for fifteen years and then went off and married a girl thirty years younger and they've recently had a baby whom he has named Augusta."

"Have you ever talked to this stepfather?"

"No, I haven't."

"Talk to him, you might get more detailed information about Angela and Ludovica."

"I'm glad you agree with me. Adele Sòfia says it's pointless as he's been absent from the lives of both sisters for years. And he has a very secure alibi, the letter from the hospital confirms the date of his daughter's birth as being June 24th and there is the evidence from the nurses that they witnessed him being present at the birth."

"What I'm wondering is why Ludovica talked to you about Nando before you had discovered who he was. Had she known him?"

"I don't think so. She had heard Angela talk about him and she was curious, that was all. Then they got to know each other, given that Nando used to go brazenly to people's houses asking about Angela. He went to their mother's and won her over by talking about seagulls. Whoever meets him is enchanted by him. Probably it's because he has the look of a refined student, his attentive eyes, a certain shyness he has . . ."

"But why was Nando Pepi so interested in Angela? Was it because he wanted to make her into a high-class call girl?"

"And if he'd just been in love with her?"

"Does he seem to you like someone who falls in love when it's his profession to send women on the streets to prostitute themselves? He is more likely to have one here and another one there who'll probably end up a drug addict into the bargain."

"According to Sabrina–Carmelina he is quite a strange man, very generous, everything he earns he spends on the girls he protects and at least to her he was kind, generous, and suscep-tible to falling in love."

"Someone like that would be an exception among pimps . . . but then it could be more the product of Sabrina's fantasies than a picture of the truth."

"He's undoubtedly an odd person, that can't be denied, I've seen it myself. At first he's a bit frightening but if you look at him a second time he gives the impression of someone who feels shy and frustrated and puts on an act to laugh it off."

"A shy person who laughs a lot doesn't exploit women."

"Why not?"

"Doesn't the fact he was in possession of Angela's keys tell you something?"

"It tells me that Angela trusted him."

"He could have taken them by force or blackmail . . . but it would be serious evidence in any proceedings against him. As I understand it, if Angela wasn't under his control she was about to become so. But is it true her mother was giving her five million a month?"

"That is what Signora Augusta says and it seems she has shown Adele Sòfia some cheque counterfoils. But Ludovica maintains they were only sporadic gifts and certainly not a regular monthly payment."

"Did Angela work?"

"She had small parts from time to time. I don't think she could have earned enough from acting to keep herself."

"If she were in need of money and he was backing her, she might have agreed to work for him under his protection. Perhaps she then thought of separating from him and he decided to make the consequence clear to her. He could have gone to see her, they might even have made love, then had an argument. She could have said something he didn't agree with, and faced with being insulted by her, he could have got hold of a knife . . . this seems to me the most likely version."

"This is what Adele Sòfia and the investigating magistrate Judge Boni think. But isn't it strange for a murderer to go back at night to the apartment where he killed a woman just to get a tape of fairy stories?"

"Why do you think Pepi valued this tape so much?"

"I don't know, perhaps because he knew Angela cared about it. This makes me think he may have really loved her."

"A delicacy of spirit that would be a little unusual for a pimp, wouldn't it?"

"She also wanted to be involved in broadcasting, to be part of the big world of voices."

"What are these stories like?"

"Not bad, very cruel and told with some sensitivity."

"I'm sure a pimp wouldn't be so thoughtful. I think he wanted to show himself in a good light to you, Michela."

"For what reason?"

"To win you over and get your support. And he has succeeded to perfection."

"Don't you believe that contradictions exist even in the most despicable people?"

"I'd call it hypocrisy rather than contradiction."

"Throughout this entire story no one is telling the truth . . . it's difficult to be certain of anything."

"If I were you I would go and talk to that sculptor Elia. It could be that he'll be able to shed some light, given that he lived for fifteen years with the two Bari sisters and their mother . . ."

When I left the lawyer's apartment it was past midnight. I drove my cherry-coloured Fiat with the windows wide open through a half-deserted wind-blown city.

When I got back I found a telephone call from Marco on the answering machine endlessly repeating, "Where are you? I love you, Michela, remember this." I do not know what to make of it. Is it the first or the second head talking? Once again he has not left his phone number so I can't call him back. I can only wait for him to ring me again. Meanwhile I listen once more to the far-away voice, for once distinct and clear, as it repeats, "Where are you? I love you, Michela, remember this, I love you Michela, remember this."

During the whole evening I have only had one glass of milk. Now I am feeling hungry. I open the fridge but it is empty. I have forgotten to do any shopping. All I can do is to go to bed on an empty stomach after drinking a glass of water into which I put ten drops of valerian.

43

I am lost, but in my hand is a small piece of paper with directions.

"Take the motorway to Velletri, turn right by the train station. At the first set of traffic lights go along Via Rondanini to the cross-roads, then take Via Roma. At the Agip petrol station turn left down a small, unsurfaced road. Go along it for five kilometres, take a right turn and you are there."

"It's a little bit complicated but you should be able to find the way; if not, ask for directions." The smooth, caressing voice of Glauco Elia has stayed in my ear.

At this point I should follow his suggestions and ask the way, but who is there to ask?

The street is deserted and only the occasional car goes hurrying past. With one hand I keep hold of the piece of paper, with the other I steer. On the road no signs are to be seen. I think again of the voice that answered me on the phone: easy, tolerant and ironic with little spikes of mockery.

I go back to the railway station and to the beginning of the street. At last I discover the Agip station, its sign hidden by the branches of a giant eucalyptus tree. I stop to ask for information but the kiosk is closed, the roof is toppling to one side, the plaster peeling, the pumps are broken and pulled out of the ground. I turn back to check the name of the street but find nothing.

I look around, hoping to see someone but not a soul goes by. In the middle of the road I see a wounded tortoise limping along, leaving a trail of blood. I stop the car and get out. I look at it close to, it appears to have been hit with a hammer; pieces of shell are missing and it is bleeding from one side. It is being closely followed by a cloud of flies, some are sticking to the wound with such greed that even when I take the tortoise in my hand, they show no sign of flying away.

I pick it up. It moves its feet and manages to push out a wrinkled head. I clean it with some leaves, I open an old newspaper and I lay it on the back seat of the car after having driven off the flies.

I resume my search for the house of Glauco Elia. A left turn, but where? So far I have seen three tracks that turn off the main road into the fields. I go back, I turn into a small road, which after several snake-like bends, brings me back to where I started.

I catch sight of a public telephone. Who knows what state it will be in? I go inside; by some miracle it is in working order. I dial the number of Elia's house. I am answered by the voice I know already. "Yes, it's difficult, I'm sorry; it's a bit of a labyrinth but with a little patience you'll get here."

I go back into the car and on to the road. "When you see a sign advertising a restaurant called Avello, slow down. After ten metres you'll see a big maple tree and immediately afterwards a narrow track. Go down it and you'll see a white gate. There I will be."

I don't have the courage to ask him what a maple tree looks

like, and I'm not sure of being able to distinguish it from a beech tree or a lime tree. I drive slowly, scrutinising the trees one by one. At last I think I see it, the maple tree has star-shaped leaves of a very tender green.

I go down a dusty lane; on each side are hedges of brambles that reach out and scratch my car. It is a fine day; through the open car windows gusts of hot air blow in, smelling of cut grass, broom flowers, cow dung and cabbages.

Out of the corner of my eye I catch sight of a length of white wood half-buried beneath the brambles. I stop, turn round, and there is the gate. I push it open enough to drive my car through; the dust has turned my little Fiat into a strange shade of grey streaked with pink.

At last, in the distance, I can see a house, a solid 19th-century building with a few decorations that attempt to lighten its appearance; fake crenallations on a fake tower, ogival windows bordered by Corinthian columns.

I arrive at the front of the house in a cloud of dust. I stop the car underneath the branches of another maple tree. I get out and walk towards the house, which looks uninhabited. But didn't he tell me he would be at the gate? The shutters are closed, the door bolted. Have I come to the wrong house? Around me there is a profound silence.

While I stand there wondering what to do, I see a man slipping out of a small side door I had not noticed. He comes towards me holding out his hand. He is tall and thin with a look of pain that makes him appear rather bent. His forehead is sunburned with a receding hair line, clear, shining blue eyes, a smile which is youthful and seductive. He is wearing loose fitting jeans that look smart, and white trainers.

"I am sorry you've had all this trouble getting here. Come inside and have a cold drink; mint tea?"

I take the tape-recorder out of the car and follow him in. He pushes open a black mosquito net that serves as a door, and goes ahead down a long dark passage. After a sharp bend we come suddenly to a spacious veranda flooded with light and with a view over the valley. The floor, of old Neapolitan tiles, is scattered with pots of lemon trees, cane chairs and Indian cushions.

"What a lovely spot!" I say, dazed by the unexpected view that opens in front of me like a fan, embracing the hills that slope gently down the valley. The house clings to grey rocks that interrupt the flow of the hill like a natural terrace.

"I only like to see fields and pasture land around me. No houses, no roads, I had to look at quite a few places before I found one like this, it wasn't easy . . . I need to be able to look up and see only green, I don't want anything sophisticated like ancient woods or lakes or gardens, just fields and meadows . . ."

"Would you mind if I record our conversation? You know that I'm doing a programme for Italia Viva on unpunished crimes against women and the murder of Angela Bari seems destined to remain a such a crime."

"Do as you want, machines make me feel uneasy but I'll do my best."

"If you ask me to stop the recording, I will."

"Is the programme going out soon?"

"No, a great deal more has to be done. I've had to spend a lot of time getting hold of material, listening to the voices of all the people in this story."

"Am I one of the characters? How interesting!"

"Well, you were married to Angela's mother for fifteen years and I know you were fond of Angela."

"Yes, I suppose that without wishing it, we are inside the stories of whoever we have loved . . . these are all things which now are very far away from me. You know I got married again and haven't seen Angela or her sister for years, and I've just had a baby daughter."

"Can you tell me what Angela was like as a child? I have very contradictory information about that."

"She was a difficult child, very difficult."

"Why?"

"Because she was so restless and angry, always discontented, always on the alert, provocative and aggressive."

"That's strange because everyone says she was such a shy, quiet child."

"Shy perhaps, but too intelligent and strong-willed to be quiet. Shall I get you some tea?"

A swallow flies out from underneath the roof into the afternoon sky, filling the air with its shrill cries. A crow answers it in a grave, sonorous voice.

"Your wife isn't here?"

"No, she went to see her mother for a few days, in Brianza."

"With the baby?"

"Yes, with Augusta. She was born on the day Angela died, an almost miraculous coincidence; one woman who leaves the world, another who comes into it. I shan't be surprised if they look alike."

"When was the last time you saw Angela?"

"Oh, I haven't seen her for years, I don't remember how many . . ."

"Yet the porter's mother in Via Santa Cecilia told me she'd seen you in May." I throw this in quite casually, hoping he won't tense up.

"I must have a double because other people have also said how they saw me at that time. And do you know where? In Naples, think of that! Yet I was here, occupied with the important task of becoming a father."

"Where did your wife have the baby?"

"At the Sant'Anselmo Hospital."

"And you were there for the birth."

"I certainly was. I believe that today a father should share in the birth of his daughter and the pains of the mother. Unfortunately did not see Angela being born, but I always looked on her as if she were my daughter."

"Why didn't you come to her funeral?"

"I detest funerals. I didn't even go to my mother's. I don't want to be involved in funeral rites, I'm repelled by all the flowers, the candles, the music . . . I prefer to keep my eyes on the image of a living person who walks, talks, laughs . . ."

"Ludovica says Angela was afraid of you."

"Ludovica isn't always to be believed, perhaps you haven't had a chance to notice this . . . since she had an abortion she has suffered from depression, she got better in the clinic with electro-shock treatments, I think about a dozen, but since then she hasn't really been herself."

"Ludovica told me it was Angela who had an abortion after her husband left her; they'd planned to go to America together and then he went off by himself."

"She told you that? Astonishing! Do you want to know the truth? Angela's husband left her for the simple reason she pushed him out after having discovered he was making love to her sister . . . they had only been married for two months . . . Ludovica is a dear girl, let's be clear about this, and intelligent and generous but not always to be believed. She adjusts reality to her own way of thinking and doesn't always know what the truth is."

"So Angela was never in a clinic, didn't have shock treatments, didn't suffer from depression?"

"Angela was always in good health. She was quite an assured person who was strong-willed. She was sometimes moody I'll agree; she always wanted both the sun and the moon. She really was her mother's daughter, less beautiful, but as tenacious, wilful and intelligent as Augusta with the same incredible capacity to adapt to difficult situations."

"Did you ever hear that Angela sometimes worked as a prostitute?"

"I don't know anything about that. As I've told you, I haven't seen her for years. From time to time I'd meet up with Augusta when I was in Florence, she always behaved very well towards me, never reproached me and I'm still very fond of her. Augusta always told me Angela worked as an actress, without much success but enough to provide her with some money over and above what she gave her."

"Signora Augusta told me she gave her five million a month but Ludovica denies this."

"Angela squandered everything her father left her without a moment's thought. Augusta is very generous, she has always helped her. I don't know how much she gave her a month but she certainly wouldn't have left her without money."

"Have you ever heard of Carmelina Di Giovanni who also called herself Sabrina?"

"No, who is she?"

"She was a prostitute. One day she stated on a radio programme that Angela worked as a prostitute from time to time."

"I don't know. To me it seems highly improbable given Angela's character, although it's true her mother said she was worried about her very free and easy behaviour, but to me it sounded more a provocation than anything else."

"Is it true that when Angela was between eight and thirteen you and she were inseparable? Your former wife said this."

"That's true, we were very fond of each other and we went everywhere together, to the sea, up the mountains, down the rivers. She was a little girl burning with the desire for life, full of energy and a spirit of adventure. She used to confide in me about her adolescent sweethearts, you know she was always falling in love with rather unsuitable boys. I used to chastise her but she couldn't have cared less. She was always fiercely independent; she didn't listen to anyone."

"When Angela got to be thirteen, something happened between you, according to Signora Augusta, and after that you stopped going out together."

"Nothing happened; it was simply that she grew older and preferred friends of her own age and needed to put the trusted old stepfather on one side. That's quite usual, isn't it?"

"After you and Augusta separated, you didn't see any more of Angela, but did you ever talk to her on the phone?"

"No, nothing like that, I never saw or heard from her. She didn't like my wife Emilia and Emilia didn't like her."

"Did you know that Angela wrote fairy stories?"

"No, what kind of stories?"

"Stories which tell obsessively of fathers who want to devour their daughters."

"I know she was very upset by her father's death when she was eight. For both sisters it left an empty gap that couldn't ever be filled. It seems he was a very loving father if at times authoritarian . . . So Augusta told me, she also said how a man like him was one of a kind."

His voice sounds frank and sincere. If he is lying it is so perfect that he himself is mistaking a lie for the truth.

"Your wife is thirty years younger than you?"

"No, actually twenty-seven."

"So she is like a daughter to you?"

"Yes, a child wife . . . have you ever read *Rien Va* by Landolfi where he writes in great detail about the 'child wife'? The solitary man in love with card games . . . do you know he went to live in San Remo to be near the Casino? He lost regularly, of course, like his idol Dostoievsky did . . . he translated him, studied him, he loved him so much he wanted to be him . . . Hasn't this ever happened to you? It has to me . . . take Bach, for instance, the Chaconne . . . once I used to play the violin. I would have given ten years of my life to know how to play the Chaconne as Bach wrote it, with those perfect geometric lines, those sublime repetitions, that diabolical clarity . . . enough to make me lose my head!"

So he too wants to lose his head. Other horses come galloping to meet me from the bottom of the valley, with their load of human heads greased with oil of cedarwood.

"So you have a child wife who in her turn has brought another little girl into the world."

"Exactly . . . so it can be seen how I am fated to live surrounded by women. But I'm happy with that; they have all taught me so much . . . my wife, for example, if you could see her . . . she is such a small creature, yet she has an unsuspected inner strength . . . she is a child mother but in some ways much more mature than I am . . . and that other real daughter of mine, she too promises well . . . I'm very content with my little household of women."

He smiles with satisfaction and real happiness. His voice has taken on a musical tone; I have only now become aware of it, as if he were singing an internal melody that only the greatest seducers are able to put on at will. "Well, if you have no more to ask me, I'll go back to my work, if you don't mind." He says this without ill-will and with a fatherly kindliness. Meanwhile he has got up and is lightly tapping the tiled floor with his trainers as if following some internal rhythm of thought.

I turn the tape-recorder off, finish the tea and go towards my dust-covered Fiat.

44

As I lean out of the window to say goodbye to Glauco Elia, it occurs to me that I haven't asked him about his sculpture.

"Are you preparing for an exhibition?"

His smile broadens.

"Would you show me some of your work?" I ask hesitantly.

"If you like," he says without seeming displeased. "I'm not a professional sculptor you know . . . I'm an architect and I make sculpture for pleasure. A few people take my work seriously, although I don't. Drawing plans of houses is my profession, it's something I know how to do well, but it bores me to death."

Meanwhile he leads me to the studio which is at the bottom of the garden, between a rose bush and a bed of cabbages. On one side there is also a chicken run.

"You see, here we always have fresh eggs," he says as if excusing himself. "I wouldn't kill one of these hens for all the gold in the world . . . they've all got names, look, that one is called Banana, this other one here is called Umbria. My wife gave her that name . . . she lays the best eggs."

"I'd like to meet your wife."

"She's shy, she doesn't like strangers, but if you want I'll see what I can do when she comes back."

He is being vague and evasive. I realise he does not want me to talk to her.

Meanwhile we have reached the studio; a large, wide, bare room with tall windows.

Blocks of marble of different colours lie scattered on the grey cement floor as well as shapes of clay covered with damp cloths.

In the centre of the room is a life-size statue placed upright, mysterious, covered in soaking wet rags. Elia goes up to it and gently peels them off. As he uncovers it I see appear a naked young girl in a sensual, languid pose. She has narrow hips, on her head is a bulging cap, her shoulders are soft and yielding, her breasts barely formed. She looks as if she has just emerged from a forbidden dream.

"It's a sculpture of my wife Emilia," he says quickly.

"It looks like Angela."

He stares at me in surprise but his look is straightforward, almost hurt; how could I be thinking such a thing?

"Did you know her?" he asks.

"She lived directly opposite me."

"Ah, and how is it we never met each other?" he says unthinkingly. But he immediately corrects himself. "How stupid of me!" he says casually, "I was thinking of another house where I used to go sometimes ten years ago. Of course I know her last place was in Via Santa Cecilia, I knew it from the papers but I'd forgotten . . . Then you lived in the same building. What was Angela's apartment like, beautiful?"

"It was simple, full of light. Angela seemed to dislike having much furniture around, it was quite empty, no objects, no pictures, no flowers or curtains."

"Do you like this sculpture?" he says, changing the subject.

"One can feel the tenderness," I say, "but didn't you tell me your wife was small?"

"Well, portraits are never the whole truth, photographs are better, aren't they? Sculpture has to catch the essence of a person rather than faithfully reproduce the exact proportions of a body . . ."

"In its whole essence this statue makes me think of Angela," I repeat rather crassly.

"It was a challenge inspired by Degas after passing through the filter of Emilio Greco . . . as I've told you I am an imitator and I like going back to the old masters . . . I don't make sculptures to sell but for my own pleasure. Indeed, to tell you the truth. I'm not at all sure that I want to accept this offer of an exhibition in Milan. Once one enters the market place, everything gets fucked up."

He laughs, throwing back his head. Actually I think the statue has something lascivious and mannered about it but I do not tell him this.

"Come with me, I want to give you some green salad for your wounded tortoise."

He walks in front of me through the cabbages, striding with

big steps across the furrows of the kitchen garden. Beyond a row of tomatoes supported by interwoven canes, there is another row of lettuce plants over which he bends lovingly.

"My wife busies herself with all this," he says casting his intense blue eyes up and down me. "She is a very prudent housewife ... at the end of the summer she makes jam and preserves tomatoes ... it's such a pity she isn't here ... she would have liked the tortoise ... my wife loves animals especially when they're ill or wounded."

As he walks in front of me I notice he has a slight limp. He is aware of me looking at it and starts to explain patiently. "I've had a slipped disc that has kept me in bed for a few days but I'm better now. It's because I'm always having to lift great lumps of clay ... I ought to try to get an assistant but I don't want to take on professional airs." As I turn my head before going through the gate, I catch sight of his tall figure watching me from a window on the second floor. He no longer has a welcoming smile on his face, but a rigid enigmatic expression that freezes his features.

45

I am thinking again about yesterday: the exhausting labyrinth, the meeting with Glauco Elia, the return home with a wounded tortoise, the visit to the vet who extracted a dozen pale, swollen maggots from its side. "It will get better, keep it in the shade, give it some lettuce, disinfect the wounds every day, keep it away from flies because they bring the maggots."

I turn on the tape-recorder and listen to Elia talking. On the tape, his voice sounds artificial, like iron heated and beaten again and again until it can be moulded into the desired shape. When we met his voice seemed more direct and sincere, obviously his body was sending me different signals. On its own the voice is expressing what I would have heard if I had closed my eyes, a circumspect and studied voice with a desperate effort of seduction.

When I got home I found there was a call on the answering machine from Merli and also one from Adele Sòfia sounding jubilant. "We've arrested Pepi!"

I telephone her. She answers the phone.

"Michela, have you heard the good news?"

"Where was he found?"

"At the airport, just as he was about to leave for Amsterdam with a false passport. It was the ring that gave him away. Do you remember, I have a similar one with a tiger's-eye. Well, I sent photocopies of my ring to all the police stations and it was through this they recognised him. He was in disguise, can you guess as what?"

"I wouldn't have a clue!"

"As a mullah, with a white robe and a kefia on his head! He had a Kuwaiti passport . . . he does have something Arab about him. He'd forgotten to remove the ring."

"Have you taken a blood sample?"

"That has been done but we haven't got the results back yet, we're expecting them the day after tomorrow. He is in prison."

"And the others? Have you examined the blood sample from Mario Torres?

"Yes, it doesn't correspond, it's a different blood group, but I did say to you he wasn't the type. We've also found that Ludovica lies; she's quite pathological even when she knows we can verify what she says. She has lied about her sister, about her fiancé, and even about her mother. We have discovered she was in a clinic and has undergone a dozen ECTs . . . I said she wasn't a credible witness. Well, I am sorry for you, Michela, you'll have to start from scratch."

When she is being sarcastic, her voice doesn't sound cruel, only slightly derisory. Underneath it I am aware of her usual good-natured motherliness.

I tell her about my visit to Glauco Elia at his country house near Velletri. She listens politely but without much interest.

"You've done the right thing, after all you're a journalist. We have our hands full of other matters. I will let you know the report on Pepi's DNA as soon as possible. You'll see I was right!"

I telephone Merli. A woman answers cheerfully, her voice ringing like a bell. "Yes, he is at home. I'll pass you on to him." So he has found someone to take care of him. He isn't abandoned and alone any more and I don't have to be the Good Samaritan. That's fine, it is better like this, although I feel rather sad. What if my vocation to look after people goes deeper that I realised? Is it the need at all costs to be a mother towards someone who could be a father to me?

"Signor Merli, how are you?"

"I'm much better, thanks . . . they've sent me a companion, did you hear her? It's my niece Marta, my sister's daughter. She looks after me devotedly and she's great. However at six o'clock she takes off and goes out dancing. Might I hope to see you this evening?"

"Yes, I must talk to you about my visit to Glauco Elia."

"Ah, how did it go?"

"I want you to hear his voice on the tape-recording."

"Then come over. I'll be expecting you."

"Would you like me to bring anything?"

"No, don't trouble yourself, except if you pass a dairy you could get me some milk. You know how much I drink and my niece only goes to the shops once a day."

"And some biscuits and two yoghurts?"

"Why not, why not?"

Today all the objects in my apartment are strangely silent. Could it be because the weather is changing, the total lack of wind, this smooth, sultry calm?

I think of Marco. At this time, in Angola, he will be going out to have supper. Will he be carrying his head with him, or will he be leaving it in the hotel?

So Mario Torres is not the killer, so Ludovica lies "in a pathological manner", and Nando Pepi has been arrested. If his blood matches that of the blood in the lift, the Angela Bari case will be resolved. All the voices I have recorded will be called upon to give evidence. So many articles have been written about the mysterious death of Angela Bari and are still continuing to be written, but as soon as the culprit is found, the mystery will be solved and the sphinx will remain dumb and motionless until the next "savage crime by unknown hands".

46

The tortoise is cured. I can tell from its energetic scratching against the sides of the cardboard box I keep it in, well supplied with leaves which I pick fresh each morning from the pots on the terrace.

On my way to the radio station I meet many famished cats. I look for the cat lady but I do not see her. Could she be ill? I don't know where she lives, I have never asked her.

At the radio station I find Tirinnanzi sitting at my table, eating a large ice-cream.

"I was waiting for you," he says, "have you heard the news? Pepi isn't the murderer, his blood test is negative."

"How do you know this?"

"That woman Sòfia rang a short time ago. As you weren't here, she wanted the director and then he told me. She was in a really black rage, your lady police commissioner."

I dial Adele Sòfia's number at the police headquarters. They say she is not there, but I can hear her shouts in the room.

"Could I please speak to her?" I insist.

"Who is it wants me? I'm not here for anybody," I hear her yell. But then, the police sergeant having repeated my name, she asks me down the telephone, "Have you heard the result?"

"Tirinnanzi has just told me."

"That Cusumano can't be trusted! I told him not to mention it to anyone. But we've got to go on and we'll do the examination again in another laboratory, though I don't trust the others . . . no one can persuade me that . . . I'm sorry but I've got to leave you," and she slams down the phone.

"Do you want some ice-cream?"

"No."

"They'll never find the murderer now, it's too late. It's all been camouflaged. Do you know Welmer's theory about how murderers take the colours of what obsesses them. When they kill they change colour for a few minutes, but once the crime has been committed, they are assimilated back into the landscape and aren't seen any more; they can camouflage themselves to perfection."

"Are they chameleons then?"

The door is violently pushed open and the director appears, giving Tirinnanzi a surly look. "An ice-cream at this hour? We're not at the seaside, isn't there any work to do this morning?"

"I was wanting to talk to you," I say timidly.

"Yes, Canova, I've been wanting to talk to you too." And he leans both hands on the table as if to stop them flying away, then he spouts out all in one breath. "I have transferred your programme on crimes against women to a top journalist. Don't be offended, believe me, I'm very sorry, but . . . there's a need to get to the bottom of events, scrutinise them, give sociological and maybe philosophical interpretations, otherwise the series will be undermined. We need a prestigious name which will give us credibility, and we need good publicity . . . You'll hand over all the material you have prepared, and then we'll make a challenging report out of it. Naturally you will be helping, you will act as adviser and assistant. I'm grateful for all the work you've done, don't think I'm not appreciative, but you must understand how things have got out of hand here and we have need of more considered work, more . . . more . . . how shall I put it . . . more comprehensive . . . it needs the expertise of a highly professional journalist supported by a first-class producer. If you want, you can continue your work on unsolved crimes . . . in fact I'd like you to know I'm saying this to you because I've seen how these unresolved cases nearly always involve women, and you could do a good mini series on the secret hopes and loves of these women. Would that suit you, do you think?"

"It wouldn't suit me at all," I say, astonished at my daring.

"What doesn't suit you, Canova? You will be paid for this, I don't expect you to do it for nothing."

"I'll leave you the Nagra tape recorder, the small Sony and

I'll also leave you the tapes I've made, but I don't want to do a series along the lines you suggest."

"Signora Canova, you have no sense of proportion; if I may say so, you don't have any humility. I understand your reaction, after doing so much work, but you must understand that it is I who decide here, and at this point I have to say to you that to work in broadcasting a more professional collaboration is required. This is not to belittle you, but to defend the interests of the listeners who have the right to be well served with the utmost professional skill."

I have either to accept his terms or to leave, there is little to discuss. I decide to leave, even if it is with a lump in my throat. I turn off the computer. I put in my bag the wooden jar with the spider clinging to its web and I leave. On my way out through the door, I catch sight of Tirinnanzi hurling his ice-cream on to the floor in a gesture of rage.

47

Without work, without a computer, without a tape-recorder, I feel a lot lighter but also battered and empty. When I was finally leaving my office for the last time I thought I heard a suffocating scream. Was it the tape-recorder or the desk?

I go to see Adele Sòfia who gives me an abrupt, off-hand welcome. I want her to listen to my conversation with Glauco Elia. It is the only tape I have kept for myself, together with a few discarded lengths of the other tapes and my notes.

It is one o'clock. A sultry wind blows in through one of the open windows and ruffles my hair. Adele Sòfia is busy talking with a police inspector and seems vexed I am there, but when I make a move to leave she calls me back.

"Wait, let me listen to that tape. You may be right, after all we're getting nowhere just . . . where did that man say he was? The fact is that we have the evidence of two nurses who say he was in the labour ward on the evening of June 24th . . . anyway, we'll ask to do an analysis of his blood as well."

We go out of the police station together and slip into a small wine bar where we eat bread and butter with anchovies.

"Shall we have some white wine?"

"Why not?"

"A sparkling '89? It was a wonderful year for Trentino grapes."

"So we can celebrate my dismissal!"

"You've been fired?"

"Well, it was me who left, but only after he'd removed me from my programme."

"I'm very sorry, it's not fair to take you off the programme at this stage . . . However one's also got to understand his point of view . . . the radio station isn't doing well, there are fewer listeners and he's afraid of losing his job . . . he's not against you, Michela, you have to see it as Cusumano having to do an acrobatic turn to keep himself afloat . . . but for whatever you may need, I am always here."

"I shan't be needing you any more seeing that I'm not doing the programmes."

"I'll keep you informed, if you're interested."

"Thank you."

I don't want to go home and so I wander round thinking about my problems. How can I live without a salary? As I go down the narrow street of the Tabacchi I realise I am being followed by two cats with dirty, bristling fur.

"I don't know where your cat lady is," I tell them, waving my arms. But they keep following me.

I stop in front of a shoe shop. I am delighted by the sight of sandals in various colours, they look so fresh and bright. How long is it since I bought myself a new pair of shoes? Every morning without thinking I put on old dirty ones, not realising how shapeless they are and how worn at the heels.

I go in. I sit down in front of a mirror and let the shop assistant try different sorts of shoes on my right foot, with heels, without heels, with laces and without.

I feel she is starting to get anxious.

"Do you have a lot of walking to do? Why don't you try these?" she says, showing me a pair of blue tennis shoes, light and soft. I look at them for a moment overcome by emotion, then I choose a pair of cool and comfortable sandals.

As soon as I leave the shop I see the cats are now three. I seem to recognise the third, a small creature, pitch black with a clouded eye.

I hurry to the butcher's and buy a kilo of mince. I walk along the Via Anicia where I last saw the cat lady distributing food.

In the distance I see a small group of cats stretching out their necks. I get close to them and without my doing anything, without my calling them, I see them running from all directions, lifting up their tails, all greasy and dirty.

I am about to open the packet but the two largest cats jump on my arm and get hold of the meat, fighting each other; the bag opens and the meat scatters all over the pavement. The smallest cats are overjoyed and throw themselves headlong on to the booty tearing with their teeth at the last shreds of paper and plastic.

"Look how she can't get it right, look what she's doing! Who is this stupid bitch?" I hear a grating voice in my ear. I turn round and see in front of me a small bent woman, almost a dwarf, with a red handkerchief knotted round her head,

"Really I . . . do you know where the cat lady lives? She always used to be around here."

"You mean crazy Maria? She died, didn't you know that?"

"When?"

"About a week ago. Maria Cini was her real name but everyone knew her as crazy Maria because she really was not all there. Once she got herself arrested in the supermarket. They kept her inside for two days and then they threw her out. Do you know why? Because she stank so strong of cats!"

She laughs, opening a wide mouth with four long, lonely teeth.

"Do you know what she'd stolen? Two small tins of stew for a sick cat and a scented soap for herself."

"And have you taken Maria's place?"

"I'm boss for the neighbourhood. Maria is dead so we've got to find a replacement. You're not someone who'd get it right, you seem more crazy than she was. See the blood ... they scratched you, eh? You'll be all right but if they scratch you, you deserve it because there's a skill in looking after cats. You have to know what you're doing, the same as everything else. You strike me as being pretty useless, like that one with the chestnut hair and the sky-blue tennis shoes ... well, she was another one who didn't know what to do and she hasn't been here any more, thank goodness! But you're no use, much better for you to stay at home, you can clear off. I think of the cats as mine, they're all mine and that's how it is. And they'll be saying look at this crazy woman who doesn't even know how to hold a packet of mince. What's your name?"

"Michela."

"You're all mad ... mad ... you don't understand anything about cats, this is no place for the likes of you."

48

I continue to wake up at seven o'clock even though I no longer have to go to work.

Last night for the first time I felt cold; summer is ending and I have not had one day's holiday. As it has recovered and I want to let it go free, I'll take the tortoise into the country today.

As I get into the car I see in the distance the new cat lady. "Good morning!" I shout from the car window but she hardly turns her head. Crazy Maria was kind and friendly but this one is just the opposite and very scratchy, more alley cat herself than the animals she feeds.

"Be off with you, you stupid cow! Can't you see how you're disturbing the animals?" Her disagreeable voice pursues me down the street with a sharp, hammering sound.

I go by the river along the Portuense and across the Testaccio, then down Via Ostiense in the direction of the sea looking for somewhere with trees where I can leave the tortoise. But it is not easy. The first oak wood I come to beside the road has been invaded by electric saws and men in big rubber boots.

"We're thinning it out," one of them tells me when I ask them what they are doing. It seems as if they are destroying the trees rather than pruning them. The saws are being driven into the tender pulp of the oaks with a deafening noise and a great spattering of sawdust.

Further on towards Castelporziano, I come across another small wood beside the road, but just as I am about to leave the tortoise, I notice that at the far end of the wood something is burning with clouds of white smoke. Is it only stubble or could it really be a fire? All Italy is burning; in the newspapers there are harrowing photographs of twisted, skeletal trees, ravaged fields, terrified animals in flight. "It's all because of those fools who throw cigarette ends out of car windows," someone says. Others say it's land speculators. "It's crazy people who commit arson for fun!" or, "It's the same people who are paid to put out the fires, they set them alight so that they can keep their jobs putting them out again." The fact remains that the trees burn and no one is able to stop it.

In the distance I can hear the noise of sirens, there really must be a fire, and soon the fire engines arrive. The firemen send me away because the road is being invaded by smoke which every moment grows denser and more acrid.

Finally I see a line of trees at the top of a small hill. I leave the car, climb along a goat track and find a large umbrella pine tree. Beneath its shade, on a cushion of dry, scented needles, I place the tortoise next to a moss-covered stone. It seems scared. Then, slowly, it protrudes its wrinkled head and looks around with watery eyes. It has learned that I am not a dangerous presence and with phlegmatic calm it slowly pushes its clawed feet into the ground and goes off towards a clump of large ferns.

I sit down and watch it walk away, clumsy and solitary. Who knows what will happen to it? I seem to be watching myself advancing determined and sad towards my new life as unemployed. Meanwhile spinning round and round inside my head are the addresses of private radio stations to which I can offer my work. I know already that I will have to face painful humiliations, goodness knows how many. So I keep putting it off.

According to Merli I should go back to Italia Viva. "Why don't you make it up with the director?" he says to me over the phone, "you know that the well-known journalist has asked for too much money for Cusumano to agree to. It's him who is wavering and wringing his hands. It wouldn't surprise me if one morning he didn't phone you begging you to come back. Adele Sòfia is manoeuvering for your return. I've heard her saying wonderful things to Cusumano about your professional capabilities. And Tirinnanzi has been saying clearly and loudly how much more together the radio station was when you were there . . . for instance, without your direction Professor Baldi loses it."

Merli and I still talk with a polite formality, using *lei* rather than *tu*, in spite of our quite intimate chatter. He knows about my difficulties and problems, including the story of Marco "losing his head" in Angola and how he can't decide to come back.

"In matters of love, it's the person who runs away who wins," he says to me in a voice of concern. "Why don't you run away a little as well?"

One morning as I am doing my sums to try and work out how long I will be able to survive without a salary, I hear the telephone ring. It is Adele Sòfia.

"This evening the best *canederli* in broth and a chocolate tart that'll make you lick your lips. Will you come and have dinner with us?"

"Thanks, but I'm afraid I can't. I've got to look for work."

"At dinner time? Don't be difficult . . . we'll expect you. I also have some news for you."

So in the evening, tired and demoralised by the day's events, I find myself once more in the Tyrolean sitting room.

"A second test of Pepi's blood has given exactly the same result as the first," she says suddenly. She seems disheartened.

"So this means he can't be the murderer?"

"It isn't him."

"So what can you do?"

"We must examine the blood of everyone who is in any way involved in the case. And this time, Judge Boni agrees."

"I thought you'd already done this."

"With Carlini, Ludovica, Torres and Di Giovanni, for the others the examining magistrate didn't think it opportune."

"So now you'd include Signora Augusta Elia and Glauco Elia as well?"

"Yes, them too."

"Let me know the results, even though I'm not working on the programme any more."

"You've got a sackful of material, you have the gist of a story. Why don't you write a book, Michela?"

"But I handed over all the tapes to the director . . ."

"If you want, I can make sure you get copies. Write a book and stop all this running after voices. I felt really sad to watch you walking around with that tape-recorder always dangling from your shoulder, to see you always having to walk bent over to one side . . . sheets of paper weigh a lot less . . ."

"But I only know how to work with voices."

"You'll learn. You're up to the neck in this story where everybody is telling lies . . . don't you think it's worthy of being told?"

"But I wouldn't know where to begin."

"Begin with things . . . *rem tene, verba sequentur*, do you remember? Your own style would emerge through your close connection with the subject matter."

"My connection with this subject matter is totally cloudy and unclear."

"A good start. Clarity will come later, logic will trace its own geometric lines even if too clearly. It's better to emerge from the fog with a grain of certainty than to find one is in the middle of a sunny piazza if that piazza is nothing but a product of one's own imagination."

"You are in a philosophical mood this evening."

"The crime in Via Santa Cecilia will probably remain unsolved. No one among the people who might have had a motive for killing her appears to have done so. There is always the possibility of an unknown person who used some strategy to get her to open the door, killed her for no apparent reason and went off!"

"Angela wasn't the sort of person to open the door to someone she didn't know. I still remember how she used to lock the door of her apartment, turn after turn. She must have known her murderer and trusted him to the point of calmly turning her back . . . to the point of undressing and carefully folding her clothes on the chair before giving herself to what she probably thought would be a loving embrace."

"Don't fantasise too much, Michela. It's proofs that are needed, not fantasies."

"The folded clothes are what disturb me most of all. They make me think of an amorous ritual, a repeated habit."

"We have so many unsolved cases and so many people as curious as you are to find a motive for every crime, a recognisable explanation, a signature. But often there is nothing whatsoever, only shadows, suspicions, gossip. No judge will be willing to keep open a case based on gossip for very long. Meanwhile there are other victims demanding justice, other cases about which public opinion demands an explanation. We have to recognise our defeats and go forward with that recognition. And they're not only ours, believe me; when you think that in New York there are at least two murders a day, and of these 60 per cent remain undetected . . . Have a slice of this chocolate tart and stop crucifying yourself. Things will settle themselves as they always do."

I lift a piece of the chocolate tart to my mouth while thinking of other things, but the perfumed, faint bitterness of the chocolate brings sensual, pious consolation.

"What's my tart like?"

"Exquisite."

"The chocolate must be of really excellent quality, not the stale stuff that comes from goodness knows where. One should hardly be aware of the bitterness of the grated chocolate and the butter must not be too greasy nor the sugar too sweet . . . and the almonds have to be fresh, the flour should be hard grain, and the eggs newly laid, the milk fresh from the cow. Only when all the ingredients are really fresh and of prime

quality will the tart emerge like a piece of the night sky, dark
and soft and delicate . . . chocolate tart is a cure for many ills,
I think. Do have some more."

49

The days have become endless and empty, with long
gaps which I spend walking, reading, or looking for work.
Without my intending it, Angela Bari's blue tennis shoes continue to tread lightly inside my slow, dismal thoughts.

Every so often I turn on the tape-recorder and listen again
to those voices that have kept me company for more than two
months; I hear Angela telling her fairy stories about cruel kings
and daughters in flight. Without the sophisticated loudspeakers
of the radio station, it sounds hoarse and childlike; the voice of
someone who dislikes the sound of her own voice and is trying
to offer it as a cautious gift which negates itself at the very
moment it is made.

"Once upon a time there was a king who had a daughter . . ."
and when she pronounces the word "daughter" she distorts the
final syllable and almost makes it disappear, as if part of her
tongue was refusing to say that word aloud. When she uses the
word "king" a light vibrating sound comes from her throat like
the whistling of a bird imprisoned in her lungs. Her voice
seems to have a premonition of disaster at the same time as it
is asserting a wish to succeed. What can it be trying to tell me?

After listening several times, I hear terror alternating with
outbursts of happiness. Terror of what?

The phone rings. It is Adele Sòfia. "We've done a blood test
for Signora Augusta Elia but, as with Ludovica, the result is
negative."

"That's good."

"I am now concentrating on the stepfather who is absent
from home at the moment."

"What do you mean by absent from home?"

"He's been away and gets back tomorrow."

"Good."

"Now there is only him and your friend Marco Calò left."

"What has Marco got to do with it?"

"It emerges that he knew Angela Bari, that he was probably with her on the night of the crime and that he often telephoned Carmelina Di Giovanni."

"Who told you this?"

"It was in the evidence given by Torres and Mario."

"Stefana Mario told you Marco had been to the Bari apartment on the night of the crime?"

"It seems that her mother-in-law, Signora Maimone, saw him."

"But Signora Maimone wasn't there then."

"In any case someone saw him."

"Why didn't they tell me?"

"Presumably because they didn't want to upset you. Didn't you know that your Marco knew Angela Bari?"

"No."

"But you knew he left for Angola immediately after the crime?"

"Yes, of course I did."

"The fact is that in your absence Calò went up to the top floor which surprised the porters. They expected him to come down after finding your door locked, but instead he didn't leave till very early the next morning when he stole away like a thief."

"Couldn't it just as well have been me: I fly from Marseilles on the afternoon of the 24th, murder Angela and go back the same night." I say in exasperation.

"My dear Michela, we've checked on your movements. We don't need a blood sample because there are thirty people who saw you in the Hotel de France in Marseilles on the evening of the 24th of June. And frankly I don't believe that even with a private jet you could have come to Rome, killed your next door neighbour and gone back to Marseilles!"

"So I've been under suspicion as well! Why on earth didn't you tell me?"

"In an investigation like this everyone is presumed guilty. Or presumed innocent, it's all the same."

"And have you traced Marco Calò?"

"We are looking for him but at the Italian Embassy they know nothing, nor do the consulates. Where can he have hidden himself?"

"He only told me he'd lost his head."

"It seems like that to me . . . but you didn't think that he's lost his head over your neighbour with the blue tennis shoes, did you? Anyway we'll find him, don't worry, look how we found Pepi."

I put the phone down and go to be sick. In the mirror my face looks grey and pinched. Is it possible to be in love with someone whom one doesn't know at all? Something turns in my stomach and catches me in the throat.

I lie down on the bed. My head is going round and round. I remember that for a moment I'd thought how reticent he seemed when he was talking about Angela. And him telling me he had learnt of her death abroad when in fact he was still in Rome when it happened! And the half-smiles between him and Angela that I caught sight of in the lift. And the statement he made about "having lost his head" without specifying over whom. And what about his obstinate refusal to reveal where he was, and the way he put off giving me his telephone number?

Yet I have known him for years. I know him very well and I know how he is, I am sure that even under threat he would never be able to kill anyone. At least that is what I have always thought.

I go and look at the photographs which we took when we were together in the mountains; standing in front of gorse bushes in flower, with skis on a snow-covered slope, on a lake in summer.

I pause to look at a very clear photograph where he is wearing a pair of gentian blue shorts and a white tee-shirt. His sunburned face, his narrow, elongated eyes, something delicate and ethereal about his long neck, the slightly sarcastic smile on his thin lips, the firm hands resting on his knees: is this the portrait of a murderer?

There is another taken at home in my apartment. He is reading a book with his legs stretched out on a table gazing at me with a look of surprise as if he were saying, "Have I deceived you, Michela?"

There is nothing in these photographs to suggest a gap in my knowledge of him as a man who is kind and decent and passionately involved in his work; admittedly rather selfish, but incapable of violence.

On the recorder I put a tape which he once sent me long ago from Australia.

"Dear Michela. As I'm not able to phone you, I'm sending this cassette through my friend Giampiero who is returning to Italy. I realise how much you like to listen to voices, even when you are not working. As you know, I am distracted by all sorts of sounds and don't pay attention when I am listening to them, but you focus on voices as if they were microbes to be analysed . . . By the end you have a vision of them that is precise and analytical, even if it is possibly distorted . . . I would rather respond to the pure musicality of voices. I'm not interested in knowing where they come from, what interests me is the result . . . To me your voice which I listen to so happily when I am able to telephone you, is dense, heavy, full, it neither cracks nor sags, there are no breaks: it is a voice that has been trained for all the subtleties of radio transmission. What I like most is not its perfection but its sweetness, and that in spite of any technical doctoring, it remains the indestructible basis of who you are. So I want to tell you how much I miss your voice, with all its sweetness and its concern. There is an eternal capacity for surprise in you that never ceases to astonish me, and which (this will seem strange to you) always amazes me. It is as if the things that happen to you are always unexpected and your charm arises from this astonishment. This sweetness is not a sweetness of surrender but of surprise. You know I am laughing to think of your astonished expression whenever you see me arrive, as if you didn't know I was coming to see you, to have dinner together and make love.

"But what is this wondrous surprise? I've so often asked myself this, what is it that comes over you so many times? It's as though you were Monsieur Candide with new shoes and white breeches having just at this moment come down from the moon . . . I love that wonder you have, even if I don't always understand it. It is as if you were being reborn each morning and each birth is painful . . . most of us want to tell the world that we know we have been here for a long time and have a long time to go . . . who wants to keep on being born and having to start again at the beginning? But instead you lift that little bird's head of yours and each morning you are astonished when God sends you down to earth, you have the same expression of amazement that you'd have had if you'd never seen your apartment, the view out of the windows, your coffee pot, and the body of the man who has loved you for more than ten years . . .

"Michela, I want to tell you how much I desire you for your sense of wonder. It is so good for me, it makes me so happy to know I can experience myself as new and unexpected each time I see you . . . Only on some evenings when I am tired, I have to confess that a suspicion comes over me. In a cowardly way I ask myself whether there could be some sort of game in all this. Could it be an act? I can't totally believe in your naïvety which at times seems to be self-destructive. Yet in the end I love you as you are: in you there is a solitary aspect, I have always thought that. Perhaps it's better when I'm away and you are able to think of me with all the calm and distance of separation. There are moments when I think you don't know me . . . and don't even want to because if you did, how could you maintain your capacity to be surprised?"

I stop the tape with trembling fingers. He says himself that I have not known him and have not taken him seriously. Who knows what profound and secret aspects of his character I have not wanted to enquire into. He was courageous in revealing how it was I who obtusely did not want to understand.

Even his voice as I force myself listen to it again with cold concentration, says much more than his words. He talks about the separation that has happened in terms of who knows what and who knows why, using a tone of voice and a rhythm that bear no resemblance to what I have known and loved. But when did this break happen? A very tired voice that is covering up its tiredness. A voice which was my age has become too like that of a father. I have not noticed this change.

Yet I know for certain that Marco could not have murdered Angela Bari. Even if they knew each other and met in secret, even if he went to see her while I was away on the evening the crime was committed, it does not mean it was him; he would not be capable of it.

50

I am still thinking painful thoughts about Marco when the door bell rings. I go to open it. I am confronted by the pale and anguished face of Ludovica.

"Can I come in?" she says, but she is already inside, shutting the door behind her with a quick, sudden movement. She is wearing a long white dress with blue tennis shoes.

"I'm sorry but I no longer have anything to do with Angela's case," I say. "I've left the broadcasting station."

"That doesn't matter, Michela, I've got to talk to someone."

"I can't really help you."

"They don't believe me whatever I say. On the other hand I have the impression you do give some credibility to what I have to say."

"Why did you say all those things that weren't true about your sister and yourself?"

"The fact is . . . I get confused between her and me. I always have . . . whatever happened to her happened to me as well and vice versa . . . so I really have to make an effort to make a distinction."

"You could at least have warned me . . ."

"I know, I'm sorry but I do need someone to believe me."

"You told me that your sister Angela had to have an abortion and that after it she suffered from depression, and in fact it was you who had the abortion and then suffered from depression."

"But it's like that, believe me, it really is. Angela suffered the same, even if in a different way."

"You made me believe Mario Torres beat you up and instead . . ."

"There you are, even you don't trust me! But if you'd seen all my bruises . . ."

I can only assume she is telling the truth. Her voice expands, grows fuller and stronger, with breaks when the sound falters. But suppose that instead she is presenting me with more deceptions? Duplicity appears to live inside her against her will. I decide to put my doubts to rest and listen to her unconditionally.

"Do you want some coffee?" I ask in an attempt to gain time.

"Then you believe me?"

"With my heart I believe you. I'll try to believe you with my head but you haven't got a good track record."

"For you to understand the truth, I must tell you my whole story, Michela, my own true story, my deepest and most secret story, not the police version . . . It all began when I was four years old and my mother gave birth to Angela. The world collapsed about me with a terrible crash that was unbearable to the ears of a child . . . all the love I had experienced suddenly became split, fragmented; some for me and some for her, a bit for me and a bit for her . . . I began to grow twisted and deformed, full of envy and jealousy . . . but Angela, my beautiful sister who made everyone fall in love with her, reacted outside all the rules. She didn't play the game: the more I hated her, the more aggressive I was to her, the more she loved me, looked for me, covered me with kisses, hung on to me, expected me to keep her with me . . . She ended up conquering me, would you believe it? She flooded me with love and I drowned in it, not only did I love her but I wanted to be her . . . The price of my failure was to become even more ungainly and stupid whilst she shone like the sun. Our father had some sense of fairness and never showed any preference, while my mother . . . turned against me on account of my thin lips, the eternal frown on my forehead, because I laughed too much and cried for no reason.

"After my father's death everything began to go downhill for my mother. You've met her, she is a woman who appears quite self-assured but it's all pretence, inside she's still a six-year-old girl. She has always needed a man to take care of her, to whom she is bound hand and foot. Everyone takes her to be an emancipated woman who knows her own mind, but she's scared of everything. Under the appearance of being a professional woman she conceals a timid, dependent character; she simply ceases to exist when she hasn't got the attention of a man.

"When my father died, she seemed unable to go on living, she wept in despair, she threw herself on to his coffin, she refused to eat or drink. She was sincere, I know that. Without my father she was lost, she felt totally isolated and lost. But after a few months, she was introduced to Glauco the handsome architect and sculptor, and he fell madly in love with her. Unable to live on her own, she immediately thought that getting married to him and being loved by him would make her feel secure and happy again. In some ways Glauco was like my father; he was extrovert, kind, in control of himself at times, ambiguous, protective. Although he was capable of much tenderness and generosity he could at times be cruel. He loved her without respecting her; I suddenly understood this. He knew how dependent she was and he gloried in it and treated her as if she belonged to him. Little by little as the years went by, he became more protective and less respectful."

This is the Ludovica I encountered the first time I went to interview her. She is being lucid and precise, but could it be all a mask? Is it possible that behind this passionate yet coherent voice she is escaping into a labyrinth of fiction?

"One evening when my mother had gone out to work, he slipped into my room with bare feet . . . 'shush, shush,' he said, 'don't talk. I know how you're afraid of the dark, and I'm afraid of being alone, can I stay with you for a while?' It was true I was afraid and I welcomed him trustingly. He began kissing my fingers one by one, it was something so sweet. Think, I said to myself, how this grown-up intelligent man, so serious and self-assured, has come to be with a small, insignificant creature like me! At that time, I used to bite my nails and make them bleed,

I had protruding teeth, and thin lanky hair pulled back into a single plait. I had legs like sticks and a huge bust of which I was very ashamed.

"That evening he told me several times that I was beautiful. No one had ever said that to me and I was overcome with gratitude. I imagined we would go to sleep in the tenderness of the newly discovered affection we had found in overcoming a common fear . . . Instead he suddenly threw himself on top of me with all his weight, suffocating me, squeezing me, lacerating me. I screamed, he gave me a slap and covered my face with a pillow, and then . . . and then . . . I thought I had been killed. Instead I was still alive, but it was no longer me. I was someone else I didn't know, someone who was a stranger to me, and from whom I tried to distance myself without success . . . I can still recall his terrible words 'If you talk, I'll kill your mother and your sister, remember that!'

"I walked in circles as if I had the plague. If anyone touched me, I'd let out a scream. I dressed like a nun, I cut my hair very short, I hid myself inside big, clumsy jumpers, inside shapeless coats. I was afraid of everyone and everything. My sister was the only person I wasn't afraid of and I used to hug her, holding her tight and shutting my eyes, wanting to be like her more than ever. I could have thrown myself out of the window, what could I do with this body of mine, now forever dirty and diseased?"

"And your mother was aware of nothing?"

"My mother was blind and deaf, a mole could not have been blinder than she was. She used to say 'that girl hasn't got the will to study, it's puberty, that's what it is.' Or she would say to him 'What's the matter with Ludovica?' She didn't ask me, never! She'd say it to him with an affectionate look, 'What's the matter with Ludovica?'"

"What did he do?"

"He used to shrug his shoulders. 'What should I know about it?' he'd say. Meanwhile he went on coming to my bed. For two whole years he continued to come to my bed – it had become a ritual. 'I've come to keep you company, don't be afraid, I'm here, you're papa's little girl . . .' I used to close my eyes and clench my teeth, I had got him not to put the pillow over my face any more, I'd lie there stiff as a piece of wood waiting for him to finish."

"Would you like some water?" I see how she is perspiring, her hair falling down on to pale cheeks as lifeless as a corpse.

"One evening, while I was having a bath, I heard his voice, he was talking to my sister Angela who was then ten years old and starting to develop. He was saying to her 'you're afraid of the dark, I know that but don't you worry, I'll come and keep you company, it's true you're a frightened little girl, but I'm here.' Without even putting on my dressing gown, with only a hand towel round me, I rushed to my mother and told her everything. What do you think she did? She gave me a slap and said, 'You're jealous because he spends more time with Angela than with you. You were used to being his little darling and now she's taken your place. Grow up, Ludovica, you're not a child any more, forget it!'

"That 'forget it!' took my breath away . . . it seemed as if she knew everything and accepted it as inevitable . . . and with us all living together, she must have been aware that he often slept with me with the excuse that 'the child has had a nightmare, poor little thing!'

"It was as if my mother had wanted me to understand that this sacrifice was necessary to keep him in the family, to keep his protection, his benevolence. It was a sacrifice never spoken of, hidden and secret, dark as the darkest of nights . . . nothing must ever be said about it, only a blind and absolute agreement to surrender our bodies to his paternal greed. That evening I heard them talking in low voices in their bedroom, he and my mother. She was plaintive, whilst he laughed sarcastically.

"'You're mad,' he was saying. 'You're utterly mad and your daughters are mad as well. Complete invention!'

"Then I heard them noisily making love as if they wanted us to hear them and let us know how justice unfolded through thunderbolts and flashes of lightning . . . he was the husband, the father, the head of the household, and his magic kept us isolated . . . there was nothing to rebel against, to get angry about ... the facts spoke clearly like the springs of the bed which creaked to the rhythm of a dance.

"I talked to Angela and told her to throw him out because he would do her harm ... and you know what she said? 'Ludovica, it's too late.' Do you really believe me, Michela, you must believe me."

"I try to believe you, Ludovica."

"You must believe me because it's all true even if I did have ten ECTs, even if I have been in a psychiatric clinic tied up like a salami, even if I've often lied, you have to believe me."

"I do believe you, Ludovica."

I watch her move to drink the water I hand her; she looks relieved but shuts her eyes as if the effort were too much. Her chest rises and falls with the rhythm of her breathing.

"Would you like to lie down?"

"No, I want to go on. Wait a minute, I'm sweating like a fountain, could you give me a handkerchief? Do you realise it's the first time I'm not crying, I'm talking about such awful things and I'm not crying, it's extraordinary. Through crying I've freed myself of everything, I've let go of the pain, annulled it. I don't want to cry any more and I want to be believed. Thank you so much for having faith in me, I'm so grateful."

51

"Do you think that Glauco Elia could have killed Angela?" I ask Ludovica when I see her calm down.

"No, it couldn't have been him ... he loves his own life too much, his sculpture, his villa in the country, to risk everything."

"Do you think that Angela and Glauco kept on meeting?"

"Yes, he came to see her from time to time, or they met in some hotel ... yes, they were lovers even if I don't have any proof of it. He was sick and tired of his child wife who knows how to do everything ... while Angela was so beautiful and unpredictable and lonely."

"But why should he have wanted to kill her?" I ask myself rather than Ludovica.

"He didn't have a reason, Michela, because he didn't do it. After all we were his children, in his own way he loved us. You know he was so jealous, above all of Angela. When we went out with some boy or other, he'd come and follow us down the street. When we got back he'd make terrible scenes, 'paternal' as my mother used to say. The more despotic and questioning he became, the happier she was. In this way the family was strengthened, we formed a blind, unbreakable nucleus."

I see she is wiping the sweat away with the handkerchief. I go and look for another. She thanks me with a nod of her head. And then she begins again with even more intensity, "I got pregnant without even knowing what was happening to me. And this time he was really worried . . . 'Don't get upset,' he said, 'we'll settle it all with gin . . .' He made me swallow half a bottle, I could easily have died . . . I believed I'd lost the baby but it was still there; then he took me to a midwife who performed the abortion on a dirty little bed without anaesthetic. Then, as a reward, he took me to Paris with him. Everyone said what an exemplary stepfather he was, so affectionate, so considerate, and he was when he wasn't insulting me, he was very affectionate and everyone envied me such a father."

"How old were you when you got pregnant?"

"Me, I was fourteen. A year later I knew that Angela was pregnant too. She was only just eleven and had started her periods that year. But he didn't take her to a midwife, he got her aborted by a doctor who used an anaesthetic. As you can see, we both knew what an abortion was. Yet when he wanted, he could be so caring: on Sundays he used to take us to the seaside, we'd hire a boat and he would row and row, he'd hand us each a towel as soon as we were out of the water, he'd buy us cold drinks, he'd tell us fairy stories about a king who had bad daughters whose hands he cut off, who then became good out of love for him . . . Relations and neighbours used to say how blessed we were to have such a loving stepfather . . . if only they'd known. But we kept our mouths shut, not letting anything seep out, in order to protect him and our mother. It seemed that without him she would have collapsed quite miserably. I thought and believed that was the painful due which had to be paid: by night a wolf in the bed, in exchange for by day a kind and affectionate father in the home . . . As soon as I had the opportunity, I got married . . ."

"Ludovica, you have never been married."

"That's true, I always get so muddled. It's Angela who got married, in spite of his prohibitions and scenes. He got to the point of sending an anonymous letter to Angela's future husband saying how she suffered from nervous disorders, a hereditary illness that could be transmitted to her children . . . the curious thing is that the man didn't give in to the blackmail of the letter and wanted to marry her all the same. But after some time he began to accuse her of being weak-minded, and irresponsible. My own story really; I was the one with depression, mental illness, cures in a clinic . . . and he got confused between us when it suited him . . . Then Cornelio went off to America by himself and Angela . . ."

"Isn't it true that Angela wanted to separate from her husband when she discovered he was making love to you?"

"Yes, that's true . . . it's so difficult for me to think of myself as another person . . . for me, my sister's husband was my husband too . . . I didn't distinguish, I couldn't distinguish between them. Hadn't we shared a father-lover for years? It's true that it was me who had the ECT, me who couldn't think rationally any more and screamed all night, screamed without knowing why . . . Angela suffered from anorexia, she didn't eat and her weight went down to forty kilos . . . I believe that even Glauco Elia was fed up with these two sickly daughters . . . it was during that time he found another woman. She was very young and he would disappear from the house for whole days and mother took was taken over by atrocious headaches and the eczema on her hands . . . Do you know that as soon as I could I had all my teeth taken out because he'd told me so often how irregular and ugly they were . . . I seem much older, don't I, with false teeth? I know that but I felt so ugly and awkward before . . . You know, Michela, I believe I did love him because you can end up loving someone who spends nights in your bed, even if he is your torturer. Can one really love one's torturer? . . . one can't go on hating the person who mingles his breath with yours . . . kill him perhaps, but not hate him. And on the one hand he was a loving father, as I've told you. How could I not love him? He was handsome, cultured, esteemed and . . . I was a small scorpion as he used to say and I should be grateful to him for having 'initiated me into sex' as he once put it in a loud, assertive voice. Then I don't know what happened, I don't know, everything began to fall apart; love went rotten inside me, I felt I was a corpse . . . I clung to another man so I could feel alive again but it didn't last long . . . I had too little self-esteem to make him value me . . . Perhaps I have forgiven him, I'm talking about my stepfather, he was a young man you see, forced to live with two seductive and badly brought up girls . . . while she, Angela, didn't forgive him and went on seeing him only to prove she was still able to make him lose his head . . . she needed to know that . . . it was enough to see how she dressed like a siren. She had no shame . . . she'd get someone to fall in love with her and then she'd escape, hide and in disgust watch others get roused. I believe she hated him as much as I did but her hatred was hopelessly mixed up with her desire for him. . . . see if you can make any sense out of it!"

"Couldn't he have killed her out of jealousy?"

"Angela is dead, I am dead, my mother is dead . . . what's the point in killing a dead woman?"

"Angela was very much alive when she was murdered."

"I don't know . . . she opened the door to him, that's certain, she opened the door to her killer because she wanted to seduce him, that's certain. She wanted to show she was the stronger. 'Female beauty is something that vanishes in the flicker of an eyelid,' he used to say and he'd make a movement with his finger as if he were squashing a fly. And you know I believed him, I thought my beauty had either never existed or had disappeared or was about to vanish, and I wept with grief that I would lose him . . . On Sundays he would bring us a plate of little cakes fresh from the oven. They smelled so good and they were hot and we ate them sitting on the bed. He had to be the one who put them in one's mouth as if we were two little babies. Once he put two chocolate cakes on top of the swelling bulge in his trousers and ordered us to eat without using our hands: who finished first would be the winner. Angela still believed she was playing a game, she played the game, she ran after him through the house for a ride on his back. For him these were all preludes to future possession . . . I know that daughters often seduce fathers, want them for themselves, taking them away from their mothers. They do that, I know they do it. But while it all remains a game, albeit cruel, you don't feel you are being killed. Only at the moment when his body weighs you down like a mountain, only at that moment when a pillow squashes your face and stops you breathing has the game ended and turned into horror."

Her voice has lost its uncertainty, the cracking, the faltering sound it has had before. Now it gushes out like a river in flood and even if I wished, I would not be able to stop it.

"I saw myself as dead, to myself and to other people . . . and I accepted this death as a necessary sacrifice to keep the family united, the only thing that could save the horrible shipwreck of feeling – what a responsibility for a child! I almost gloried in it, it was on me alone that the integrity of this small Christian family depended . . . wasn't this my duty? I assisted, the corpse I was, in the birth of a kind of sensuous poison, the savage pride of my mission, the presumption that I alone, a small unacknowledged god, would save my mother and my sister from catastrophe. My presumption collapsed the moment I realised how he was fooling Angela. So my sacrifice had been in vain! All that silent suffering, clenching of teeth, had been as nothing, useless. I wanted to kill him, I really thought that, I would have done it but then I knew that in the end I would kill myself because deep down I was convinced it was all my fault . . . When my mother said to me 'as usual, Ludovica, you're a liar and a story teller,' I thought it was she who was right. I was her guilty child, given to deceitfulness and disgrace, my tongue had gone rotten in my mouth forever . . . Why didn't I kill him? I've asked myself this so many times . . . I could have done it . . . if only I had . . . I thought of doing it with a pillow or a knife but I ended up putting it off. After so much thinking, I believe I have understood only now why I didn't kill him. The fact is I loved him, I loved my humiliation. I was in love with the horror and all I wanted was for it to continue . . . I've spoken the truth down to the dregs, Michela, the sickening dregs . . . I remember one evening to going to the cinema with a boy, and suddenly seeing him in the dark behind me and starting to shake all over . . . I was eighteen then, no long a child but I still trembled . . . When he grabbed hold of my arm and dragged me out of the cinema, I let him have his way . . . once again I stupidly let him have his way . . . Pale as a corpse, as soon as we got home, he started to hit me and still I let him have his way . . . He shouted that I was a slut, a bitch, that I went swinging my hips down the street, that I flirted with everyone. Yes, yes, I told myself that it was exactly as he said. But when I heard him saying the same things to my sister, that she was a whore, 'a harlot in her soul', that she deserved to be raped a thousand times, I became rebelled. . . . I went out in the street and went to bed with the first man I met and made sure I was paid . . . it was to make him angry, I think, I don't know, perhaps I wanted to confirm what he'd said and show myself that he was right . . ."

Now she is crying so desolately that I don't know what to say. I stroke her hair which is damp with her tears, as if her whole body is weeping.

"Please believe me, Michela, say you believe me."

"I do."

"Why have I been such a coward?" The pain has dug a furrow across her smooth forehead.

"Don't torture yourself."

"I can't sleep because of Angela's death . . . it's my fault, you see I know she did not have much of a will to live but it was me who agreed to the way she was destroying herself . . . wouldn't legal punishment have been better than the complicity of my silence . . . a silence that included the terrible love for our torturer?"

Not knowing what to say I offer coffee, biscuits, but Ludovica doesn't take any notice. Then suddenly she asks me, "Have you got any perfume?"

"Yes, I think so."

I come back with a little round bottle. She takes the bottle from my hand, pulls out the frosted glass stopper and lifts it up to her nose, half-closing her eyes. As if by magic the tears dry on her cheeks, her lips curl into a veiled smile.

"Essence of bergamot," she says. "Can I pour myself a little?"

"Of course."

She cups her hand and pours. Who have I seen making a similar gesture? Of course, it was Sabrina—Carmelina putting the cigarette ash into her cupped hand. And all at once I discover how many features Ludovica and Sabrina have in common. Is it the conviction of being blame for their own sexual humiliation?

Like a child Ludovica undoes a button on her dress and puts a few drops of the perfume on her chest and on her neck; a light scent of olives and green lemons.

"I feel better now, thank you," she says slowly.

"So do you think Angela could have been killed by a madman who turned up by chance?" I persist stubbornly.

"I don't know. Angela had relationships with men that were so intense, so unpredictable, like with Marco."

She stops, putting her hand to her mouth as if to say, "Oh God! I've made a blunder!" I reassure her that I already know about it. I ask if she can tell me when it all began between Angela and Marco.

"I don't know, I don't know much about it. I've told you how she admired you, Michela, and that she wanted to have a job like yours on the radio . . . she wrote stories which she'd read aloud, but inside herself I'm sure she valued her ambitions very little. Marco was part of you, Michela, and she wanted to get closer to you so she found the quickest way and one she was good at, involving the use of her body."

"A rather contorted way of getting close to someone."

"Angela didn't know any other . . . she was too unsure of her thoughts, of her words . . . but she knew she could count blindly on her body . . . she'd even seduce the tobacconist at the corner shop or the clerk at the post office to get something that was ahead her legal right . . . it was her way . . . And I have to confess it has often been mine . . . only I haven't got the confidence, the marvellous spontaneity which she had."

She bites her lip. She looks so unhappy that instinctively I hand her the little bottle of perfume because it might give her some relief. She takes it from between my fingers, lifts it up to her nose and takes a long, deep breath as if it were a drug.

"Perfumes are what make me feel better. Michela, do you really believe me? I've told you the whole truth without leaving out the smallest detail. Do you believe me?"

"Yes, I believe you," I say, and it is true.

52

It is night. Along the street can be heard the clanking of the garbage collectors; a garbage bin is lifted up, emptied into the truck and deposited on the ground. One bin, two bins, three bins, and the truck moves down to the end of the street. The noise grows more distant.

I turn on the light. Now I am fully awake, I pick up a novel by Conrad and with swollen, watery eyes, I try to get into the extraordinary story of 'The Secret Sharer': a ship's captain who, unknown to his own crew, fishes a shipwrecked man out of the dark waters of the night. The man, young and naked, looks exactly like him, almost a double of the captain who decides then and there to hide him in his cabin.

They find themselves facing each other in silence, the captain, a man who is an upholder of law and order esteemed by everyone and a naked man who is outside the law because he has killed a sailor in a drunken brawl, a wanted man entirely alone. Yet the two discover they are close, intimate, in agreement. In each of them there is something of the other and their mutual recognition is an act of profound humility but also of pleasure, almost a forbidden happiness to be concealed.

To free the shipwrecked sailor, the captain has to bring the ship in close to the rocks and risk it being broken to pieces. Close enough to the shore for his double to get into the water without being seen and close enough for him to find refuge without drowning.

In the experience of Conrad's captain, I seem to recognise something of my own. I would not be so curious about Angela Bari if I did not recognise in her some of my own loss and my own confusion, my fears and my lack of assertiveness.

I too am carrying out a dangerous manoeuvre to bring myself as close as possible to the rocks with the risk of shattering my future. To let down gently into the water the corpse of the blue canvas shoes so it can swim to safety in the darkness of the night and reach another landing place that will at least be tranquil even if not happy.

In the silence that follows the moving off of the garbage truck, I hear the telephone ring. I run to answer it, knowing it is Marco. And indeed it is him.

"Why didn't you tell me you knew Angela Bari?" I ask immediately and all in one breath so as not to lose my courage. I hear an apprehensive silence at the other end of the phone and then a sigh.

"Now when I'm ill you go and bring up something that is of no importance . . . you really are monstrously selfish, Michela!"

"It's not something of no importance . . . Marco, whether you like it or not, you're implicated in a crime; they suspect you because you were with her on the evening she was murdered, and went away immediately after her death . . . they want to test your blood to see if it corresponds with that of the murderer."

"If you think I murdered Angela you're an absolute idiot . . . you know very well that I'm incapable of hurting a fly! So why do you say these idiotic things, you know me, Michela, don't you believe me?"

"Just tell me when you're coming back, Marco."

"Right now I can't. Try to understand me . . . you make no effort to try and understand me; you're too taken up with yourself."

"Marco, they're looking for you, the police are looking for you."

"They can go on looking for me, I'm innocent and you must believe me."

I put down the receiver. He rings back and tells me I'm being idiotic. Suddenly I feel so tired, I don't seem able even to bear the weight of the telephone. I throw myself on the bed after having unplugged it and fall into a deep sleep.

I dream that Marco is lying stretched out on the bed, quite naked. A very small girl is sitting on his chest; she opens her legs wide, she is wearing a little snow white shirt and a pair of blue tennis shoes.

I wake up with a bad headache. I get up and put away the clippings of crime reports from the newspapers, women ripped to pieces, ripped open, children massacred, girls butchered, raped, drowned. I experience a sudden feeling of disgust, I want to reject all these horrors. I do not want to hear or to see anything that speaks to me of female bodies that have been ripped, violated, slashed to pieces.

I am on the point of throwing it all away when I am stopped by remembering what Adele Sòfia said, "It's necessary to give form to one's own obsessions, for which there are always profound reasons; don't shut your eyes, go ahead."

I pick up some American statistics on violence in the family. I look at the statistics without taking them in. I need to sit down to clarify my ideas a little. I feel the coldness of the floor beneath my feet.

I read how cases of violence occur more frequently in Catholic families than among Protestants and Jews. I read that violence does not occur only in poorly educated, deprived families as is generally believed, but among all classes, even in the rich and professional classes. The research indicates that 30 per cent of violence occurs in families of high academic status. It shows that the majority of cases of incest between fathers and daughters occurs in middle-class families (from 52 to 56 per cent). And that the majority (77 percent) of wives who become victims of assault are not in waged work and are full-time housewives. According to the author, cases of incest tend to repeat themselves down the years and are very rarely isolated incidents. Frequently the father becomes involved with one daughter after another. Alcoholism is often present, but more as a way of obliterating the feelings of guilt than as a reason for violent behaviour.

I read how among girls and small children who have been raped by their fathers: 60 per cent suffer from depression as adults, 40 per cent from a deep sense of guilt, 37 per cent from suicidal drives, 55 per cent use alcohol and drugs, 35 per cent suffer from sexual problems such as frigidity and vaginismus, 38 per cent have a tendency to promiscuity and 60 per cent suffer from a lack of self-esteem.

In front of me I have the photograph Ludovica gave me the first time I interviewed her for the radio. It shows her and Angela as children walking along the street: Ludovica thin and angular with heavy breasts which she seems to be trying to hide by hunching her shoulders, and Angela small and shapely, with her loose chestnut hair reflecting the sun.

The two sisters do not look alike yet there is something which they share; a painful anxiety, almost like an invisible mutilation that makes them both accommodating and fiercely defensive. A defence that is also a need to negotiate surrender with the least pain.

Two children who walk hesitantly together towards a hell that is familiar to them both and in which they are so used to living that possibly they no longer want to leave it. Anyway where else could they go?

Angela gazes in front of her as if she knew the right road and is aware she can confidently set out on it. Ludovica inquires of her sister whether there might be a way out, even if it is difficult and full of thorns, so they can escape together without being seen.

53

"What are you doing? Don't say you're still asleep at this hour!" It is the voice of Adele Sòfia.

"I've got nothing to do, I've been asleep."

"Do you know that we haven't been able to find your Marco Calò? He's been seen in Luanda, but there is no response from the hotels in the city. He's been reported at Cuanza Sul, but even there the authorities know nothing. The last hotel where he left information is at Matanie but he departed a few days ago without leaving an address. Has he telephoned you?"

I say yes although I want to say no.

"And why didn't you let us know immediately?"

"He didn't tell me where he was, he didn't leave me a phone number, he only said I was a stupid idiot and totally selfish to suspect him."

"I should have continued to have your telephone tapped."

"And Glauco Elia?"

"As soon as he gets back we'll do a blood test. The judge agrees, all we are lacking is the agreement of the person concerned."

"Shouldn't he be back by now?"

"Not yet. But all the same he has a solid alibi. He was at the hospital on the evening his wife gave birth, it is written down in the hospital register and we have the evidence of two nurses."

"So, by a process of elimination, it can only be Marco?"

"By a process of elimination I agree, but logic has to be supported by scientific evidence. We have to analyse his DNA. The next time he phones, put his voice on to the tape recorder. I'll see your phone is monitored again, provided Judge Boni authorises it."

"What else?"

"Have you found work?"

"No, I haven't."

"They who sleep catch no fish. Goodbye, Michela, don't

lose heart, you'll find another job, you know how to do the work. Do you remember my idea of a book?"

I get up. I decide to go and check on the alibi of Glauco Elia: there is something I find unconvincing in this almost too perfect coincidence: the death of Angela, the birth of the baby. Did it all really happen on the same evening, at the same time?

I get into my Fiat and drive to the Sant' Anselmo Hospital. Once there I am sent from one office to another. "But who are you? What do you want?" They don't seem able to understand that I am asking something very simple: to know at exactly what time Glauco Elia's daughter was born.

Finally, in the maternity department, I find a kindly young obstetrician who takes me to see the register of births. She is called Rosa, she is small and well built and wears her hair very short. Underneath her white shirt I catch a glimpse of two small flat breasts; strong wrists and large, delicate hands emerge from her rolled-up sleeves. They look very able to deal with the mysteries of the female body.

"Augusta Elia was born on the 24th of June," she tells me.

"At what time?"

"The time, wait a minute, it isn't there. That's strange. It could be that . . . yes, after 11 o'clock at night the register is closed and the girls fill it in on the following day."

"So really she could have been born on the 23rd of June, around midnight?"

"Actually it could be so. Even though they're obliged to write down the precise date and time of birth, if it is written in on the following day they should put the date of the previous day. And usually they do. But in the case of Augusta Elia, the lack of an exact time makes me think it is like you say; it's possible she was born late, between midnight of the 23rd and the morning of the 24th. And so the next day they wrote it up as the 24th without specifying the time."

"Two nurses have testified that the father, Glauco Elia, was present at the birth and that it was at night."

"That's true, I was around and I do remember him standing behind the glass screen."

"And was it late in the evening?"

"Yes, almost midnight."

"So the nurses' evidence is correct except that it could be the 23rd and not the 24th?"

"They remember as I do that he was here, but we didn't go and check the date on the register. The girls who wrote in the date must have been on the morning shift and would have thought that if the baby was born after midnight they had to write the date as the 24th."

"Thank you very much, you've been so kind," I say, feeling feverish.

"I've done it because of your voice," she says unexpectedly. "When I heard you talking to the ward sister I said to myself, I know that voice, and then I remembered having heard you on Italia Viva. Isn't that so?"

"I'm not working there any more."

"I'm sorry. I enjoyed listening to you. You have an unusual voice, it makes me think of peaches in wine."

"Peaches in wine? In what way?" I don't know whether to take it as a compliment or a criticism.

"I'm not sure, something that slips down the throat with a fresh sweet sensation."

She comes with me to the car which I have parked beneath an enormous lime tree. The bonnet is covered in small soft flowers that only need a breath of wind to send them whirling away.

"Summer is ending," she says, picking a withered flower and smelling it. "The scent of these lime trees reaches up to me in the labour ward and consoles me for the pains I have to witness every day."

She too loves lime trees. I tell her how I also follow their scent, and how it saddens me to know that in a short while the tree will lose its feathery clusters and put its scent to sleep until next year.

I ring Adele Sòfia from the first phone box I see and tell her what I have discovered.

"Good, you've done the right thing, we had too much faith in the hospital register . . . although I still can't see the motive, I simply can't understand the reason for this homicide."

Two hours later I receive a call from Lipari. "He's disappeared."

"Who?"

"Glauco Elia."

"When did he go?"

"After we had notified him of the summons, when we told him we had to do a blood test, when he knew we were checking on his alibi at the hospital."

"I thought you'd put him under police surveillance."

"We were going to do that, but he forestalled us . . . the fact is . . . what reason did he have to kill a stepdaughter he hadn't seen for years?"

"Signora Maimone said she'd seen him in the courtyard of Via Santa Cecilia but you didn't believe her."

"Someone who has seen the Madonna, you must be joking!"

"In this case she was telling the truth."

"Goodbye."

54

This morning in the passage outside my apartment I find an envelope with a cassette inside it. It has my name on it written by hand . . . someone must have delivered it, the postman never comes upstairs and neither Giovanni nor Stefana know anything about it.

As soon as the tape starts to run I recognise the sensuous, full-bodied voice of Glauco Elia.

"You will be surprised at my disappearance, dear Michela, but don't be upset. I am by nature resistant to interrogations and to examinations in general. When I was a child I used to hide in cupboards on the days I had to take part in gym competitions. Everyone would be looking for me and I'd stay there in the dark, without saying a word until the uproar was over. I was excellent at hiding and they never used to discover me.

"If I am turning to you, it is because when I met you I had

the impression of an inquiring mind that was also sympathetic and tolerant. I realised you wanted to understand me rather than to judge me and for this I am grateful, although I didn't cut a very good figure with you on that day . . . I was too involved with my work . . . But I felt we could have really understood each other. Isn't this true? You so acutely attributed the memory of Angela to my statue. Well, I have to admit to you that the small girl modelled by me is really Angela, and if one wants, also in part her sister Ludovica: two little children who have been close to my heart for years even though they were not my daughters in the biological sense of the term.

"Ludovica was twelve when I married their very beautiful mother, Augusta. She was an awkward girl, afraid of everyone and everything, a small wild cat who hated her mother because she had all the beauty and there was none left for her. She hated her little sister because she was convinced she had taken all her father's attention away from her. How could I not be touched by a child so full of self-hatred? How could I not feel tenderness for a small wounded creature who felt so alone and despairing? I began to talk to her as if she were a grown-up person and she was grateful for that, I began taking her with me in the car when I went out to work and she was happy with this. She felt she was being treated as a woman, accepted for herself and respected as she had never been by her own father, or by her mother who neglected her. Their father had died prematurely and the whole family recounted fantasies about him; however, you should know that Augusta confided to me that he was never faithful to her; a month after they got married she discovered he was going out with his assistant nurse. She got him to send her away but some time later she found out he was involved in another relationship, this time with an anaesthetist. As you know, human material is never lacking for anyone sexually anxious.

"When, after months of courtship, Augusta decided she loved me, she had not recovered from the nervous disorders that resulted from her husband's treatment. At dinner, she would begin to cry and the tears would run down on to the plate. I loved that woman so much and I tried to provide her and her children with a family. I re-established timetables that had never been respected, I created the priorities and rituals that are important to every family that wants to call itself one.

"Every day, come what may, I came home to have lunch with them, I never left them alone and I never betrayed my wife with office girls or secretaries as he had done with nurses and anaesthetists. I spent the evenings at home; even if I had important work to do. We had a Somalian maid educated in a Parisian family who prepared wonderful dishes. At mealtimes the children could talk only if they were questioned just as my father had taught me. They were not allowed to shout, get up from the table, pile food on their plates, make a noise when they were eating, drink without wiping their mouths, crumble up bread, and so on.

"I still remember the first time I ate with them. They seemed like two savages; they did exactly what they wanted, talked with their mouths full, stretched across the table to help themselves to wine, spilling half of it on the tablecloth without ever apologising, while poor Augusta rushed to and fro from the kitchen. "No, you must stay sitting down," I told her. "We will find someone to serve at table but you must stay seated beside me and set a good example to the children who are growing up like animals, dishevelled, dirty, never washing their hands before meals . . .

"I can say I have been a really good father, giving them a good upbringing and teaching them respect for others.

"From time to time I took them to the opera, at first they protested because they were ignorant as goats but then they learned to love music and afterwards . . . I can still hear Angela's voice saying, 'Papa, they're putting on *The Barber of Seville*, will you take me?' And the same with books, it was I who taught them to read. When I came into that house, there wasn't a book on the shelves, the girls roamed the fields all day and come back home dead tired with their legs all scratched and covered in mud, to sit down at table screaming and shouting 'I'm famished!' and throwing themselves on the food like two starving little dogs.

"Before supper I got them to read aloud: together we read

Oliver Twist, Pinocchio, Robinson Crusoe. Ludovica didn't give herself much peace, she was a rebel. She was always wanting to go out and her mother used to say, 'She's stronger than I am, I can't get her to do anything, I can't restrain her.' 'Leave it to me,' I said. 'You'll see, I'll tame her.' Indeed after two months of small rebellions, sulks, complaints and tears, she ended doing what I said; she could only go out on her own with my permission and she had to be back at an agreed time. She took on more feminine ways, she was gentler and showed more humility, in fact she became more manageable as I had predicted, even if every now and then I'd see her lift up her head in her own inimitable way with all the furious grace of a serpent to say to me, 'You aren't my father, you're only my stepfather!' But I replied with irony, with conviction and sometimes with a slap (though I was never violent), that she had to refer to me as 'papa' and obey me. But don't think I was all that severe or really tyrannical, I was capable of great forbearance and infinite tenderness when I saw they needed it.

"Augusta was grateful that I had educate those two girls. 'You've transformed them into young ladies,' she used to say. She'd laugh contentedly and I felt pleased with their educated voices, their elegant ways, their natural good sense. They studied when they had to study, they never had to resit examinations or fail them as they were when I first came into the household. Before that time they would be floored by exams and were described by their teacher as 'uncontrollable.'

"But things began to break down at puberty. Ludovica developed late at fourteen and she became flirtatious and unruly. She would take off her bra and let her large breasts hang loose. I told her she was being terribly provoking in ways almost intolerable. At first I tried giving her good advice, talking to her of the dangers she was running but it meant nothing to her, she didn't see I was right. Then I tried severity. When she came home with some friend from school, I'd shut her in the dark for hours and she'd beg me to open the door as she had always been afraid of the dark. In the end I took to hitting her, in particular on the day I met her by chance at the cinema with a horrible boy, a real thug. You should have seen how they were fondling each other, it was despicable, absolutely disgusting.

"In the end I made the decision to leave her to her own fate, even though her mother was entreating me not to abandon her. 'That child has qualities and you are so good at bringing out the best in people,' she'd say to me, but obviously with Ludovica it wasn't possible. She rebelled against me with so much fury, saying I had done her more harm than anyone else . . . I think she came to accuse me seducing of her . . . but fortunately everyone knew she had developed a capacity for lying that was almost pathological. She lied effortlessly without ever blushing, or showing any embarrassment. She became the most hardened of liars, at times simply for the pleasure of doing it.

"When she began to hate me because I stopped her behaving like a prostitute, she invented the most despicable things about me and she went on doing this because her mother believed her.

"How can one describe the depths of dishonesty which a child corrupt in her soul can reach when she pursues her own pleasure at any cost? She didn't want anyone to come between her and her wish to enjoy every possible freedom.

"When at this point, a man appeared on the horizon, already married, but in love with her and with a strong character, we encouraged her to go and live with him. This was Mario Torres, and he turned out to be full of contradictions, at times very affectionate, at times violent. I know he beats her up but I think with good reason. Ludovica is a headstrong woman, wayward and capable of doing anything to get her own way.

"Fortunately there was the other daughter, the younger sister Angela . . . you know that there was four years between them, yet they seemed so far apart, the day and the night. Angela was so docile, simple, so open and full of joy . . . she was very fond of me in spite of my having insisted when I first knew her on behaviour that seemed strange to her. But Angela was quite different; a tender, pliable girl, sensuous and wanting to please. With her I never felt I was wasting my time as I did with Ludovica; she was faithful and companionable till the end.

"I confess to you that I used to see her although I told you the contrary. We continued to have a very sweet, affectionate relationship. If we met in secret it was because of my wife. She was very jealous of Angela. If she knew I was going to see her, she'd start crying and I can never hold out against a woman's tears, it pains me too much. My wife is so young and so devoted, I have to avoid hurting her for I am her whole life and it would be stupid to upset her.

"So I went to see Angela without telling anyone and I tried not to be seen even by the porter. Only once I caught the eagle eye of the Calabrian mother-in-law, that shrew with pig's eyes, always stuck in her chair.

"Luckily there were times when she was away and I was able to slip into the lift without being seen. Stefana and her husband Giovanni Mario are very vague, perhaps because I knew how to nourish their vagueness with appropriate gifts."

The telephone interrupts my listening. "Didn't you have an appointment with our director at six o'clock?"

"Yes, excuse me, it's just that . . ."

"If you can get here within five minutes you'll be able to see him. Otherwise we'll have to put it off till next week."

"No, I'll come at once, tell him I'm on my way."

The director of Vox Populi is about seventy and has a slow and courteous manner. He asks a whole heap of questions about the series on crimes against women, "I know Cusumano is in difficulty. I could propose buying the series as a whole, what would you say to that? Would you feel able to do some more work on it?"

I feel an urge to throw my arms round him but instead I stand dazed and stupid, staring at the white hens on his blue tie.

"But if you aren't interested . . ."

"Oh no, it's my work, I've been working on it for months."

"Then that's fine . . . I'll talk to Cusumano and let you know. Goodbye, Signora Canova, I hope we'll be working together, I really need professionals like you at my station."

5 5

I rush back to my apartment to listen to the voice of Glauco Elia, a voice that becomes more and more obsessive. What else will he have to say?

"Angela and I were friends, more than friends, a father and a daughter who were companions, who looked to each other, who understood each other immediately, it only needed a look ... She confided in me about her love affairs, like a child and I'd tell her about my wife and my sculpture and the baby I was expecting ... Actually I'd like you to know that I wanted to call my daughter Angela, my little girl like her ... but my wife opposed this so decisively and obstinately that there was nothing I could do. I named her Augusta, a small consolation ...

"Angela loved her sister in spite of the tyranny she always imposed on her ... their relationship was a strange one. Angela valued her sister and had unlimited faith in her in spite of knowing how wild her talk, her capacity for fantasy, her stay in a mental hospital. Not to speak of her husband; on whom, as I see it, Ludovica used seduction and intrigue in an attempt to take him away from her. When Angela learnt of this, instead of turning against her sister, she was furious with her husband and chased him out of the house ... Wasn't that unjust? I believe that in revenge Angela thought about stealing Torres from Ludovica. In any event, Torres was madly in love with her although he didn't think of leaving Ludovica, he only covered her in bruises.

"The elder sister was frustrated at seeing how unique her younger sister was, and with fiendish intent tried to imitate her. She copied everything her sister did without adding anything of herself. She had all her teeth taken out because they were crooked and she wanted them to be regular and white and perfect like her sister's ... she wanted to be equal but

Angela's teeth were real and hers were porcelain: you could see this a mile away.

"Lately Angela spent time, too much time on her own. I don't know why she was so alone, she had a gift for making friends but when she asked for anything more, they all turned away as if they were afraid of the weight with which she might burden them . . . She was both fragile and strong at the same time; if she wanted something she would get it but she never used aggression or blackmail like her sister did. With her submissiveness and gentleness she would end up getting just what she wanted. She knew how to take everything, giving you the impression of bestowing on you something she had no intention of conceding . . . her body was there to entice you, to cajole you. It was hard to resist, and indeed no one did resist it . . . the body of a little girl starved of love, a body so soft and yielding it invited a kind of cannibalism of love . . . Anyone looking at her body clothed or naked, would be overcome by an excruciating desire to touch her, caress her, to penetrate her, even to rape her because in some way she was really asking for this, she wanted the thrust of being possessed, the invasion, to push you away with a childlike rejection. She'd say 'no' with her head while her lips, her heart were saying 'yes', offering herself and denying herself at the same time with a sensuality that brought out the wish to kill her.

"So perhaps I have arrived at the moment of confession; I could have killed Angela because I loved her in spite of everything, because she called me and rejected me, because she promised without keeping her promise, because she wanted to destroy, because her seduction was all powerful and deadly. But I didn't kill her, someone else killed her for me . . . I don't know who it was and I don't want to know . . . I imagine that they would have been impelled by the same reasons; a profound desperation, anger at how she was continually running away from the tie of love, from feelings of tenderness, from demands for trust and faithfulness, whilst offering up gentleness, tenderness, docility and absolute surrender . . . I never found her to be a rebel like her sister Ludovica, never saw her irritated, angry, bad-tempered; her despair was so deep that no one was ever able to capture it, the painful joy of existence that held her spellbound. In that joy she played with all her powers of enchantment: a sad joy, if one can put it like that, a lacerated joy. I never heard her protest, never say no, never give a sharp answer, never show her claws. She knew how to be very sweet . . . 'soft to the touch and smelling of roses', as Don Giovanni says . . . she was utterly without defences, tender and solicitous . . . she never pretended, absolutely never . . . she was incapable of pretence, her vulnerability was such that it made you feel anxious, what will she do to get out of all this, I would say to myself. This is why I followed her, even after so many years, even after my second marriage, even when I was about to be a father. I felt bound in some way to stay near her, to keep her company and protect her.

"And she was grateful, and she would show it by seeing there were fresh flowers whenever I visited her or a home-made cake, then she'd say 'Papa, tell me everything!'

"But in reality it was her telling me horrible stories of men who fell in love with her and then wanted to shut her up at home, forever imprison her, lock her up . . . men who wanted to put a chain round her neck, show her off to friends, eat her up little by little, leaving her even more solitary than before. I know she had once tried to sell herself, she confessed it to me herself with great candour. 'Papa,' she said to me, 'I went with a man who gave me five hundred thousand lire all at once, only to be with him for an hour and he wasn't ugly, he smelled of freshly laundered clothes.' But the second time the man who paid her was a sweaty youth and she couldn't stand the smell. 'You know I couldn't ever be a prostitute because my nose is too sensitive, I can't stand strong odours and a naked body has strong smells that make me feel quite sick.'

"I believe she didn't ever try it again but from those times kept strange friendships. There was Sabrina, a prostitute in the Tiburtina district and her pimp Nando whom Angela thought was a good person, in spite of being a pimp . . . two rough characters if you ask me, indeed I believe both of them ended up in jail . . . But that is how she was, a strange girl, solicitous, docile, with an intense melancholy and a tendency to be self-destructive ... it wouldn't surprise me if it were she who provoked her murderer, pushing him towards the crime, naturally with great gentleness, with the most gentle passivity, with the most terrible, veiled submissiveness. I have never known a more dissolute or more ferocious softness than hers ... a softness that welcomed you like the night in the darkness of its womb and then abandoned you to meditate alone on the poverty of the human body ...

"And now I have to make the gravest confession and I hope you will believe me, you must believe me, Michela. I don't care about the police, they will never believe me, but I need you to believe me.

"My daughter was born on the night of the 23rd of June at one minute past midnight ... At the hospital they registered it as the 24th but without the time; therefore when the nurses testified that I was present at the birth, which occurred late at night, they thought it was the night of the 24th rather than the previous one. I blessed this mistake because it made it possible for me to have a secure alibi.

"On the evening of the 24th of June I was with Angela and I don't believe anyone saw me arrive. The porters were asleep and the gate into the courtyard was open ... I went upstairs without using the lift and when I tapped on the door of the apartment she opened it. She was wearing tobacco brown trousers and a white silk shirt that slid over her shoulders and her breasts. I realised at once that something was the matter; perhaps she had quarrelled with somebody, although she never picked quarrels ... and I'm sorry to have to say this, dear Michela, but I believe the person with whom she had quarrelled was Marco Calò ... He must have left a short time before and perhaps she was waiting for him to come back. I noticed she had taken off her blue tennis shoes and had put them beside the front entrance, perhaps she had come on tiptoe to the door thinking or hoping, I don't know which, that it might be him, Marco.

"Actually I hadn't said I would come round at particular time, I'd just told her I might come round one evening ... I didn't think she was in love with Calò, it was a manoeuvre to seduce him like the many others. She wanted to possess him, make him 'lose his head' and then throw him out, or perhaps she was wanting to make a friend of him so as to be able to reach you because she was very interested in your work as a radio journalist; and she longed to enter into that magic world of voices . . .

"Angela didn't know and couldn't conceive of any other way of interesting people except through using her body: and it was easier for her to use it with him than with you, but I see this as an innocent manoeuvre. There was no wickedness in her, only an inveterate need to make use of her physical fascination, even to get in touch with you and the radio station.

"She said she was hot and she took off her shirt. Between us there was a great intimacy but not a sexual one I assure you, so that I found nothing strange in her undressing.

"She stayed wearing her bra and her trousers . . . she came close to me and looked at me in a way that sent shivers down my spine. I don't know what was in her mind, she seemed strange . . . Then she took off her trousers and folded them on the chair, giving me a sly look. 'I'll do as you tell me,' she said, 'as if I were a nice ordinary girl, isn't this how you want me, Papa?' And she seemed so serious and sensible that she touched me deeply.

'But what are you doing?' I said to her . . . frankly she seemed to be going too far.

'I'm hot,' was her reply and she went back to her trousers and her shirt, folding and refolding them obsessively in a precise, provocative way. I stayed looking at her, thinking she was quite mad, a mad, perverse child.

'Do you want a coffee?' she asked me, going towards the kitchen almost naked, wearing only her pants and bra.

'Why are doing this?' I asked her and she shrugged her shoulders.

"She was so beautiful and gentle and there was nothing vulgar in the way she undressed, Botticelli's *Primavera* could not have done it more gracefully.

"When she started to remove her bra, I said, 'I'm going . . . you want to be alone.' And she began to laugh, but very delicately, without any malice.

'Are you afraid of me?' she said . . . you can understand how horribly tantalising she was being as she stood there completely naked, yet she'd taken off the last garment with a naturalness, a childlike innocence without malice.

"Meanwhile the coffee was done and she poured me some into a little cup and asked 'How many sugars?' She seemed a chaste little girl who has just emerged from a sea shell. But she didn't serve the sugar, she left everything on the table and went to the window, turning her back on me. She looked out of the window as if she were waiting to see someone down in the courtyard . . . I thought, 'she is expecting someone' . . . I said to her, 'Cover yourself because you'll be seen from outside.' But she did not answer and with her back turned towards me and completely undressed, she started to say horrible things to me . . . I was aghast because she'd never done that, it just wasn't in her character, in the way she behaved . . . I immediately understood that it was Ludovica talking . . . it was as if the elder sister had momentarily taken possession of that tender body which I had always known in its mute, sweet blindness . . . She told me I had ruined her life, that her body was dead, forever dead.

" 'As a corpse you are very seductive,' I said, simply to say something . . . I understood she was angry but not with me; she was beside herself with rage, I had never seen her like that . . . and this rage that was not hers expressed itself through exhibitionism and provocation, weapons of Ludovica. It was only she who could have brought her to this point with who knows what lies and untruthfulness.

" 'Look at this naked body, look at it,' she said to me, 'do you know that you have made it completely alien and absent?' It was exactly Ludovica's voice, yet it was all nonsense because I had never touched her body and God knows the temptation . . .

"She talked for a long time about herself and Ludovica . . . it was terrible seeing her standing there, naked and calmly weeping, without desperation, without rage, with the tranquil composure of a ghost. Then I went up to her to take her in my arms, to tell I loved her, that she was still my little girl even if . . .

242   *dacia   maraini*

"At that moment she gave a start as if she had seen someone in the courtyard, as if she had heard a footstep, I don't know which it was.

" 'Go away!' she said.

" 'Are you expecting someone? Who is it? Tell me who it is,' I asked . . . she shrugged her shoulders as only she knew how, with such complete disinterest and such passive gentleness that it wasn't possible not to go along with her.

"So, I left her at around eleven on the evening of the 24th of June. This is the truth. I left in a hurry, I didn't see her again, I didn't want that 'someone' to find me there. I didn't meet him on the stairs so I thought perhaps she had been lying. But then when I knew she had been knifed, I realised she really had been expecting someone and that this someone had killed her.

"I couldn't tell the judge the truth because he wouldn't have believed me. If they had found the murderer I would have told them what happened that evening, but since he hasn't been discovered I can't risk being charged with homicide.

"This is the truth, Michela, I swear it. I am telling you because I like you, because you are neither a judge nor a police officer. Make what use of it you want. I am going where they won't ever find me. I'm used to hiding, I did it as a child as I told you, and I'm doing it again now . . . I hope that in the meantime they'll find the murderer, then I can come back and tell the truth.

"With this I say goodbye hoping you will believe me, I am worthy of being believed and I hope you will also understand my resistance to being analysed, questioned, suspected. It would make me feel like butcher's meat, like *bétail*: my mother, who is French, often used that word with contempt, wrinkling her full upper lip a little as she said it. I found that raised lip in Ludovica and then in Angela, almost a sign of destiny.

"I thank you from the bottom of my heart for having had the patience to listen to me. I'm setting off for another continent, I won't say where because of a reticence that both animates and calms me.

"With much affection, Glauco Elia."

56

A cassette with a confession. I must take it at once to Adele Sòfia. Although it is camouflaged and incomplete, what more can he reveal? Even if Glauco is insinuating that at the last minute "someone" else has killed Angela instead of him, even if he is suggesting that this could be Marco Calò, it is all quite clear and obvious. I dial police headquarters but the number is continuously engaged. I decide to go there.

I have parked the car in Via della Lungarina. On the corner of Via Titta Scarpetta I see the dwarf cat lady with her red handkerchief tied round her head walking briskly, carrying two heavy plastic bags.

"Good morning," I say, slowing down and putting my head out of the window.

Her reply is to throw herself dangerously right in front of the car so that I am forced to stop suddenly. I can see from the angry curve of her mouth that she is going to shout abuse at me. All I can do is to listen while she stands with the bags and lets fly at me.

"The cats are being killed and poisoned and strangled, and you go round sitting ever so comfortably in your cars!" and she spits at the car window. "This morning I found a sack with three dead cats in it, all poisoned. Who did it, eh? And they weren't only killed, they'd been tortured too . . . Animals, they say animals as if they had a bad smell under their noses, when the real animals are you . . . any animal is better, far better, even rats, they don't spend their time torturing, poisoning and putting animals into sacks . . . it's only human beings, only you pestilential motorists with faces like full moons, only you know how to do these horrible things. These aren't drawing-room cats, oh no, of course they aren't, they stink and they show their claws, but how can street cats be sweet and graceful, they're forced to look for food in rubbish bins, hunted by everybody, always in danger of being squashed under the wheels of your fucking cars?"

Now she is alone in the middle of the street busily gesticulating and she seems to have forgotten me. Her black skirt full of spots of grease waves round her thin legs.

"All you motorists killed crazy Maria by forcing her to breathe your pestilential exhaust fumes . . . she really was crazy and didn't know anything about anything . . . but one thing she did know was how to cook aubergines with parmesan; the way she used to do them was a miracle, oozing with mozzarella that went down a real treat . . . a real pity she's dead: once a month she'd invite me home, she'd say come and eat some aubergines the way you like them . . . she wanted to be forgiven because she had a house, cooking pans, a son, when I've only got a park bench to sleep on."

Suddenly she begins to jump up and down in the middle of the street, kicking up her feet and swinging round and round with an agility one would never expect from a woman of her age. I watch her with amazement, amusement, and then with admiration: there is elegance and dignity in those jumps of despair.

I am about to say something to her but she is already occupied with a crowd of famished cats, so I drive off to the police headquarters.

They tell me Adele Sòfia is not there and that she is waiting for me at my apartment. I rush back.

Adele Sòfia is there by the open door of my apartment, her tooth-brace gleaming more brightly than ever, her grey hair all flattened to one side, a black skirt fitting closely round her ample hips, a well-cut jacket with the pockets stuffed full of papers.

"You've forced the door, why?"

"We knew you'd received a cassette from Glauco Elia and we wanted it at once, but you weren't here."

"How did you know?"

"Through Stefana Mario."

"But the name of the sender isn't written on the envelope."

"She must have guessed . . . But did you or didn't you receive this cassette?"

I realise that Elia must have brought it here and that Signora

Maimone would certainly have recognised him. It is even possible he left the envelope with the cassette in the hands of Giovanni Mario, trusting in his vagueness.

"Yes, and I went to see you in order to hand it over."

"Then please give it to me."

I hand it to her. She slips it into a portable tape-recorder and starts listening, walking up and down beside my front door. Meanwhile I go to answer the phone ringing in my bedroom and I hear the far-away, affectionate voice of Marco announcing his arrival on Sunday.

"I want to see you, Michela, will you meet me at the airport?"

"Have you found your head?"

"It's back on my neck again like it's always been."

"You know they're looking for you, they want to do a blood test."

"I'm coming back for that too. I don't want them thinking I'm a murderer . . . you don't think it, do you, Michela, you believe I'm telling the truth?"

"Tell me just one thing. What were you talking to Carmelina —Sabrina about on the phone from Angola?"

"About nothing: it was she who rang me to talk about Angela who'd been killed and about Nando who'd disappeared. In all she rang me three times while I was in Luanda. I'd given the number to Angela before she died and she had passed it on to Sabrina, that's all."

"You never gave it to me!"

"Don't tell me you're jealous of Sabrina!" he says laughing, and I am reassured by all his deviousness. He is a liar but he is not a murderer.

As I say goodbye, I see Adele signalling her departure. She has not realised who it was on the other end of the line, and did not hear what I was saying as she was too absorbed in the ambiguous confessions of Glauco Elia. It is better like that. I am sure I shall see her at the airport on Sunday.

57

Adele Sòfia's sonorous voice wakes me up in the middle of the night. I put on the light and look at the time. It is just on four o'clock.

"He's gone and shot himself in the mouth," I hear her saying.

"Who has?"

"Glauco Elia, of course."

"Where did he do it?"

"In the field next to his house. We'd already taken a blood sample and rushed through a test . . . it was him without a doubt. At long last we know who killed Angela Bari!"

"And the cassette?"

"We've got it. If you want we'll return it as soon as everything has been seen to; after all it belongs to you."

"He seemed so convincing."

"But his blood has been more truthful."

"So he was lying about the last part of his visit on that night . . . the way he was asking to be believed really touched me, even though believing him probably meant finding Marco guilty."

"When he talks it's as if he were talking about someone he doesn't know, someone who without realising it makes use of the same mannerisms as himself . . . there's a lot of truth in the cassette and a lot that's left out . . . the voice is beautiful and persuasive; it seems as if he is trying to protect that other inhabitant of his mind, his vampire brother . . . an intention that fails. Let us say the intent or the force behind his aggression isn't at all clear. The whole story could be described as an ugly mixture of rage, jealousy, pride, prejudice, frenzy, fear, cowardice, desire, sexual frustration as well the anger of Achilles, of the hero who has been betrayed. I don't really know but it's probably all of this together with the rapacity that is so characteristic of gifted eccentrics. Let's face it, he was a man of talent. Have you ever seen his sculpture? He was preparing for an exhibition in Paris . . . how sad it all is . . . Oh, did you know that Cusumano has given up on those forty programmes about crimes against women? The owners didn't like it. And Vox Populi is wavering . . . it seems the theme frightens people off. I think you should make a book out of it. If you want I can get hold of other documents for you. So do come and see me and we can talk about it."

"Thank you."

"And then on Monday when he's rested from the journey, bring your Marco along. We'll have to question him."

"But you've found the culprit!"

"It's only a formality . . . Calò was in Rome on that evening, he hasn't got a very good alibi and it is possible he went to Angela Bari's apartment either just before or just after . . . one could presume some complicity . . . it's an idea of Judge Boni's and one can't be absolutely certain he's wrong."

It does not seem possible to get away from this crime even after an obvious and patently clear solution. Complicity? But what if Marco and Elia didn't actually know each other? Can I be sure of this? Am I certain of it? Reason demands sacrifices but for how long? There is a sly smile on the face of the sphinx.

The friendly sound of Glauco Elia's voice persists in my ear. "Michela, you've simply got to believe me. I deserve to be believed."

Marco's voice hammers at me down the phone. "You've got to believe me, Michela, you've got to."

And in my other ear I can hear Ludovica's voice telling me insistently, "I need someone to believe me, I'm asking you to believe me. You do believe me, don't you?"

Each voice has a ring of truth that does not seem to match up with the logic of cause and effect so dear to Judge Boni and to Adele Sòfia, the police commissioner. The voices are moving bodies with all the intricacy and ambiguity of living organisms, beautiful or ugly, weak or strong, they are criss-crossed by long veins, blue and tender, strewn with dark blemishes like constellations in the sky at night. It is difficult to get them to be silent as one can with the paper words of a book.

Should I get away from the fascination of the voices to enter into the logical geometry of written signs? Would this be wise action or only a way of escaping from the sharp-eyed and chattering bodies of the voices?